Collision Bend

Collision Bend

✿ ✿ ✿ ✿ ✿ ✿ ✿ ✿ ✿

*A Cleveland novel
featuring Milan Jacovich*

✿ ✿ ✿ ✿ ✿ ✿ ✿ ✿ ✿

LES ROBERTS

*St. Martin's Press
New York*

A THOMAS DUNNE BOOK.

An imprint of St. Martin's Press.

COLLISION BEND. Copyright © 1996 by Les Roberts. All rights reserved.
Printed in the United States of America. No part of this book may be used
or reproduced in any manner whatsoever without written permission except
in the case of brief quotations embodied in critical articles or reviews. For
information, address St. Martin's Press, 175 Fifth Avenue, New York, N.Y.
10010.

Library of Congress Cataloging-in-Publication Data

Roberts, Les.
    Collision bend : a Milan Jacovich mystery / Les Roberts. —1st ed.
      p.   cm.
    "A Thomas Dunne book."
    ISBN 0-312-14570-5
    1. Jacovich, Milan (Fictitious character)—Fiction.   2. Private
investigators—Ohio—Cleveland—Fiction. 3. Slovenian Americans—
Ohio—Cleveland—Fiction. 4. Cleveland (Ohio)—Fiction. I. Title.
PS3568.O23894C65   1996
813'.54—dc20   96-20201
                                        CIP

First Edition: September 1996

10 9 8 7 6 5 4 3 2 1

For Jane Bauschard,
the indomitable "Tig,"
whose imagination inspired this book,
and whose courage inspires its author.

Acknowledgments

The author wishes to thank Wilma Smith, news anchor for WJW-TV, for sharing her knowledge of the television news business as graciously as she shares her talent and insight with the viewers of Cleveland. If I got anything wrong, the fault is all mine.

Thanks, too, to Dr. Heather Raaf of the Cuyahoga County Coroner's Office for her expert advice on what is and what isn't.

My appreciation to Jerry and Harriet Zelman, and to Carole Carr, for the use of their names.

And my thanks to Nikki Scandalios for allowing me to not only use her name but to change her gender. She is much prettier and much nicer than her namesake in this book.

And once more, love and gratitude to Diana Yakovich Montagino and to Dr. Milan Yakovich.

Collision
Bend

CHAPTER ONE

Virginia Carville was, as usual, right between my bare feet.

That's because she was the special reporter and sometime coanchor on the eleven o'clock news on Channel 12, and I'm generally lying on my bed when I watch her.

I met her once or twice several years ago when she was an eager college intern at the station and still known as Ginger. It wasn't until after she'd progressed to newswriter and then to full-fledged reporter that she began insisting everyone call her Virginia because it was more dignified.

I opened my feet a little wider, the better to see her, and the side of my foot touched that of Dr. Nicole Archer, neonatologist extraordinaire, from whose bed I was watching the news. My toes are always cold, no matter what the weather, and her bare skin felt good against mine. Warm. Cold toes don't seem to bother her; she murmured softly deep down in her throat and drew a little closer to me without looking up from her book.

Reading and watching the news doesn't sound very romantic, I know. But Nicole and I had been together for ten months and had finally passed beyond that initial fevered leaving-a-trail-of-discarded-clothing-in-our-heated-rush-from-the-front-door-to-the-bedroom stage. It was comfortable now.

Virginia Carville was doing what they call in the TV news business a "stand-up," this one in front of the control tower at

Cleveland Hopkins Airport, which meant little except that she was more visually interesting than someone sitting behind a desk in the studio. She was going on about a commercial plane that had crashed three hundred miles from Hopkins and saying that the liner's "black box," which automatically records all flight information, had survived the accident and FAA officials were in the process of determining the cause.

I've always wondered why they don't build airplanes out of the same apparently indestructible materials they use to make the black box.

Ginger had reinvented herself since becoming a "personality." I remembered her as an intern, mousy and drab; now she was almost pretty, at least in her television makeup, and obliquely sexy. She'd always been ambitious, right from the start; without drive and fire no one would last a month in the TV business. She had done it the hard way, working her way up through the ranks fairly quickly, earning the respect of her peers with an in-depth piece on an old woman whose two drug-dealing sons had been murdered and dumped in Lake Erie by the local crime boss. Virginia had talent and instinct to go along with the ambition, and more than one local politician had suddenly developed a case of tight collar when Virginia Carville called and said she wanted to talk to him on the air.

There was no way for me to know, when I'd first met her years before, and as I watched her now from Nicole's bed, that she would indirectly turn my life upside down.

She finished her report from Hopkins and the broadcast cut back to the studio, where longtime anchor Vivian Truscott, the reigning queen of the Cleveland media, was nodding in a fascinated way. "Thanks, Virginia, keep us informed," she said as if she really gave a damn, and gracefully segued into a commercial, promising to return with the sports report and the wrap-up in just a moment.

In the commercial, which was local, a small business entrepreneur dressed like a circus acrobat did what apparently was meant to be a comic wrestling act with a bear, for reasons I couldn't discern. I had no idea what he was selling and couldn't imagine why he thought anyone would want to do business with a terminally cute man who wrestled bears. He, however, seemed to be having a good time, and what the hell, it was his money.

Nicole threw her left leg over my right one and shifted next to me on the bed. "Is the news over yet, Milan?" she said sleepily.

"All but the sports."

"Is it going to snow tomorrow?"

"They said no. Partly cloudy and cold."

"They always lie," she said, putting the book on the nightstand. "I'll probably have to call a snowplow in the morning to get the partly cloudy off my driveway."

She switched off the bedside lamp so the only illumination in the bedroom was the bluish glow from the TV screen, and rolled onto her side, facing me. "Maybe we'll just have to stay home, then. Snowbound."

I kissed her under the ear, pushing her blond hair out of the way first. "They won't find us until the spring, arms around each other, starved to death. I hate it when that happens."

"We won't starve. I've got stuff in the freezer."

"Klobasa and pierogies?"

She gave my chest a mild slap. "Milan, I'm a doctor!"

"Oh, yeah. Cholesterol. Beer, then?"

"Ever since you came along I always seem to have beer." It was the mildest of rebukes, and I rightly ignored it. "And sliced ham and turkey."

"Well, that's okay then. We can be snowbound. What'll happen to your patients, though?"

"What'll happen to your clients?"

I waved a hand cavalierly. "They'll live."

She screwed up her mouth. "My patients might not," she

said. "That's why I'll call the snowplow." She rubbed the inside of her foot up and down my calf. "Being snowbound might be okay otherwise, though."

I put my arm around her shoulders, drawing her close so her face was nestled against my neck. She wore sweats to bed in the wintertime, and I threw my other arm over her and sneaked my hand up under her sweatshirt to feel the warm skin in the hollow at the small of her back.

"Besides," I said, "being snowbound might get boring."

"After a while, maybe."

I took her earlobe into my mouth and sucked gently. "You think?"

She stroked my leg more insistently with her foot. "No," she breathed.

I moved my hand lower, down under the waistband of her sweatpants and did some stroking of my own. Her feet might be warm but the perfect twin globes of her buttocks were icy to the touch.

I switched off the TV. With all the astonishing inventions and miracles of science that have come along in the last fifty years or so, without a doubt the most important one is the TV remote. Even though I didn't get to hear the latest sports news.

When the clock radio alarm went off at seven A.M. Nicole and I were sleeping nude, spoon-style, closer to her side of the bed than mine, probably because she's a notorious hogger of covers and I'd simply followed them over there. She rolled toward me and nuzzled my neck for a few minutes, and I thought it would be a lovely way to begin the morning if I started something, but she whispered that she had to go to work. She got up, put on the coffee, and disappeared into the bathroom. I lay there a while and listened to the sounds of John Lanigan, John Webster, and Jimmy Malone do the zany "Knuckleheads in the News" shtick they do every Thursday on WMJI-FM. This morning they were recounting the sorry tale of a bank bandit who'd called first and alerted the bank that he was planning a robbery. I stayed in bed and chuckled until the coffee was ready.

I went home to shower and change before going to the office myself.

"Going to the office" is something fairly new for me. For years I'd run my business out of my apartment in Cleveland Heights where Cedar Road and Fairmount Boulevard come together to form a triangle. The building is right across from Russo's Stop-'n'-Shop and the Mad Greek Restaurant at the top of Cedar Hill, which, I'm told, is the first official foothill of the Alleghenies. My line is private investigations and industrial security, and I call my business Milan Security. I gave it my first name because I figured damn few people are able to work their tongues around my Slovenian last one: Jacovich, with the *J* pronounced like a *Y*. For that matter, not too many people get my first name right. It's MY-lan—long *i*, with the accent on the first syllable.

However clients might mangle my name, working at home had been damn convenient. My desk was twenty-six feet from my bed, I didn't have to get dressed up every day, and unless I had to actually go somewhere, I didn't worry about traffic or the weather or where I was going to eat lunch. But last summer all that changed.

My aunt, Branka Jacovich, widow of my father's brother Anton and the only relative to whom I was at all close, had died at the age of eighty-two and left her entire estate, consisting of a small savings account, some insurance, and a little three-bedroom house in Euclid just off Lake Shore Boulevard where she'd lived for sixty years, to her two surviving children and to me.

At the urging and with the assistance of my old high school chum Rudy Dolsak, who was now senior vice president of the Ohio Mercantile Trust and was always after me to do something better with my money than simply sticking it into his vault, I had used my share of the inheritance to purchase an old building down on Scranton Road in the belly of the Flats, about a mile away from the restaurants and nightclubs that draw hordes of young drinkers and dancers even on the coldest of nights. It was on the bank of that peculiar and difficult-to-navigate kink in the Cuyahoga River known as Collision Bend, because of the many shipwrecks that had occurred there in the nineteenth century. They've since rerouted the river, but Collision Bend is still a navigator's nightmare, and it still requires some skillful ship handling to avoid aquatic fender benders.

Once a warehouse serving Cleveland's booming iron ore industry, my building had been converted to office space in the seventies and had languished half empty ever since. With Tetka Branka's bequest, I'd taken it over and spruced it up a bit, and I now occupied one of two sprawling office suites on the second floor. A bank of floor-to-ceiling windows afford an absolutely splendid view of the busy water traffic and the handsome skyline of downtown Cleveland beyond, dominated by the proud facade of the Tower City shopping center and office complex right across the river.

People who haven't been to Cleveland for thirty years would be surprised by the Flats. Once a barren, weed-choked riverbank, it became a shipping mecca when the steel industry was in full throttle, then reverted to a rusty collection of derelict warehouses. It wasn't until the early nineteen-eighties that someone got the bright idea to turn it into the fun-and-frolic center of northeast Ohio. Restaurants, bars and nightclubs sprang up first on the east bank of the Cuyahoga, later on the west. Even the venerable Fagan's, which used to be the only place to eat on the east bank of the Flats, turned trendy, catering to the young hip crowd. In the old days, if Fagan's didn't have a seat for you they'd find one, even if it was behind the bar or in a telephone booth. Now the Generation X-ers, the ones who wear their baseball caps with the bill pointed toward the back, stand in long summertime lines to get in.

Collision Bend, though, is about a mile upriver and hasn't been invaded yet by the hip-slick-and-cool crowd. You can still taste the river and the rust on your tongue, still feel the ground vibrate beneath you with the pulse of the nearby steel mills, still hear the raucous caw of the gulls and experience in your viscera the ponderous passage of the great ore boats on the river outside your window.

The entire first floor of my building is occupied by a long-time tenant, a company that sells and installs ornamental iron doors and railings. My second-floor tenant is a surgical appliance and supply house. The rent I charge them both more than covers the mortgage payments, and of course I was financially better off than when I worked at home.

But now that I had a legitimate office and plenty of space, Rudy Dolsak and another pal, Ed Stahl, the Cleveland *Plain Dealer*'s gadfly columnist, had prevailed upon me to take a quantum leap into the late twentieth century and purchase and install a complicated computer I can barely operate. I have not, however, gone on-line so I can meet people and make new friends on the Internet, get e-mail, and get myself hooked on the electronic bulletin boards that have proved so addictive to so many people. I do, after all, have a life.

I also beefed up my business inventory with a plethora of security cameras, listening devices, concealed microphones, electronic bugs, and other arcane paraphernalia of the security trade. I can take photographs around corners. I can practically listen in on what's going on clear across the river. And to record conversations held in my office, just in case I ever have to prove who said what when, I'd let a smooth-talking salesman sell me a recording system I can activate by kicking a little switch under my desk, something I'd had no occasion to use and rarely even thought about. Suddenly I'm high tech.

Me, a guy who has to have his teenage son program his VCR. And although I've kept my answering machine in my apartment, at my business I now even have voice mail, a term that always seems to me to be an oxymoron.

I unlocked the wrought iron security gate my first-floor tenant had installed for me as a suck-up welcoming gift when I bought the building. Then I opened the big, heavy oak door, which has done yeoman service for at least fifty years and creaks like the door of a medieval keep, and went up the stairs to my office.

On sunny days I rarely turn the lights on in there until late afternoon because of the bank of windows, but this morning the weather prognosticators had been right and the sky was partly cloudy—more than partly, if the truth were known. It was that ominous gunmetal gray that Clevelanders grow used to in the wintertime. So I snapped on a little faux Tiffany lamp Nicole had bought me, to make it more cheery.

A bank of white steel filing cabinets that I'd bought used stand against one wall, and in one corner is a storeroom, to which I'd added a steel security door, where I keep most of my sophisticated snooping equipment. I even have my own private john with a shower. Against the far wall is a den-size little refrigerator designed to look like an old-fashioned Wells Fargo safe, and it amuses me to think that if burglars ever did manage to get through all the security, they'd think they'd really scored—until they opened and found, instead of cash or negotiable securities, two six-packs of Stroh's beer in bottles, a half-empty jar of Stadium mustard, and several cans of Diet Pepsi.

Nicole and I had spent several pleasant weekends combing antique stores to find the two oil paintings I'd hung on the wall. One was of a bucolic rural landscape that looked a lot like south central Ohio farmland, and the other a Depression-era painting of a location not far from where I sat, showing the Terminal Tower as seen through the billowing smokestacks of LTV Steel.

I hung my coat and scarf in the closet and made myself a pot of coffee. At home I have an old-fashioned Mr. Coffee brewer, but Nicole had bought me a space-age-looking Braun for the office, and even the way it hissed and burped and bubbled as it brewed sounded vaguely European to me, and ever so sophisticated. I was not only high tech, but getting high class as well.

My morning was spent devising a grid for a motion-sensitive security system for a company out in Solon that manufactures plumbing fixtures—and save the jokes, because I heard them all from Ed and Rudy and some of my other buddies when I'd first accepted the assignment. Consistent with human nature, they'd waited until there had been several break-ins at the factory before they decided they needed some protection. I had the floor plans of their plant and offices, and since the very first thing the president of the firm did was moan about the cost, the trick for me was to place as few devices as possible where they would be most efficient, so that a mouse couldn't make it across the office floor without alerting the police. It might sound comical, but I've been around long enough to know that people will steal anything, even toilet bowls.

At a few minutes before twelve my stomach started to growl. All my life I've been a three-meals-a-day man; when you're as big as I am—around six three and two hundred twenty pounds at my best weight, which is about eight pounds less than what I currently weigh—you need a lot of fuel to keep that engine running. But I'd skipped breakfast that morning, something I did often since I'd been staying so many nights at Nicole's house, so I activated my voice mail and walked downstairs and over to Jim's Steak House on the corner of Scranton and Carter at the western end of the Eagle Avenue Bridge.

Jim's is a Cleveland fixture, having occupied its strategic

site on Collision Bend for so long, I can't remember a time when it hadn't been there. In the summertime you can eat on an outdoor patio, and all year long the dining room offers a stunning view across the river. But it's basically the same one I see from my office windows, so when I eat lunch there I prefer having a steak sandwich and a beer at the bar of the cozy, masculine lounge, where there's always a conversation to be struck up with the bartender or one of the customers. It's the kind of place where you get into heated discussions about sports and politics with strangers.

I'd just swung my leg over the barstool and was ready to order when the Channel 12 noon news came on. I was startled to see Vivian Truscott sitting beside the regular daytime anchorman. I was surprised to see her even awake at noon, much less on the set; she usually does the news at six and eleven o'-clock. Ordinarily the fashion plate of Cleveland television, today Truscott was wearing a severe black suit and simple makeup. She looked tight-lipped and tense.

"This is a difficult story to report," she was saying, and the quiver and strain in her voice were completely at odds with her usual cool, almost glacial professionalism. "But this morning our Channel Twelve colleague and my personal friend Virginia Carville was found dead in her home on Edgewater Drive on the west side of Cleveland. The police believe . . ."

Her voice broke, and she shook her head and put her face in her hands. "Damn!" she said.

Her coanchor leaned over and patted her arm, then turned to the camera. "This isn't easy," he said. "Virginia was a good friend to all of us. The police are saying there was foul play."

And suddenly I wasn't hungry anymore.

✢ ✢ ✢ ✢ ✢ ✢ ✢

CHAPTER TWO

✢ ✢ ✢ ✢ ✢ ✢ ✢

Y ou wouldn't expect a Cleveland bar to take its name from a James Joyce novel, but there Nighttown is, about two blocks from my apartment, right at the top of Cedar Hill in what is actually Cleveland Heights. I don't know all the customers there the way I do in Vuk's Tavern down on St. Clair Avenue, where I had my first legal drink on my twenty-first birthday; Nighttown isn't that kind of a bar. The TV set down at the end of the room is small, and the volume is kept low so it doesn't intrude on conversation or on the live jazz they feature on selected evenings. Nighttown is almost equidistant from my place and Ed Stahl's big sprawling house on Coventry Road, so occasionally we meet there for a drink, as we did on this cold February Friday.

Ed, with whom I frequently play penny-ante poker and attend ball games and who is a neverending source of inside Cleveland gossip, is the embodiment of the hard-bitten reporter and resident city-room curmudgeon; the measure of the man is that I'd been his friend for more than three years before I ever knew he'd won a Pulitzer Prize—and I found out from somebody else.

"Why would I mention it?" Ed said when I'd questioned him about it. "It was years ago, for God's sake!"

Ed constantly smokes a foul-smelling pipe, and his habitual expression is a cynical scowl that tells you he's heard everything and believes only a small fraction of it. He sports horn-rimmed glasses that make him look like Clark Kent at the end of a wasted life, and on all but the hottest days of summer he wears one of his collection of disreputable tweed suits with one of his two ugly ties.

The TV set was tuned to the Channel 12 six o'clock newscast, and of course the lead story was the murder of Virginia Carville. We stared at the screen morosely, and while I drank my Stroh's, Ed sipped his Jim Beam-on-the-rocks and made a sour face as it went down into his stomach and no doubt lit up his ulcer.

"They're killing reporters now," he said, turning his palms upward in supplication. He was trying to keep it light, but over his many years of tough, in-your-face newspaper work Ed has encountered more than his share of problems; a county commissioner once took a swing at him, he's received several death threats, and once a mob punk put a dead rat in his mailbox. The killing of a journalist was far from funny to him. Or to me.

"They have any leads?" I asked, sure that Ed had been one of the first journalists to talk to the police and had gotten more out of them than any other reporter in town. Some of his jealous colleagues believe the cachet of the Pulitzer is what makes the most important people talk to Ed more than to anyone else, but I know how Ed can wheedle, cajole, and if necessary, bully even the toughest cop, the most autocratic city official, the haughtiest industrialist or corporate attorney until he gets the information he wants.

He shook his head. "They found her in her bed, strangled with a pair of her own pantyhose. And they think she might have been raped. At least, there were signs of recent sexual activity." He cleared his throat and shifted around on his barstool.

"Did you know her well?"

"I knew her," he said. "Naturally. This is too tight a community for any of the press not to know all the rest. She started out as kind of a Twinkie, but she worked and learned, and in the past few years she finally convinced those clowns at Channel Twelve to let her do some of the hard stuff. She handled it like a champ. And she was good. She knew how to ask the hard question. I had respect for her."

I was somewhat surprised. Ed normally shared the opinion of most print journalists, and voiced it loudly and often that television reporters of either gender were strictly cosmetic, hired for their bone structure and hairstyles rather than for their journalistic skills.

"She was a local girl," he said. "Her parents live in Bainbridge Township."

"And she went to Kent. I knew her just to say hello to, through Mary." That was Mary Soderberg, the top sales executive at Channel 12, whom I'd loved and lost several years earlier.

We sat quietly for a while, not speaking. Sadly, we've all grown inured to sudden and violent death, and what that says about us as a society I don't even want to think about. But when the victim is someone you know, even slightly, the ugly fact of murder hits you low and hard.

After a while Ed said, "We don't teach respect anymore. I'm not sure half the population even knows what the word means. Nobody has respect for anything, not even human life. You kill somebody for the clothes they're wearing, for 'dissing' you, for crossing the street onto your territory—a patch of broken sidewalk you don't even own . . ."

"Ginger Carville's murder doesn't exactly sound gang related, Ed."

"It's the same principle, though. To take a human life like that . . . ah Jesus, I don't know anymore, Milan. Am I just getting old?"

"You are," I said. "But I understand what you're saying. When I grew up, we operated under the reasonable assumption that we weren't all potential victims, that rape and murder and armed robbery and carjackings were things that happen to the other guy."

"Now we are the other guys." The thought made him morose.

"Not if we're careful."

"You suppose Carville wasn't careful, a good-looking woman who was on television every night? You suppose she was listed in the phone book, that she left her doors unlocked and got undressed in front of an open window?"

"You're assuming she was killed by a stranger."

"You think she wasn't?"

"I don't think anything. I don't have enough information." I signaled the manager, a genial Irishman who sometimes fills in behind the bar, for another beer. "But most homicides are committed by people known to the victim."

"Maybe it was a boyfriend," he mused. "Or an ex-boyfriend—one she jilted."

"Could be. Thank God it's a police problem and not mine."

I usually know better than to be so stupidly optimistic.

Nicole had some sort of lecture to attend at Notre Dame College of Ohio that night. By tacit agreement I don't accompany her to things like that and she doesn't go with me to football games. So I went home and threw a couple of chicken breasts slathered with mustard, tarragon, and some honey into the oven along with a baking potato. I cracked open a beer and settled myself comfortably in front of a TV table in my den with a well-thumbed copy of *The Great Gatsby*. It's my favorite novel, and I reread it every five years or so because the older I get, the more I get out of it.

After I finished eating I turned on the TV to watch the last quarter of the Cavaliers pounding the Los Angeles Clippers, then switched over to Channel 12 for the late news. They all still seemed pretty shook up as they reported on the ongoing investigation of Ginger Carville's murder. There was a sort of thumbnail memorial tribute, a calculated tearjerker, I thought, with childhood photographs and videotapes of her and her family, and archive stuff from her earliest days at the station right up to her appearance Thursday night just a few hours before she died.

She'd been a gawky, appealing little girl without being at all pretty, and on the family videos her parents beamed at her proudly as she did cartwheels in the back yard and squealed at being squirted with a garden hose by some unidentified little boy. It all seemed very normal and ordinary, and it hit me all the harder that she was dead, and how she got that way, and when I looked at the vintage images of her family, her business-executive father and plain, pleasant mother, my heart hurt for what they must be feeling now.

The Channel 12 news staff, especially Vivian Truscott, was uniformly somber, speaking in hushed tones. Vivian, whose usual on-camera demeanor was so relaxed and professional, had been Ginger Carville's mentor and supporter, and you could tell how shaken she was. The silly, self-serving banter between the anchors and the weather lady was missing. No "happy news" tonight.

I was sure their grief was sincere and genuine, but I knew there was something else at work here. Sudden and inexplicable violence had struck too close to home, and Carville's friends and colleagues all at once realized that they too were the "other guys" bad things happen to. The tragic Oklahoma City bombing had been a wake-up call to all Americans that we aren't as safe and secure in our little lives as we'd thought; Ginger Carville's murder had hammered that point home even harder in Cleveland.

Her body had been discovered at ten thirty Friday morning, and mention of the murder first appeared in print in the Saturday *Plain Dealer*. Now, of course, all of Cleveland was abuzz with it. It's a big city, two and a half million strong if you include the whole metropolitan area, but in some ways it's a very small town—lots of people know lots of other people—and the death of such a visible citizen as Virginia Carville was bound to send shock waves all across the viewing area, from Avon Lake east through Hunting Valley.

Virtually everyone was affected. Rudy Dolsak called to ask me if I'd known her personally. My next-door neighbor, a sprightly eighty-six-year-old, accosted me as I stepped out of my apartment door in my bathrobe. Mr. Maltz, who insisted on staying in his Cleveland Heights apartment by himself despite the protestations of his married daughter who lived in Beachwood, pointed an outraged finger at the headline in the morning paper as I picked it up. What a terrible thing it was, he said, a beautiful young girl like that. When I went across the street to Russo's to buy a bottle of wine for dinner, I heard two different sets of people lamenting in the checkout line that if something like that could happen to a celebrity like Virginia Carville, none of us were safe in our own homes.

That was the key, of course. Everyone in town felt as if they knew her because she was in their living rooms and bedrooms on an almost daily basis. The ugly fact of senseless murder had now become personal, and as a result very terrifying indeed.

Even my older son, Milan Jr., now seventeen and starting to be aware of things besides girls and football, called me just before heading out to the Euclid Mall to engage in the mandatory Saturday ritual of hanging around with his buddies and vying for the attention of the teenage girls, to ask me if I'd ever met the victim. I told him yes but I didn't know anything about what had happened and sternly expressed the hope that he wouldn't discuss it with his younger brother Stephen; eleven-year-old kids should be worrying about soccer practice or long division or snowball fights, not murder.

Nevertheless, Greater Clevelanders of all ages were talking about Virginia Carville.

Even Nicole.

Saturday evening we were sitting side by side on my new living-room sofa, listening to a terrific new Shirley Horn CD, our plates of veal and wild rice before us on the coffee table.

I've turned into a not-too-bad cook since I redid the apartment and started entertaining a little more. Nothing fancy, but respectable.

"I can't believe it," Nicole said. "She was on TV Thursday night, Milan. She was so vital, so pretty." She shook her head sadly. "She didn't know she only had a few hours left to live."

"Not many of us know the exact hour we're going to check out. Death is almost always a surprise."

"You must have known her."

"I met her a few times," I said. "Several years ago. I can't ever remember our saying much to each other beyond a casual hi."

"Does it make you feel sorry you never got to know her, Milan? Now that she's dead?"

"People die every day that I never got to know."

She took a sip of the merlot I'd bought that afternoon. "I'm sorry, it was a dumb question."

"No it wasn't. When something like this happens to someone we know or have seen regularly on TV or in the movies, we don't quite know how to deal with it, because it seems suddenly personal. So we cope any way we can."

"I hope they get him," she said fervently, waving her wineglass in front of her. "The killer. I hope they hang him on a meat hook." She sat back against the sofa cushions. "I went to school for eight years because the practice of medicine is life-affirming, and I wanted to be a part of that. I bust my ass all day long trying to keep little premature babies alive. Some of them weigh less than two pounds. Some of them become addicted to crack while they're still in the womb. Every time I save one of them, give one a chance to grow up strong and healthy, it's a victory. So when some sicko takes a life needlessly like that . . ." She smiled at me, but there was sadness and pain behind it. "It pisses me off."

"It pisses me off too," I told her. "But they'll get whoever did it."

"Sure. Like they got the Mad Butcher of Kingsbury Run," she scoffed, referring to our most famous unsolved mass murders, the case that back in the thirties cost Cleveland's safety director, the "untouchable" Eliot Ness, a future political career.

"We've got a good police department now. I know—I used to be part of it. And probably Marko's on the case."

I was speaking of my oldest friend, Marko Meglich. We've been almost like brothers since grammar school. Now he's the number-two man in the CPD's homicide division, a lieutenant, and while his gold badge relieves him of having to pound the pavement anymore, Virginia Carville's killing, which happened within Cleveland city limits, would certainly find its way to his desk. And he would probably take a personal interest in such a high-profile case. Marko, in recent years, has become more politician than policeman.

"Marko, the cradle-snatcher!" Nicole snorted, rolling her eyes. She doesn't like him very much and only tolerates him on rare occasions for my sake. He and I had gotten divorced within a year of each other, and while I'd led a relatively quiet social life since then, Marko had made the wooing and winning of a long series of inappropriately young women his second career.

"It doesn't mean he isn't a good cop."

She sipped her wine silently, sort of grudgingly conceding the point. "You think the killer was someone she knew?" she asked after a few moments.

"That's the way most homicides go, yeah."

She shuddered. "That's something to think about in the middle of a dark and lonely night."

"Don't go getting suspicious about your next-door neighbor, now."

"My next-door neighbor is an elderly lady with four cats and a rose garden," she reminded me.

"Look out for her when she's got those pruning shears in her hand."

"And your neighbor is Mr. Maltz."

"A real suspicious character. So I guess we have real reason to worry. Look, could we talk about something else? When I have the most beautiful woman in Ohio sitting on my sofa and drinking my wine, murder isn't exactly my topic of choice."

"What do you want to talk about, then?"

"I don't know," I said. "How's the veal?"

She patted her lips with her napkin. "It's delicious, but you're not supposed to ask, you're supposed to wait for me to say so. Ever since you learned how to cook you've gotten to be a real pain in the ass, you know that, Milan?"

"Does that mean you're staying for breakfast?"

"Depends."

"On?"

Her eyes did their mischievous little dance that always makes me crazy. "On whether I'm too worn out to go home."

Breakfast, such as it was, consisted of coffee, juice for Nicole, and two bagels each. She took hers with strawberry jam, but I'm more traditional and less health-conscious, so I spread mine with cream cheese, much against her better judgment. I don't worry about my cholesterol. They keep changing their minds about what's good for you and what's not. For years they told us that eating pasta was healthy; now it's a dietary no-no. Then they came out with a warning that peanut butter wasn't good for you; if it were true, I'd probably have been dead fifteen years ago. I can't keep track of what's healthy and what's not anymore; therefore I just ignore it all and hope that the cholesterol cops who mind everyone else's business for them won't make a citizen's arrest in broad daylight when I'm having a klobasa sandwich from a vendor's wagon on Public Square.

Nicole went home at eleven and I drove over to my ex-wife's house to pick up my sons for the day. Lila and her live-in consort, Joe Bradac, were at mass, probably to confess their unmarried state and absolve it with a couple of Hail Marys and Our Fathers, so we were saved the ordeal of talking to each other, and Joe was spared having to hide in the upstairs bedroom as he usually does when I come over. For a change a visit to my former home was easy.

After some discussion it was decided that we'd take in a movie. Do you know how hard it is to get two boys, one eleven and one seventeen, to agree on a movie that won't send their parent screaming into the parking lot for a cigarette? Sylvester Stallone, who wound up entertaining us that afternoon, is no Spencer Tracy, but his films are usually watchable. Afterward we drove down the hill on Mayfield Road to Mama Santo's in Little Italy for pizza and Cokes. I was grateful there was no table talk of Virginia Carville.

Stephen was full of bubbly conversation about the Cavs and how high he'd scored on some bloodthirsty interactive video game at the mall, and Milan Jr., just four months away from his high school graduation, was concerned about college. His mother wanted him to go to Cleveland State, so he could live at home. I preferred Kent State, less than an hour's drive from Cleveland, where I'd spent five wonderful years and where my elder son had a shot at making the freshman football team. Just one more issue over which I would lock horns with Lila, who thought football was a sublimation of the male of the species' worst instincts.

All pretty normal, mainstream American, I thought. I didn't know that starting the next day, things weren't going to be normal at all.

The boys slept over, as they usually do on the alternate Sundays when I have them, and I dropped them off at their respective schools on my way to the office, thinking that working away from my apartment was kind of pleasant at that, mainly because I didn't have to clean up the detritus of the boys' visit right away in case a client walked in. Besides, I was finding that going to a real live office with my name on the door made me feel just a little more legitimate.

The morning was a bright sunny one, rare for an Ohio February, and teeth-aching cold. Outside the windows, sunlight danced on the surface of the river. I fired up the computer, and was preparing the formal presentation for the plumbing fixture plant's security system, when someone walked in the office door.

It would have been a surprise in any case, because my business is not the walk-in kind and I wasn't expecting a visitor. The sight of this visitor made me feel as if I was on an elevator that had suddenly separated from its cable and was plummeting a hundred stories.

"Hi, Milan," Mary Soderberg said.

CHAPTER THREE

Coping with loneliness is something you learn how to do when you've been alone for a while; you don't ever really accept it, but you get to where you can manage it on a daily basis. Still, there are times when seemingly without any reason at all, without any incident to trigger the memories, you miss a specific person so badly that everything inside you begins to hurt, like the pain of a malignancy spreading outward from the heart.

I'd had a lot of those times after Mary left me. Every once in a while I still had one.

I scrambled to my feet, feeling like an oaf, the chair legs noisily scraping against the hardwood floor. I was all at once aware that my big, aging, football player's body was thick and awkward and ungainly, and I automatically sucked in my stomach and tried to stand up straight and tall.

"Hello, Mary," I said. I'd seen her once in almost three years, about two years after we'd parted company, when I caught a glimpse of her from clear across the Ohio Theatre at the Great Lakes Theatre Festival's production of *The School for Wives.* I don't know if she saw me or not; we'd both been with other people, and saying hello and making introductions would have been awkward in any case. The sight of her, however, had seriously affected my enjoyment of what otherwise would have been a pleasant evening. Seeing her now standing there five feet away was seriously affecting my Monday morning.

She looked beautiful, as always, even though on this particular morning she seemed tense and tired, and there were dark smudges beneath her eyes that I knew meant she hadn't been sleeping well.

Her gaze swept the room. "I like your new office. Great view," she said, unbelting her leather coat and shrugging it off. She put it on one of the client chairs. "It suits you."

"It's good to see you, Mary. Please, sit down." I came around the side of the desk and unnecessarily held the other chair for her, feeling foolishly chivalrous. She sort of glided into it and gracefully crossed her long legs to the soft accompaniment of a nylon whisper. Her perfume was still dizzyingly familiar.

"I was sorry to hear about Auntie Branka," she said, looking up at me. "I know how much you loved her."

I nodded sadly, remembering the vibrant, skinny old woman in widow's weeds, her blue-eyed gaze fierce as an eagle's. "She was the last of the Mohicans. The last of my real family. Now it's just me and the boys."

"Does that scare you?"

"Sure. There aren't many people you can count on unconditionally. It's hard to lose one."

Her eyes got stony for as long as it takes a seabird's shadow to cross the sun, and she examined a red fingernail.

"It's been a while, hasn't it?" I said, sitting back down in my own chair, regretting my banality. Why can't people really talk in brittle, crisp witticisms the way Carole Lombard and William Powell and David Niven used to in the movies? "How've you been?"

"All right."

"Just all right?"

She shrugged. "All right's better than most people can claim, I guess."

"You look great."

She lowered her eyes demurely. "So do you. You've lost a little weight."

"And a little more hair," I said. The Slovenian curse.

"How are the boys?"

"They're good. Milan Jr.'s graduating in June."

"Wow. He was just a little guy when I met him. And Stephen?"

I indicated his approximate height.

"I probably wouldn't recognize him." She sighed. "Time has a way of tumbling by, doesn't it?" She glanced away, out the window.

"Mary," I said gently, "you didn't come here to ask about the boys."

She chewed some of the lipstick from her bottom lip. She always did that when she was nervous. I remember her doing it in a hospital room several years earlier when I was recovering from a concussion and she was about to tell me she was dumping me for someone else.

"No," she said. "No, of course I didn't." She was having trouble getting the words out, doling them out stingily like a small child who'd been forced to share her small stash of M&M's with all the other kids.

I waited.

She laughed suddenly, too loud. "I don't know where to start."

"Just start," I said, and waited a long while for her to do so.

Rubbing the side of her index finger with her thumb, she said, "You've heard about Ginger Carville?"

"Of course. I was really shocked. Everybody was. I'm sorry."

She took a deep breath. "This is very hard, Milan . . ."

"It shouldn't be," I urged. "We're old friends, Mary."

"Is that what we are?"

I leaned back in my chair and didn't answer.

"I'm not the one," she said. "Who needs help."

Taking up a pencil from the old Cleveland Indians mug on my desk—now that I had an office I'd gotten an electric pencil sharpener, and I keep my pencils sharp as stilettos—I began doodling on a yellow pad. It was my usual doodle that I've been doing since I was in middle school—an empty gallows. Don't ask me why; it's something buried deep in my psyche. "Who, then?"

"Milan, the police spent the whole weekend questioning Steve."

The point of my pencil broke, and I put it down, embarrassed. "Steve Cirini?"

She nodded.

"Why?"

She looked down. "He knew her. Ginger. From Channel Twelve."

"Two hundred people who work at Channel Twelve knew her. Why are they questioning him?"

"He'd been—seeing her," she mumbled.

"Seeing her?"

Her head snapped up. Her face was flushed, her eyes wet and angry. "Fucking her! Did you want to hear me say it, Milan?"

The ugly word was like the snap of a bullwhip in the quiet room. "No. I didn't want to hear you say it." I tried to take a deep breath, but the large stone building sitting on my chest made it difficult. "So you and Steve aren't . . . together anymore?"

She fumbled in her purse for a tissue. "Yes, we're still together. I guess."

Irretrievable seconds of our lives ticked by in roaring silence. Finally I said, "I still don't understand why you're here, Mary."

She dabbed at her nose with the tissue. "Steve needs a private investigator."

"Why?"

"His attorney said that right now he's the only logical suspect, but that the heat would be off him considerably if there was another one. And he suggested hiring an investigator to find one."

I picked up the pencil again, just to have something to hold in my hands while I asked the next question. The hard question. "How can you be sure he didn't kill her?"

"Because you can't be close to someone for three years without getting to know him," she said sharply. "And Steve simply isn't capable of . . . that."

"Everybody's capable of 'that' when they're cornered."

She shook her head. "Not Steve."

"But he's capable of cheating on you."

She drew a ragged, shuddering breath. "It's hardly the same thing, though, is it?"

"There are people who would think so," I said. "Is he in custody?"

"No. They questioned him on Friday and again on Saturday, but they let him go home both times."

"That's a good sign," I said. "It means they don't have enough for an arrest warrant." I took a new pencil and began making notes. "Who questioned him? What were the cops' names?"

She shook her head helplessly.

"If Steve is still walking around free, why didn't he come here himself?"

She uncrossed her legs and recrossed them. I tried not to let it distract me. "He thought you might not want to talk to him."

"Talk to him?" I tried to laugh but it came out more like a dry cough. "I would've thrown him down the stairs."

She blinked. "Even after all this time?"

"Twenty years from now, if I'm still alive."

"I forgot who I was talking to for a minute there."

"That's a mistake," I said. "Mary, I'm sorry you're in the middle of this, but I'm the wrong guy for you to come to. Business has been pretty good since I moved down here, and I've got a full plate already. And I'm sorry, but I'm not one for picking at old scabs. I don't want the best part of Steve Cirini. I can recommend somebody else if—"

"I'm not interested in somebody else." Her look bored into me like a laser. "Mark Meglich has the case. You and he are friends. He'd listen to you."

"I can't do this," I said, putting the pencil down. "It'd be too hard on both of us."

"Please? Don't make me beg, Milan. I hate it."

"Why is it so important to you?" I said, trying without much success to keep the nasty edge from my voice. "The guy's been seeing another woman behind your back."

She stood up abruptly. "You haven't mellowed a bit, have you?" she said, and the edge in her own voice could have cut steel. "You're still the same rigid, moralistic, judgmental son of a bitch you always were!"

I had to agree with her. "Some things don't change."

"I didn't think they had," she said, more quietly. "I suppose that's why I trust you."

"Trust is overrated. I trusted you, once. It didn't work out so well."

She jerked back as if I'd slapped her. "That's a little cold. An elephant never forgets, is that it?" she said.

"Elephants don't have a hell of a lot to remember."

Her mouth tightened into an unattractive slash, and she went to the window to watch the gulls swooping low over the water, looking for breakfast. "Would it mean anything if I said I was sorry?"

"That's really nice of you, Mary, but sorry just doesn't cut it."

"Does money cut it then?" She turned to face me, backlit by the morning sky, the light creating an aura around her blond hair. "I'm offering you a legitimate job. Nobody's asking you to work for nothing."

"I can't take your money."

"It's not my money, it's Steve's. He's willing to pay you whatever you want."

"Strictly business, huh?"

She lifted her chin and squared her shoulders, and I could almost see the strength flowing through her. She was having a rough time of it, but she'd pull through, she'd persevere. You don't make a living selling TV advertising in this town if you aren't tougher than hell. "Strictly business."

"One of the nice things about being my own boss," I said, "is that I get to pick who I work for. And I don't want to work for Steve Cirini."

The starch seemed to go out of her again, and she leaned back against the windowsill as though she'd crumple onto the floor if she didn't. "Then for God's sake," she whispered, "do it for me."

"All right," I said, and the suddenness of it surprised her, I think. I didn't like myself very much when I realized that's what I'd been waiting to hear.

Lieutenant Mark Meglich was putting on weight. The custom-tailored three-piece suits he'd taken to wearing ever since his divorce were starting to look a little tight across the middle, and his thick, football player's neck now tended to bulge out of the collars of his expensive shirts.

It was all those good restaurant dinners. Marko only goes to the best places, like Johnny's Bar, Johnny's Downtown, the Caxton Cafe, and Sammy's, in the Flats. He rarely stays with the same young woman more than a month, and while there's excitement in variety, one of the downsides of romancing a new love every few weeks is that you have to wine and dine 'em a lot. Thus the extra roll of flab at his middle and the Elizabethan ruff of suet around his collar as he sat behind his desk at the old rock pile that is the Third District police station on Payne Avenue and East Twenty-first Street.

We've been friends since we were ten years old.

Years ago the top police brass moved downtown to the new Justice Center, which always feels more like an office building than a police station to me. I much prefer Payne Avenue, where I worked when I wore the Cleveland PD uniform. They call it "the Old Central" now with a certain gritty affection, but once upon a time it had been known citywide as "the Roaring Third," because of the high incidence of crime within the district.

It's still a pretty rough neighborhood, but the lawlessness was more fun back in the old days—and better dressed, too. You got a classier variety of crooks then. Bootleggers, high-ticket hookers, gamblers, grifters, and members of the organized families from Collinwood and Murray Hill all came out on the town to strut their stuff in the downtown area. Now the Roaring Third doesn't roar anymore. The crime is mostly of the street variety—dark and violent and depressing in its hopelessness.

The brass nameplate on Marko's desk read LT. MARK MEGLICH; he'd decided the Americanized first name was more fitting for one of the city's top cops. He was in shirtsleeves and wearing the vest of his pearl-gray three-piece suit; the jacket was hung behind the door on a thick wooden hanger. He lit a cigarette, which made me want one. Since I started seeing Nicole I've been trying to cut down, because as a doctor she obviously disapproves of the habit. And I'd been doing pretty well, too, down from a pack and a half to about eight cigarettes a day. But seeing Mary Soderberg in my office had shaken me more deeply than I'd realized, and as the smoke wafted across Marko's desk toward me, I reached for his pack of Winstons and shook one out.

"You smoking OPs these days?" Marko said.

"I left mine at the office."

"Yeah, right. Let the lowly paid civil servant keep you in cigarettes." He rocked back in his chair. "So how the hell did you get involved with the Virginia Carville business?"

"I have a client who asked me to look into it."

"Well, look right out of it again. It's a homicide, Milan, and you know damn well it's against the law for a PI to investigate a capital crime." He gestured at the smoke-yellowed walls, the white acoustical ceiling tiles that had long ago gone gray, the faded and buckled linoleum on the floor, and his own scarred desk. "And the law happens to be what we sell in our cozy little store here. Who is this client, anyway?"

I pondered for a moment before answering, but then I figured what the hell, it's Marko, and if you can't level with your oldest friend, there's no one you can trust. "Steve Cirini."

He coughed out a jet of smoke. "You're kidding!"

"Alas, no."

"He's our number-one poster boy right now." He narrowed his eyes at me. "Isn't he the one that Mary . . ."

"He's the one."

"The son of a bitch stole your girl! What do you want to help him for?"

I understood why he was asking. Marko, like me, is a Slovenian, and Slavs don't easily forget a wrong. They're killing each other right now in Bosnia over tribal grievances hundreds of years old. "Because Mary asked me to."

He covered his face with his hand in disgust. "Give me a break," he said through his fingers.

"I know it'd be a lot easier for you if Cirini was your perp. Save your people some legwork. But I'm signed on anyway, and I'd be remiss if I didn't do everything I could to clear him."

"You want to know what I think? I think it sucks."

"I didn't come here to ask for your blessing, Marko." It irritates him when I call him Marko instead of Mark; I usually try to remember not to, but old habits die hard.

He took his hand away from his face, which was red and

angry. "No, you came here for confidential information that you're not supposed to have."

"Do I get it?"

"Why should you?"

"Because deep down underneath the politics and your precious clearance rate, you're a decent human being who wouldn't want an innocent man to take a murder rap."

He glared at me while he thought it over. After a while the anger turned to a childish pout. "Ask nice."

I sighed. "Who're you dating this week?"

"What's that got to do with—?"

"Just tell me."

He scowled. "Her name's Brittany," he said belligerently.

Brittany. Jesus. "If you don't play ball with me, I'll tell Brittany's parents she's sleeping with you and they'll ground her."

"Very funny!" he spat. "She happens to be twenty-four years old."

"Twenty-four. Think of that, Hedda! Why, she's the dowager empress."

"This is how you ask nice?"

"Come on, Marko, we've helped each other out in the past. It goes both ways. Cut me a little slack here."

Regarding me narrowly for a moment, he finally took a file out of his bottom drawer and laid it on the edge of the desk in front of me. CARVILLE, VIRGINIA was written on the tab in black felt-tipped pen.

"I'm going to the john," he said, stubbing out what was left of his cigarette and picking up the morning *Plain Dealer.* "And I'm taking a newspaper with me, so I'll be gone a while. Don't be here when I get back."

"Thanks, Mark," I said, gratitude making me call him by the name he prefers.

"For what? I said no, didn't I?"

He got up and went out, closing the door behind him, leaving me alone in his little cubicle of an office. On a steel filing cabinet behind him was a vintage coffeemaker and Marko's own porcelain mug with a replica of his gold shield baked onto it. Among such quirks as the vast wardrobe of custom suits, the walrus mustache that he erroneously believes makes him look like Tom Selleck, and the string of women barely of voting age is Marko's belief that drinking coffee out of cardboard or foam cups causes cancer, and so he mail-ordered his personalized mug for the office. Woe betide anyone who touches that mug. He even washes it out himself every morning at the basin in the men's room, surely an eccentricity for anyone as high-ranking as a lieutenant.

I opened the Carville file.

The crime scene photos were ugly, the stuff of which recurrent nightmares are born, lit by glaring, pitiless flashbulbs, with no texture or shadows to soften the horrible reality of violent death. She was on her bed, on top of the disheveled covers, wearing only an opaque white nightgown that had been pulled up around her waist. Her face was discolored, her eyes bulging, the pantyhose wrapped cruelly tight around her throat. She'd been photographed from every angle. I looked at the pictures only as long as I had to.

The body had been discovered at ten twenty-five Friday morning by one Andrew Lemmons, a staff news producer at Channel 12. Carville had been scheduled to arrive at the station on Euclid Avenue at seven that morning to go out on a shoot. When she didn't show up on time, Lemmons, with a full news crew on the clock and waiting, had called her house every fifteen minutes or so, a fact attested to by the messages he left on Carville's answering machine, the first at 7:18 and the last at 9:52. Concerned that something was wrong, Lemmons and the news crew had driven out to her house on Edgewater Drive, where they found the door unlocked and Virginia Carville dead in the upstairs bedroom. Andrew Lemmons had gone downstairs and called the police from the wall phone in the kitchen and then had thrown up in the sink.

There had been no sign of forced entry.

A pair of Virginia Carville's high-heeled shoes had been found halfway up the stairs as if she'd kicked them off hurriedly on her way up. Her coat, the one she'd worn to work the previous evening, was on the floor in the vestibule.

The large bath sheet hanging over the shower rod had been damp, as was the bottom of the shower curtain itself, which would seem to indicate that the victim had showered shortly before she died. The medicine cabinet held the usual array of cough syrup, Advil, birth control pills, makeup, and a partially used plastic bottle of Oil of Olay. There was a container of scented bath beads on the edge of the tub along with a pink razor. A pump-type dispenser of moisturizing cream was on the counter, and an empty Summer's Eve disposable douche container in the wastebasket.

The police had questioned her next-door neighbor, Rosemary Kelley, who said she had gone to bed right after *Seinfeld* and hadn't seen or heard a thing. Her name sounded vaguely familiar to me but I didn't know why. I jotted it down.

A pair of beige sheer-to-the-waist L'eggs pantyhose had been knotted around her neck, and asphyxiation was the cause of death. The victim's bowels had emptied at the time of death, which is not unusual in strangulation cases.

Marko Meglich has always been a details guy, and he had trained his people well. Beige sheer-to-the-waist L'eggs. I wondered if that was important, whether it would have made a difference if the pantyhose had been Sheer Energy or Hanes, white or black or blue with a reinforced crotch, or patterned with seams up the back.

The pantyhose were identified as belonging to the victim, as there were several similar pairs in one of the drawers and in the laundry hamper. A pubic hair found in the mesh had proved to be Virginia Carville's. Hair of a different color, both pubic and from someone's head, had also been found in the bed.

There was trauma to the back of the skull as well, caused by an unknown blunt instrument, although not severe enough to kill. The coroner's postmortem had established that the time of death was between three and five A.M. Friday morning.

There was semen present in the victim's vagina, indicating recent sexual activity; some had been sent to a laboratory in Washington for DNA typing, a process, as we all know from the O.J. Simpson trial, that could take months.

Several members of the production staff at Channel 12, when interviewed by the investigating officers, Detectives Richard Haake and Peggy Farmer, stated that it was rumored that the deceased had been involved in a sexual relationship with the national sales manager, one Steven Cirini, for some time.

Cirini had been questioned at length on two separate occasions—the second time his attorney had been present—and although he admitted being at the Carville home after midnight and having sexual relations with her, he claimed he'd left shortly after two A.M. and gone to his own home in Mayfield Village. He lived alone and had no alibi for the estimated time of death.

I made all the notes I needed to, closed the folder, and went out into the hallway. Just as I reached the stairs Marko emerged from the men's room, refolding that morning's sports section.

"You still here?" he said, mock gruff. Ever since he became a big shot in the police department he tends to snarl everything. I wondered if he did that with Brittany, and if so, how it sat with her.

"Just leaving."

"Milan?"

"Huh?"

"You were never here, all right?"

"I wish."

"If anybody gets wind of a leak out of this department, it's my ass."

"Your ass is safe with me."

"I'm not kidding," he warned. "I'm not going to sit here and watch you bust my own case under my nose and make me look like a fucking idiot. If you find out anything—*anything*—I want it."

"That's the whole point, isn't it?"

"Damn right it is. What's yours is mine."

"Friends forever."

"All of it."

"All for one and one for all. I'll bare my soul to you. Cross my heart."

He doubled a fist up under my chin. "Don't bullshit me, Milan."

"Mark, I don't need credit for a homicide bust; I'm self-employed. And I don't even like my name in the paper." I put my hand on his fist and gently pushed it away. "I'll rake the leaves a little bit and I'll give you whatever I turn up. The rest is up to you."

It seemed to mollify him, but not much. "I'd still like to see Cirini swing."

"You and me both," I said, irritated with myself by the truth of it. "But if wishes were diamonds, we'd be millionaires. If he didn't do it, he didn't do it."

"And if he did?"

If he did, I'll be glad, I thought but did not say. "If he did, I'll deliver him here myself, gift-wrapped."

"And Milan"—he poked a finger into my chest, a liberty I'd allow few others—"this is strictly between us, all right? Don't let my people trip over you when they're trying to do their jobs on this thing."

"I never do," I said.

Chapter Four

I got on Interstate 90 and headed east from downtown, eventually reaching the suburbs at the far eastern edge of Cuyahoga County. Mayfield Village lives up to its name—small and quaint, solidly high-end middle-class residential and picturesque, made slightly less so by the recent housing tracts that have sprung up along SOM Center Road. The initials stand for three of the many communities the long highway passes through—Solon, Orange, and Mentor—but I've always thought that someone could have gotten a little more creative and picked a prettier name for what is, for most of its length, a lovely drive. In any case, locally everyone refers to the thoroughfare as "Som."

Steve Cirini's home was just east of Som in one of the newer developments, a modernistic split-level with lots of wood and glass that looked very much like every other house on the street. It didn't look much like what one thinks of as a home in what used to be part of the Western Reserve of Connecticut. The trees, newly planted, wouldn't afford much shade in the summertime, and denuded in February, they seemed particularly skeletal and underfed. In another thirty years they'll be lovely, if anyone is inclined to hang around and wait.

A cardinal flashed brilliant red against the gray sky as it zoomed over Cirini's front yard and lit in one of the scrawny trees. Cardinals invariably brighten my outlook, and I suppose other people feel the same way, because the beautiful creature is Ohio's official state bird. I also found out somewhere that the blacksnake is our state snake, and tomato juice is the official state drink. Don't ask me why.

Steve Cirini must have been looking out the window; he answered the door almost as soon as I rang the bell. It had been a while since I'd seen him close up, but he hadn't changed much. He was still playboy handsome with black, curly hair he'd allowed to grow a little too long. His at-home clothes consisted of beige Dockers, Nike cross-trainers on sockless feet, and a Coogi sweater that looked as if an artist had dropped his entire palette of oil paints on it, and in which Cirini would have been visible five miles away in a dense fog. Looking at him, I tried to ignore the corrosive that bubbled up inside me, peeling away the lining of my stomach.

In the course of my work I often make people mad at me. But what was between Cirini and myself had nothing to do with business. He was my personal enemy, and we both knew it.

He gave me a curt nod that I couldn't quite read. "Milan. Thank you for coming." Neither of us made any attempt to shake hands. I noticed he had two fresh-looking red furrows running down his left cheek.

He led me into a living room the size of a small movie theater, where an expensive built-in sound system was playing muted Miles Davis, not the old great stuff that broke new ground and changed forever the sound of jazz but Davis's later, screw-the-listener self-indulgences, which I can't stand. A wide floor-to-ceiling window looked out on what someday would be a stand of oak and sugar maple, and the late afternoon light battling through the cloudy sky gave a bluish cast to the several-days-old snow.

It didn't much look like a bachelor's house; everything was orderly and in its place. Some people might call Cirini a neat-freak; others less inclined to kindness, like myself, would classify him as anal-retentive. Except for the morning paper on the floor beside the designer sofa, and a red-and-yellow Channel

12 mug sitting on its cork coaster precisely in the center of the glass coffee table, it looked as if no one besides the cleaning woman had been in the room in years.

Cirini sat down on the sofa and indicated a high-backed white chair obliquely across from him. He picked up a remote control, pointed it at the wall like a medieval wizard, and the music stopped in mid-note, leaving us sitting in an uncomfortable silence.

There is an almost primal edginess about two men who know they've slept with the same woman, and unlike male mountain goats, who can butt their horns together until one retires with a headache, the mutual animosity must be dealt with some other way—in our case with a masquerade of spiderweb-fragile civility.

It makes no difference if either of the men care for the woman anymore, and it doesn't even matter if there was little in the way of a relationship to begin with, which was certainly not the case with Mary and me. The testosterone tension is always there, tacit but palpable; it hung in the airy, pristine living room between Steve Cirini and me.

"Well," he said finally, crossing an ankle over his knee, feeling as awkward, I'm sure, as I did.

"I hear you've gotten yourself in a little trouble."

"*I* didn't get into any trouble—I didn't do anything wrong. The trouble just seemed to find me."

"Poor muffin," I said.

He flinched. "Look, Milan, whatever might have gone down between me and Ginger Carville, I didn't kill her."

"You sure?"

He tossed the remote control onto the coffee table with what for him must have been reckless abandon. "What the hell kind of question is that?"

"One I ask all my clients before I stick my professional neck out on their behalf."

He made a wry face. "You certainly say what you think, don't you?"

"I'd have thought Mary would've told you that."

"Mary told me a lot about you," he admitted. "She said mostly that you were a great guy."

"Being a great guy and fifty cents'll get you a condom from a vending machine." I pointed a finger at him. "A woman you've been sleeping with is murdered and you've got two fingernail scratches on your cheek. That probably doesn't sit too well with the police."

The hand that went self-consciously to his face seemed to have a life of its own; he pulled it away and looked at it as if it belonged to somebody else. "Actually, it was Mary who did that. Yesterday."

"When she found out you'd been screwing around on her?"

He crossed his arms across his chest like an Ed Sullivan impersonator, hunching his shoulders a little. The black curls crinkled against the collar of his sweater. I'm certain that most women, Mary Soderberg and Ginger Carville included, thought those curls irresistible. I just thought they made him look like a jerk who needed a haircut.

"Since I'm number-one on your shit parade," he said, "do you think you can do this job without prejudice?"

"No. Everyone has prejudices. Show me someone without any and I'll show you someone who doesn't have any taste."

He bristled at that, looking around the room defensively as if I'd insulted his taste in furniture. He obviously thought his home belonged in *House Beautiful.* Maybe it did—it just seemed bland and without character to me.

But then I'm prejudiced.

"So what's it going to be, Mr. Cirini?" I said. "Do I stay or do I go? It doesn't matter a damn to me either way. I don't need the money."

"Everybody needs the money."

"But not everybody's willing to compromise their principles to get it."

He considered it a while, his brow furrowed as if the very act of thinking hurt. Then his face relaxed, became open, almost friendly. This was the Steve Stunning I'd always known, the consummate salesman. "You stay. Please." The smile was disarming, little-boy helpless. "I'm kind of twisting in the wind here, Milan. I need you to cut me down."

"How?"

He put both feet on the floor and leaned forward. I noticed there were a few strands of gray in his black hair, but not too many. "Because of my relationship with Ginger Carville, the police seem to have elected me America's Most Wanted," he said.

"Understandable."

"And I know how cops are."

As an ex-cop it was my turn to bristle. "Oh? How are they?"

"Once they've decided they have a likely sucker, they zero in on him and don't look anywhere else." He looked sheepish. "At least that's how it is on television."

"Television," I said, and looked up at the beamed ceiling.

"So I want you to."

"To what?"

"Look somewhere else."

"Private investigators aren't allowed to investigate homicides."

"I know that," he said as though insulted that I thought he didn't. "But there's someone else who had motive and opportunity."

"Did you pick up motive and opportunity from television too?"

He ignored my sarcasm. "The police aren't bothering to look for anyone else, so maybe you can turn up someone likely. Take some of the heat off me. Anyone even suggesting I might have done something like that—well, it's hard on me. I'm so upset I can't even go to work, and when I don't work I don't make any money."

"Your grief is touching."

"Hey, I'm sick about what happened to Ginger," he protested, and flung his arms out wide as if I could see his distress better that way. "I wasn't in love with her or anything, but we were friends." He flushed deeply. "More than friends. And nobody I know has ever gotten murdered before, and it's preying on my mind, believe me. But my main concern now is that I didn't do it, and the police think I did. That's why I want you."

"Why me?"

"Because Mary trusts you."

"We only give guarantees on toasters."

He seemed to collapse inward, and all at once he looked very small and childishly vulnerable amongst the big poufy sofa cushions. "Well," he said haltingly, "do what you can, all right?"

"Fine. As long as we understand each other." I took two contracts from my inside pocket and handed them across the coffee table. I'd filled them out before I left the office. "Who's your attorney?"

"My attorney? Bob Nardoianni. Why?"

"Give this to him and have him sign it," I said.

"Why can't I just sign it myself?"

"For your own protection. If you hire me, I can't guarantee you confidentiality. If your lawyer does, the attorney-client privilege is extended to me."

He looked fuddled.

"Work with me, all right?"

He unfolded the contracts, read the top one carefully, and gulped a few times.

"Three thousand a week?"

"Plus expenses."

He shook his head. "Jesus, I'd hate to think what it'd cost me if you *did* need the money."

"There are cheaper investigators," I said, only slightly ashamed that I'd jacked up my price just for him.

"No, no. I want you."

"Then you can write me a check for the first week before I leave." I took out my notebook and a pen. "Now, talk to me."

"About what?"

"Tell me everything you know about Virginia Carville. How well you knew her. What sort of relationship you had. When you last saw her. Everything."

Put-upon, he settled even deeper into the cushions. "I met her when she started at the station," he said. "Seven years ago, maybe. She came on board as an intern from Kent State. She used to run around in baggy sweats, no makeup, washed her hair every two weeks whether it needed it or not. I didn't see much of her; she was usually down in the studio. She was production, I was sales, so we just kind of said hello in the hallway. But everybody liked her. They thought she was pleasant, efficient, and good at her job."

"Okay."

"I didn't really have much to do with her. I barely noticed her."

"How come?"

"She was a kid, looked like one and acted like one. Not my type."

I didn't say anything. I certainly didn't want to hear what his type was.

"Just about the time she graduated," he continued, "one of the newswriters left for greener pastures—Chicago, I think—and she got the job."

"Was she good at that too?"

"Must've been, because after about a year and a half Nicky made her a producer."

The Nicky in question was Channel 12's general manager, Nicky Scandalios, an aggressive, ambitious executive who was such a tireless self-promoter that he was almost as famous in Cleveland as his on-air talent.

"That's when she dropped the grunge look, got rid of some of the baby fat and started dressing like a grown woman."

"And that's when you noticed?" I said.

"No, not really. Well, yeah, I noticed, but . . . hell, I don't know. You don't take notes about your own life because you never think someday there might be a quiz."

"All right, go on."

"After about another year she talked Nicky into letting her do the graveyard talent shift. You know, the one-minute news-breaks every hour, all night long."

"Uh-huh," I said. I'm enough of an insomniac sometimes that I'm very familiar with the late night newsbreaks.

"Okay. So she did that for a while, maybe a year, and all of a sudden she's a field jockey."

"Also Nicky's call?"

"Everything that happens at that station has to be okayed by Nicky. Ray Aylmer, the news director, certainly had input too. But I think Vivian Truscott was the one who came up with the idea of making Ginger a field reporter."

"Vivian Truscott?"

"At the time Vivian and the weather Twinkie were the only on-camera females in the news department. Vivian thought there should be more. And Nicky's not immune to affirmative action pressure either. But Vivian's was the deciding vote. And I think she pushed Ginger because she didn't consider her competition."

"How was that?"

"Look at her. Vivian's gorgeous—and mature. Ginger was just kind of cute and wholesome-looking, so I guess Vivian fig-ured if there had to be another woman doing news on-camera, she could do a lot worse than Ginger. She went to bat for her and Nicky bought it."

"I wouldn't exactly describe Virginia Carville just as kind of cute and wholesome-looking," I said. "She was a very attractive woman."

"Sure, but not until after she started doing stand-ups and anchoring on the weekends. She got herself a makeover at some swanky salon in Rocky River and a whole lot of expensive, glamorous clothes from New York."

"How did Vivian Truscott feel about that?"

His face became a blank mask. "You'll have to ask Vivian."

"Don't you know?"

He put his hands together in front of him as if he were praying and then patted them together once in silent applause. "She and I aren't exactly pals."

"Oh?"

"No."

I waited for him to elaborate, pretty sure he would. He didn't disappoint me.

"I find it hard to be platonic buddies with beautiful women," he said.

"You mean you put the move on her, she wasn't interested, and it got messy?"

"It was years ago. Before she got married." His reluctant smile made him look like a baby with a gas pain, and he shook his head with grudging respect. "That was pretty perceptive. Mary said you were good."

"You might remember that if you ever decide to try and bullshit me. So at the end was there bad blood between Carville and Truscott?"

"I wouldn't exactly call it bad blood. They just weren't as close as they used to be."

I hadn't been writing much of this down because it was neither pertinent nor, frankly, very interesting. I settled back in my chair and put the cap back on the pen. "So when did you come into the picture? With Ginger, I mean?"

He scratched his chin. "Last spring, I guess. I'd been out at a sales meeting—a dinner meeting at the Caxton Cafe with a client. You know, the whole full-court press. It ended late. I stopped by the station to get something out of my office. I was leaving at about quarter of twelve, and so was she. We talked; it was a nice night so we went for a drink at the Theatrical."

"And?"

"And ba-da-bing!" He clamped his right bicep with his left hand and brought his fist up in the classic gesture.

"Just like that?"

"Pretty much, yeah."

"What made you decide after six or seven years that suddenly you had to go to bed with Ginger Carville?"

"I didn't *have* to," he said. "But the thought wasn't unappealing. And the first time it wasn't exactly my idea."

"She seduced you."

He looked at me as if I were too stupid for him to bother answering.

"And you obliged her out of a sense of chivalry."

"Hey, show me a guy who turns it down when a beautiful woman offers it, I'll show you a guy that walks a little light in his loafers."

"But you were seeing Mary then."

He smirked. "I thought you said this wasn't going to get personal."

"It's not. I'm trying to get the big picture. So you kept seeing Ginger?"

"Yeah. Yeah, sure, every so often." His smile grew more smarmy with fond remembrance. "Ginger Carville was some wild chick, take it from me."

"How often did you get together?"

"Two, three times a month. Sometimes more, sometimes less. It was no big deal to either of us."

"Just two healthy animals in heat, hmm?"

"Something like that. Listen, Milan, you're a single guy, you understand what I'm saying, right? She was seeing somebody else, I was seeing somebody else. What we had was strictly for grins."

I wasn't grinning.

"Tell me about the night she was killed."

His face hardened, his expression grew grim and sour. "I went over to her place about midnight."

"The Edgewater Drive house?" He nodded. "Where was Mary?"

"I don't see Mary every night."

"Okay."

"So I went over there."

"Was Ginger expecting you?"

"Sure. I talked to her during the day."

"At Channel Twelve?"

"No. Well, I was at the station, she was out shooting a story. We talked on the phone."

"You do that often?"

His hands flopped loosely at the ends of his wrists, which I interpreted to mean sometimes yes and sometimes no.

"And you arranged to come to her house after she finished the eleven o'clock news."

"Yeah."

"So?"

"So we got there right at the same time, met in the driveway. We went inside and right upstairs."

"And?"

"And what do you think? We did—what we do." He bit his lip. "Did."

"No small talk? No drinks? No how-was-your-day?"

"Hell, we didn't have time for that. This wasn't a boyfriend-girlfriend kind of thing. We both knew why we were there, and we didn't play games. It was always like that. Pure sex, nothing else."

"The American dream," I said with a tongue that felt as though someone had wrapped it in cotton batting.

"You got that right." He smiled a little, lost in erotic memory. "She had a terrific imagination. Sexual imagination, I mean," he elaborated, just in case I hadn't gotten the idea. "Sometimes we screwed in the car, once against the wall in the parking lot at the station. Sometimes she liked to do it with her clothes on. Well, not *all* her clothes, but . . ."

I was suddenly cognizant that my fingers were cramping around the pen from squeezing it so hard, and I made a conscious effort to relax my hand. I had no desire to hear about Virginia Carville's sexual proclivities; I certainly had no interest in Steve Cirini's. "Did you do it with her clothes on that night?"

He nodded again.

"In the bedroom?"

"Sure in the bedroom. I mean, we started fooling around on the way up, but eventually we got to the bedroom."

I couldn't resist. "With a sexy, kinky guy like you, you never know."

He stood up, suddenly all machismo and aggression, and took a step toward me. "Knock off the wiseass, all right, Jacovich? I don't like it."

"I don't care what you like," I said quietly. "Sit down, Mr. Cirini. I wouldn't need much of a reason to choke the shit out of you, so don't give me one."

His face went pale and he sat down quickly, bouncing on the sofa. He grimaced. "This isn't going to work," he said. "You and me, I mean. It was a mistake having Mary talk to you. I just don't see how you're going to help me if you hate my guts."

"I can't remember too many clients I've had that I liked. I told you you're not buying my friendship. And I'm not looking to win Miss Congeniality. But if you want, I'll tear up those contracts."

I reached for them, suiting the action to the word.

"No!" He leaned forward and put both hands down on the contracts, fingers outspread. There was something in the timbre of his voice now that hadn't been there before. The easy, brittle charm had been replaced by what sounded like pleading. "I'm scared, Milan. Really scared."

I liked that.

He was having difficulty talking. It might have just hit him at that moment that he was neck-deep in big trouble, and the fear was tightening his throat, giving his voice an almost desperate rasp. "I'm not the world's most wonderful human being, okay? And I didn't get to be a national sales manager at the top station in a major market by acting like Mother Teresa. But I didn't kill Ginger, I swear to God." He raised one hand, as if taking an oath.

"You better be leveling with me. If I find out you're guilty— if I find out you're trying to use me—I'll bring you down myself, and smile all the way home."

"Why would I kill Ginger Carville?" he whined. "I had no reason."

"No? Let's see. Let's think the way the cops are going to. Maybe she wanted to break it off and you got mad."

"She didn't want to break it off. And if she had, frankly I would've been no more than mildly irritated. Like I told you, whatever strong feelings there were between us ended just south of the belt."

"Okay, then, how's this? Maybe Ginger decided that ba-da-bing! wasn't enough anymore. Maybe she wanted something more than just grins, and maybe she started pressuring you about it."

"No way," he said. "She wasn't that kind of chick. Besides, she was seeing somebody else."

"Who?"

"How the hell should I know?"

"You didn't ask?"

"I didn't care!" he said, his voice rising. "We kind of took the same position as Bill Clinton on gays in the military: don't ask, don't tell. Get your fucking foot off my neck, all right? I already got grilled by the police."

"I'm trying to think like they're thinking."

"I know how they're thinking," he said. "That's why I need you. To get them thinking in another direction."

I sat still, staring at him. Finally he broke eye contact.

"You've got every reason not to like me," he murmured. "But Mary's told me enough about you that I know you're a stand-up guy. You wouldn't want to see an innocent man go down—not even me. Help me, Milan, for Christ's sake."

He writhed against the cushions, twisting one leg around the other, in an obvious panic. I let him stew for about thirty seconds. Finally I said, "Write me a check, Mr. Cirini."

He got up quickly and went to a blond maplewood desk against the wall. "All things considered, you're not going to go on calling me Mr. Cirini, are you?"

I nodded. "Think of the alternatives."

I looked away while he wrote the check, hearing the scratch of his pen in the quiet room. He came around in front of me holding it out, and I took it and folded it into my notebook. Then I stood up.

"Milan, I'll be grateful to you forever if you get me out of this jam."

"If I get you out of it, Mr. Cirini, I think the first thing you should do is see your tailor."

He looked blank. "My tailor?"

I headed for the front door. "Yeah. You need to do something about that loose zipper."

CHAPTER FIVE

I might as well have told a bee not to buzz.

Steve Cirini was one of those men who approach literally everything and everyone on a sexual level. To women he was the charming and irresistible louse they looked on as a challenge; to men he was, on a subconscious and visceral level, a sexual threat they usually handled with uneasy care. He knew how good-looking he was, used his considerable charm where it did the most good, and walked around every moment fully aware of the weight of his genitals inside his Jockeys.

The kind of man who sometimes lets his gonads lead him into the Valley of the Shadow.

There didn't seem to be much point in my going all the way back downtown to the office after seeing Cirini, so I went straight home. The drive from Mayfield Village to Cleveland Heights was against the rush-hour traffic, and I made it back by about five.

I checked my answering machine but there was no little red light blinking. That's what I get for moving the business out of the apartment.

Then I dialed up my office voice mail. The manager for the plumbing supply company had phoned for what he delicately termed "a progress report." The guy from whom I subcontract all my TV security cameras had called in a quote, which from the size of it was not going to thrill the plumbing fixture guy. And Nicole had called to tell me she'd been held up and would be arriving at my place a bit later than planned, so we'd have to catch the nine o'clock show at the Cedar Lee, Cleveland's best art movie house. They were featuring one of those romantic French films that always look as if they were shot with a Kodak Instamatic.

"I'll bring some take-out chicken to save time," she said before clicking off.

Somehow tonight Nicole's voice sounded frighteningly different; I'd seen Mary this morning, talked to her, smelled the perfume in her hair, and my world had altered a little bit.

I put down the phone, grateful for the extra time. I made the bed, showered, and changed into jeans and a sweater, switching on the radio to keep me company: Terry Gross and *Fresh Air* on WCPN. Then I cracked open a Stroh's.

It still seemed strange sitting on the sofa and relaxing in my living room, which had so long served as my place of business. Until I'd redone things, I'd spent all of my at-home leisure time in the big sunporch–den. I hadn't gotten used to it yet, using my apartment for just living, and as a result I still wasn't completely comfortable with it, any more than I was feeling completely at peace working out of my office on Collision Bend.

I'll probably be one of those old farts who sits on the porch rocker and talks to his grandchildren about the good old days back when baseball was played on real grass, and each American car company made only two models, the two-door and the four-door. But I learned long ago that along with death and taxes, nothing is mandatory if not change. Sometimes it's an improvement, sometimes it's nothing short of a disaster; either way, change comes to us whether we like it or not.

No matter what you do to stop it, the world keeps revolving—and evolving. I guess one way of measuring your success as a human being is by how well you adapt to that evolution. Thus far I thought I'd earned a C-minus and was in real danger of failing the course.

So seeing Mary again, up close and one-on-one, had not only made my stomach do triple gainers but had caused a subtle change in me, creating a kind of unease that was bound to make me begin questioning a lot of things.

I didn't like it.

I opened my notebook and reviewed what I'd copied from the police file along with the jottings made during my conversation with my client, making some more notes on what needed to be done.

Obviously I needed to talk to Andrew Lemmons, the Channel 12 field producer who had found the body. And to Vivian Truscott, who had at first mentored Virginia Carville's career and then gone somewhat sour on it when her creation turned into a monster of potential competition. Then there was the next-door neighbor, Rosemary Kelley. I couldn't get over the feeling that I'd heard the name before, but it was lost in the nether reaches of my consciousness.

There was also Nicky Scandalios to be factored in. As the general manager of a network affiliate TV station, he was a pretty important guy around Cleveland—although probably not as important as he thought he was—and he was probably busy right now, scrambling to find Virginia Carville's replacement. There was a chance he might not even talk to me. But it seemed more likely that to help clear his sales manager of a murder rap and bring the killer of one of his team to justice, he'd put out the welcome mat for me.

Hard to tell, though. His station operated profitably only through the goodwill of the people of northeastern Ohio, and I could hardly blame him if he just wanted to duck his head and hope everything would go away. Me included.

I closed my notebook, put a bottle of chenin blanc on ice, and set plates, wineglasses, silverware, and napkins on the coffee table, since I hadn't yet bothered to get myself a dining table and chairs. There was a place for it, a little L off the main room, beside the kitchen door; a phony-crystal chandelier dangled over the empty space. But it had been a long time since I'd had more than one person to dinner, not counting Milan and Stephen, who usually scarfed down their pizza or hot dogs sitting on the floor. And with all the money I'd spent buying and furnishing the office and redoing the apartment, a formal dining room wasn't one of my big priorities.

I wanted a cigarette badly, but Nicole was bound to notice the smoke when she walked in. So I had another beer and looked out the window at the traffic pattern down where Cedar Road slices into Fairmount Boulevard and then meanders its way down the hill to University Circle.

It was twenty-five after seven when Nicole rang the doorbell, her arms full of bags of chicken from the Boston Market on Warrensville Center Road. I kissed her before she could put them down; it was the kind of kiss that tends to get someone's immediate attention.

"What was that for?" she said when she caught her breath.

"For being such a wonderful neonatologist."

"I am at that," she said, obviously pleased. "We almost lost a preemie today. That's why I was late."

"Almost?"

She smiled and nodded proudly. "As you so perceptively pointed out, I'm a wonderful neonatologist."

"Don't worry about the time," I said, "we'll just relax and eat and then catch the nine o'clock show. Nine fifteen, actually."

I helped her off with her coat and she sat down and began unwrapping the meal while I wrestled the cork out of the chenin blanc.

"How was your day?" she asked as I poured.

"Nothing as exciting as yours. At least I didn't save anybody's life."

"Well, everybody has slow days," she said.

"To slow days," I toasted, and we tinked glasses.

She divided the chicken between us. It was good, but I didn't have much of an appetite. I thought briefly about not telling her I'd seen Mary, but that would be sneakily dishonest. We'd always been open with each other—that's why the relationship worked so well.

Deciding how to break the news was another story altogether.

When I eventually swallowed what I had in my mouth, I said in my most offhand manner, "Actually, my day was kind of interesting."

"Tell me," she said.

And I did. I sketched it out for her, Mary's visit, my talk with Marko, my meeting with Steve Cirini, omitting any details I thought might upset her. It was like walking through a minefield in the dark. When I was halfway through I noticed that both of us had left most of our perfectly tasty chicken dinners on our plates to get cold. We helped ourselves liberally to the wine, though, so that by the time I finished talking, the bottle was just another dead soldier.

Nicole played with her glass quietly as I talked, her fingers leaving smudges all over the crystal.

"That's a lot more than you usually tell me about what you're working on," she said at last.

"I don't want to keep anything about this from you—because of Mary."

"Thanks for that."

The Streisand CD had ended long before, and in the ensuing silence the ticking of the wall clock in the kitchen was distinct.

"Are you asking my permission to do this?" she said. "Is that what this is all about?"

"No," I said, and the skin on the back of my neck prickled a little bit. "I'm not asking permission. You and I aren't about permission."

Her brown eyes were wide and confused. She didn't really look angry, or even hurt, but she seemed to be having trouble getting a handle on it all. "What did she do, just walk into your office this morning?"

"That's right."

"No phone call to tell you she was coming?"

"I haven't spoken to her in years."

"What if you hadn't been in?"

"Then she would've made the trip for nothing, I guess."

"Were you surprised?"

"That's an understatement."

"How did you feel when you saw her?"

So many feelings had gone through me when I'd looked up and seen Mary Soderberg standing in my office that describing them all was impossible. "Amazed," I answered truthfully. "Startled. Flabbergasted."

"Are you being coy?"

"I don't think I know how to be," I said with some irritation.

"Were you pleased? To see her after all this time?"

"No, not particularly. Not at all, as a matter of fact."

"But that didn't stop you from agreeing to help her?"

"I agreed to help Steve Cirini."

She nodded, staring at the wall. "Odd," she finally said.

"Why?"

"I wouldn't imagine you'd want anything to do with the guy she left you for."

"I don't—but if he's innocent he deserves all the help he can get, don't you think?" It sounded noble. And pompous. And pretty hollow, even to me. "Besides, I'm being well paid," I added.

She stood up and took her wineglass and her plate into the kitchen. She was in there a lot longer than it would have taken to put them in the sink. Then she came back out and stood in the doorway, hands on either side of the doorframe like Samson between the pillars of the temple of the Philistines, her mouth a thin incision across her face. Her already prominent jaw was jutting out aggressively. "You're doing it for her, aren't you?"

I considered a vehement denial—a lie. "I suppose I am," I said.

Now the hurt was evident behind her eyes, and in the rigid way she held her head. "I'm . . . not really sure how I feel about that, Milan."

"There is no 'that.' An old friend asked for the kind of help I'm trained to provide, and I said I'd do what I can. It has nothing to do with you and me."

She opened her mouth to say something but then hesitated. Nicole is always spontaneous and free-spirited, the kind of person who always says what she thinks and worries about it afterward, so I was struck now by how slowly she spoke and how carefully she chose her words. "So I'm supposed to cool my heels while you spend every day running around with your ex-girlfriend?"

"You don't have to cool your heels at all," I answered, becoming both more irritated and more apprehensive. I didn't like the direction this was heading. "I'm working for Steve Cirini, not Mary. I doubt if I'll see that much of her—she's not a part of the investigation. I'm sure that in all the years you've practiced at the clinic, you must have dated one or two of the doctors, and it doesn't bend me out of shape to think that you're seeing them every day."

"We're not talking about me."

"No," I said quietly. "We're not."

She wrapped her arms around herself. "Are you still in love with her?"

I took a while before answering. "No, Nicole, I'm not still in love with her. Mary came along at a low point in my life, when I was feeling lousy about myself because my marriage had fallen apart, and I was lonely and hanging out at Vuk's Tavern on St. Clair Avenue all the time. Otherwise I would've been damn near a recluse. She taught me to relax and how to laugh and how to feel like a human being again. So there are emotional echoes, sure. When you found out your ex-boyfriend had been killed, didn't you feel bad—sad—even though you hadn't even seen him in two years?"

She shook her head resolutely. "Of course I felt bad. But I was never in love with him to begin with."

"Well," I said, "I was in love with Mary at one time, and no amount of talking is going to change that. And even though she hurt me, and even though I'm not in love with her anymore and haven't been for a long time, I was then, and when she asks me for help, that's got to count for something."

She leaned against the doorframe. "Thanks for being honest, anyway."

I cleared my throat, swallowed, tried to relax. The sofa might just as well have been a bed of nails.

"Where does that leave us?"

"Right where we've always been. It's a job, Nicole. That's all it is. It'll probably be finished in a week."

"I wish I could be sure about that," she said, brushing her hair away from her face.

The half piece of chicken I'd eaten was congealing in my stomach. "I wish you could, too," I said, and felt our relationship turning to fine, powdery sand between my fingers.

It should come as no surprise that the French movie went unseen that night, at least by us. Nicole ventured the opinion that we probably couldn't save the evening and went home early. She just didn't feel as if she'd be very good company. She wasn't angry, she assured me.

I didn't believe her.

I finished up the dishes, feeling low and mean, a headache building up behind my eyes and a hollow, empty place in the middle of my chest. I don't know why I have such problems with relationships; I'm no prize, but all in all I think I'm a pretty decent guy. Sometimes I send flowers even when it isn't Valentine's Day, I don't run around with other women, I'm not abusive, I don't get drunk and fall asleep on the sofa, I'm attentive and affectionate, and I never throw my dirty socks on the floor.

But the people I love keep leaving me.

Maybe I just fall for the wrong women. High-maintenance women, as current psychobabble has it. And because of my job, and my kids, and a nature that has of necessity become somewhat solitary in the last few years, I'm a low-maintenance kind of guy. I give as much as I can, but it always seems to fall a few feet short of the fence.

Send in the clowns.

CHAPTER SIX

Nicky Scandalios, the general manager of Channel 12, was a large man of about fifty, with a former athlete's body that was losing its battle with middle-aged spread. Silver-white hair, thinning slightly and worn about half an inch longer than current fashion would dictate, framed a round chipmunk face. Judging from his ruddy bronze color, he spent time in the health club's tanning booth that he would've been better advised to use working out on the Nautilus machine.

His office, on the top floor of the station's headquarters on Euclid Avenue, was the size of a small manufacturing plant, done in varying shades of gray with black and silver accents. The gray wall covering looked like the carpet in somebody's upstairs hallway. And Scandalios, dressed in a suit of buttery gray, a white shirt with pearl links securing the starched French cuffs, and a black silk tie with a pearl stickpin, matched the decor. Very old-world. Very elegant. He looked as if he should have been squiring Lillian Russell to Delmonico's.

"Mr. Jacovich, I don't need to tell you how shocked and saddened we are here at what's happened," he said in the unctuous tones of a funeral director. "We hired Virginia Carville when she was just a snot-nosed kid with stars in her eyes, and we watched her grow into the beautiful and capable young woman she became. She was one of our own. This is an insupportable loss." He passed a hand over his eyes. "Insupportable."

Scandalios made the declaration as easily as if he was doing his on-air promotional pitches. I figured he was comfortable in almost any situation, in the way of people who are used to spending a lot of time in the public eye. He was on the boards of several cultural institutions around town, he and his wife were regulars on the benefit circuit, and he made frequent appearances on his own station, so choosing his words carefully to produce the desired effect came naturally to him. The kind of guy from whom you wouldn't hesitate to buy a used car, or an expansion of your term life insurance policy that you didn't really need. The kind of wheedler who could separate you from a large chunk of your daddy's patrimony when a new hospital wing or a season of light opera had to be funded.

A schmoozer.

"I appreciate your seeing me," I told him.

"That's perfectly all right," he assured me. "Why, when Mary called we just cleared our calendar of everything else for the next half hour. Because of course in addition to our grief about Ginger, we're very concerned about Steve Cirini. He's a vital cog here." He harrumphed and cleared his throat. "As well as being a close personal friend of ours."

I wondered if Scandalios always used the royal plural.

"Of course, it's inconceivable that Steve could do anything like this," he went on, "so obviously we're entirely at your disposal."

"That's good. I was hoping you could fill in some background for me."

He inclined his head in acquiescence. Regally.

"Was there anyone here at Channel Twelve that Ginger Carville was particularly close to?"

"Well, we don't monitor who goes to lunch with whom. We have more important things to attend to. Vivian Truscott was her guardian angel, so to speak, when Ginger came to work here. They were good friends, at the beginning."

"At the beginning?"

He shrugged. "It was a mentor-pupil relationship, the very best kind. Vivian is gracious and generous as well as being a first-rate talent, and she was very giving, very helpful to Ginger, and we appreciated it, believe me. It gave us a fine, home-grown reporter. Of course when Ginger kind of blossomed and established her own identity here on-camera, there wasn't a—need, I guess you could say, for the kind of closeness they'd had previously."

"Was there enmity?"

"No, no, no," he clucked. "But Ginger was considerably younger than Vivian, and once she grew into herself she gravitated more to people her own age. Naturally."

Naturally. "Anyone in particular?"

He rubbed his jaw, sagelike. "No one that I can think of off-hand." His dark eyebrows wiggled and he made a sour-lemon face. "Besides Steve Cirini, of course. I guess they were . . . close."

"You knew that was going on?"

He drew himself up in full huff, as if I'd asked him if he'd known his employees were dealing crack off the loading dock. "Absolutely not!"

"You sound as though you wouldn't have approved."

His smile was benign, patient. "It's not our place to approve or disapprove. These are employees. Coworkers. I'm their boss, not their father. But you know how office romances are. They're a distraction, they hurt productivity, the work suffers, and when they fall apart, as they invariably do, it puts a strain on everyone. So we don't exactly encourage that sort of thing."

"You didn't seem to mind that Cirini was also dating Mary Soderberg, who works in his own department, which is a hell of a lot more likely to hurt productivity. That's been going on for three years now—surely you weren't unaware of it."

"Of course not. But you see, Mr. Jacovich . . ." He ran both hands down across his chest, as if he were gently fondling a woman's breasts instead of his own. "The on-camera personalities here, especially in news, are really our public relations representatives. That's who the viewers see every night in their living rooms. They provide the station with a sort of neighborhood identity. So . . ." He smiled again, sadly, as if the harsh realities of the world had taken a great toll on him. "There are different ground rules for the talent. We couldn't have a reporter dating a politician, for example. There'd be a real conflict of interest there, a real problem of journalistic ethics. Our talent have to be kind of like Caesar's wife, if you know what I mean."

"Well, yes, I guess," I said.

He frowned slightly. "I sense a 'but' coming."

"Cleveland may be a pretty socially conservative community, but nobody here is naive—or stupid, either. Ginger Carville and Steve Cirini were both unmarried adults. If anyone had found out they were seeing each other, there wouldn't have been much of a scandal."

He sat back in his chair and put his hands in his lap. "I suppose not," he said.

"Let's table that for the moment. Was Ginger working on a particularly hot story, something that someone might not have wanted to come out?"

"I couldn't tell you. I don't make the news assignments."

"Who does?"

"The assignment editor. But the news director makes all the final decisions. That'd be Ray Aylmer."

"Could you arrange for me to meet with some of these people? Aylmer and Vivian Truscott, and Andrew Lemmons?"

His sparkly blue eyes grew flinty and cold. "I think not, Mr. Jacovich."

"Why not?"

His hands went to his chest again. It was a disconcerting

habit that shrieked narcissism, and impossible not to stare at. "Because we have a television station to run. Tragedy or no tragedy, we've got to fill up twenty-four hours a day with programming, a lot of it local. You don't find people standing at the water cooler talking about the weather or last night's ball game around here—everyone has too much work to do. Television is high-pressure, especially news." He glanced at his Rolex, and the band's gold links caught the rays of the overhead light and threw them back onto the ceiling. "It's eleven thirty. In exactly five and a half hours the viewers of the Greater Cleveland area are expecting a sixty-minute newscast, and another one immediately following, and all the people you've mentioned are vital to getting those casts on the air. I'm sorry, it would just be too disruptive."

I had been fighting a tension headache since Nicole walked out of my apartment the night before, and all at once it started playing jungle drums behind my eyes. "I'd think it would be even more disruptive if your sales manager got arrested for murdering one of your field reporters."

"That's not going to happen," Nicky Scandalios said with the absolute conviction of one who is used to getting his own way in all things.

"I hope not, Mr. Scandalios, because it's my job to prevent it. I'm here now, and I could get it all done this afternoon and get out of your hair."

His hand started to go to his own receding hairline, but he brought it down, glancing nervously at me to see if I'd noticed.

"I can go to their homes in the evening to talk to them," I said, "but that's going to waste a lot of time. And if you're worried about this station's image, time is just what you don't have, because the police are working hard to find a reason to put Steve Cirini away, and I'm sure that would be the kind of story your competitors would jump on with glee."

He colored beneath his ruddy tan, and there was a film of perspiration at his temples. "That's not a threat, is it, Mr. Jacovich?" he said softly, trying to keep his voice from shaking. "There aren't too many people in this town with the stones to walk in here and threaten us."

"I'm not threatening you at all. I'm just telling you what needs to be done and asking if you'll help me do it. If you want to try hindering me, take your best shot."

His mouth tightened for a moment, and then the public relations smile returned as if he'd clicked on some interior switch. "I don't want to hinder you," he said. "I'd have no reason to do that."

"Good."

He held up a warning index finger; its nail was manicured and buffed to a dull gleam. "But I'll have to insist on strict confidentiality."

"I can't make that promise," I said. "This is a murder case. I won't repeat anything I hear if it doesn't have a bearing on what happened to Ginger Carville, but other than that, I'm required by law not to withhold any evidence from the authorities. I could lose my license—and maybe worse. I'm not going to risk that."

He fingered his lower lip, squeezing it softly. It always amuses me that when people want to buy themselves a few extra seconds to think, they invariably start playing with parts of their faces.

"You've kind of got me by the nuts," he thought out loud.

"I'm not sure I care for your metaphor, Mr. Scandalios."

He stared at something totally absorbing over my head somewhere. "All right," he sighed at last. "I'll ask all of them to make themselves available to you this afternoon. But make it as quick as you can; we're a TV station and we can't go on the air at five and tell everybody we're sorry but we're not quite ready."

"I appreciate it," I said as I got up to leave.

"Just try not to fuck up our news department, all right, Mr. Jacovich?"

"I will. And you try not to fuck up my investigation, Mr. Scandalios."

So that was the great Nicky Scandalios, I thought as I made my way down the corridor. I'd seen him on the tube a thousand times, but this was my first in-person encounter. He had the same charm and charisma he showed to the public at large, but without the TV lens as a filter, they seemed false and forced. He was like a department store Santa Claus ho-ho-ho-ing and bouncing toddlers on his knee when all he wanted was to get back to his locker for a surreptitious little nip of the Annie Green Springs.

I turned the corner, heading for the stairs, and came face-to-face with Mary Soderberg. She was so startled to see me that she dropped the file folder she was carrying, and papers scattered all over the floor.

Simultaneously I said "Sorry" and she said "My fault" and we both squatted down to retrieve the contents of the file. Her trim dark-blue skirt rode up high over her thighs to the darker, reinforced area of her pantyhose. I looked away.

"Have you found anything out yet?" she said.

"No. But it's only been twenty-four hours. You have to be patient, Mary."

She straightened up, adjusting her clothing. "Maybe you remember that patience isn't my strong suit."

We just stood there in the narrow corridor looking at each other while busy people jostled us as they rushed by on their way to the studio or the copying machine or the coffee room.

"Keep me posted, Milan," she finally said, and walked off down the corridor.

I was operating on an empty stomach, and my meeting with Nicky Scandalious had given me a full-blown headache, making it hard to focus my eyes. I stopped in a new shopping mall across Euclid Avenue from the Cleveland Clinic, where President Clinton had once made a speech, and went into the drugstore to buy some Advil.

On the way to the cashier I happened to glance at the paperback book rack. I stopped short.

Now I knew where I'd heard Rosemary Kelley's name before. Her current book, *Desire With a Stranger,* which had a bright red cover featuring an illustration of a bosomy raven-haired beauty in the embrace of a square-jawed stud whose shirt was open to the waist, was currently number-two on the local best-seller list, to which Kelley was hardly a stranger. She was one of Cleveland's most famous writers, author of heavy-breathing romance novels, and as familiar a figure on the society pages as in the book-review section.

And she was Virginia Carville's next-door neighbor.

I slipped a copy of the book out of the rack and took it up to the cashier with me. Historical romances are not usually my cup of tea, but you're never too old to try something new.

CHAPTER SEVEN

Along with all the other producers and associates, writers, researchers, and the rest of the Channel 12 news support staff, Andrew Lemmons worked in a large room they called the bull pen, in the center of a flurry of activity that would be impressive to one who'd never seen it before. Chest-high partitions of acoustical wallboard that formed individual cubicles gave not even the illusion of privacy, but they reduced the insistent buzz of dozens of intense telephone conversations, and they enabled the occupants to pin up a blizzard of three-by-five cards, Post-it notes, assignments, and the occasional relevant cartoon.

A desk, two chairs, a bright red filing cabinet, and a computer were crowded into Lemmons's cubicle; with the two of us in there it was downright claustrophobic, and if anyone else had wanted to join the conversation they would have had to stand outside and holler in.

Andrew Lemmons was a light-skinned, open-faced black man whom I estimated to be in his late twenties, and in addition to the harried look he shared with almost all his colleagues in the newsroom, there was a tightness around his mouth and a weariness in his eyes, the aftereffects of shock and grief. He wore neatly pressed chinos and a checkered dress shirt open at the neck, and the knot of his blue knit tie had been pulled down to give him breathing room. His slim, muscular body was partly a result of genetic accident but also might have been attributed to his perpetual motion as he sorted through various papers and index cards, examined the labels on boxed videotapes, and took quick gulps from a cardboard cup of black coffee that could only have come out of a machine. The television news business, especially on a local level, is highly intense and as stressful as walking a tightrope, and it invariably takes its toll. Lemmons probably burned a thousand calories in a normal day just sitting at his desk.

And this was hardly a normal day.

"It's still tough for me to focus," he said. "Tough to concentrate on the work." He wrapped his arms around himself as if he were cold, and his eyes went dull and hard. "Like it matters a shit anymore." He studied the desktop. "I'm the one that found her, you know."

"That's what I understand."

"It was horrible, walking in there and finding her that way," he said, and passed a hand across his face. "We were coworkers—and friends. Good friends. I'd never seen her like that before. Naked. It was like a violation—*another* violation, like *I* was violating her."

"You had a key to her house?"

He shook his head. "The door was open when I got there."

"You mean unlocked?"

"Open. About an inch or so, I guess. I figured she'd gone out to get the paper and had forgotten to close it, so I rang the bell and waited. Then when no one answered I got kind of nervous, so I went in. I looked around downstairs for a while, then I went up to the second floor." A tremor shook his wiry body. "That's when I found her."

"You got nervous?"

His glance flicked over me. "She hadn't shown up to work, she hadn't called, her front door was open, and nobody answered the bell," he said mechanically, sounding like that computerized operator who gives you the number when you call directory assistance. "Damn right I got nervous."

"I see what you mean," I assured him. "So you and Ginger worked together a lot?"

"Virginia. She liked to be called Virginia. Sure, we worked assignments nearly all the time. Whenever she had to go out on location she always used to ask for me, until they pretty much got the idea and started assigning us together without her even asking. We were like two parts of a machine." He interlaced the fingers of both hands by way of illustration. "It was the kind of thing where you always know what each other's thinking without having to discuss it. We saw news the same way."

"What way is that?"

"We both felt that the story is always the most important thing," he said, straightening his shoulders defensively. "Neither one of us gave much of a damn for pretty pictures. Virginia was very careful about her appearance—TV news is very competitive, a real shark tank. But we both felt we were in the information business, not show business. It was a shared philosophy. That's what made it work so well. We were a team, you know?"

"Did everyone in the news department get along with her as well as you did?"

He seemed to take a little umbrage at the question. "Nobody disliked her, if that's what you mean. She was damn good at what she did. I suppose there were times when she could be a pain in the ass, but—"

"In what way?"

I could tell he was sorry he'd said it. "She was a perfectionist. That means if anybody else on the crew was dogging it on one of her stories, dragging their feet, not putting out a hundred percent, well, they'd hear from her—in no uncertain terms. Out in the field she wanted a quick setup and wouldn't stand for anything less. So there were some people who preferred working with one of the other reporters just because it was easier to slide a little. But everyone around here respected her professionalism."

"What made you decide to go to her house that morning?"

"I was worried about her," he said. "She was never late. Never. As a matter of fact she was always here half an hour or so early, to make sure she was properly prepared. If she was going to be even five minutes late, if she'd gotten stuck in traffic on the Shoreway, she'd always call, so her crew wouldn't have to sit around wondering. That was the kind of person she was."

"She had a car phone?"

"All the field reporters do, courtesy of Mr. Scandalios. All the TV news departments have scanners so they can monitor the other station's radio communications. That way we can steal a beat on the other guy. With car phones that doesn't happen."

I couldn't help noticing that he pronounced the boss's name as if it had a sour taste. "You get along with Scandalios?"

His mouth turned down a little more. "He's all right—for a suit. He works up there in the executive offices and never gets his hands dirty."

"That's why you don't like him?"

"No, that's not why. Do you like your boss?"

"Not much," I said. "I *am* my boss. No other reason?"

Andrew Lemmons lowered his voice. "Look around you. See many black faces in this newsroom? I'll save you the trouble; there are three besides me, none of them ranked any higher than associate producer. How many you see on the air?" He held up one slim finger, then curled it closed into a fist. "And they've got him doing the wake-up news and midday on the weekends."

"Are you saying Nicky Scandalios is a racist?"

His tired eyes grew a little more tired. "I don't even know what that means anymore. He doesn't ride around in a white sheet and burn crosses, but I get the idea black isn't his favorite color."

"But you're here. You're a producer."

"Sure," he said. "I was born and raised in the Glenville neighborhood, ten minutes from here. I went to Miami of Ohio and got a degree in communications, and then I came back home looking for a job. The only reason they hired me was because they make a big deal out of using local people, they think it's good PR. And they didn't bring me in as a producer, either. I put in my time pulling cable and watching white guys that I knew couldn't carry my jock get promoted."

I thought about telling him that in every business the new guy always has to start out doing the equivalent of pulling cable, no matter what color he is, but I didn't think he'd want to hear it.

He rubbed his face again and shook his head as if to rattle loose some unpleasant pictures. "It was Virginia Carville that got me the producer gig. She requested me, went to the mat for me with Scandalios and Aylmer." He looked at me. "It's been a singularly lousy weekend."

"What about Steve Cirini?"

"Another suit." He allowed himself the ghost of a smile. "An Armani suit."

I smiled too. "Did you know that Cirini and Virginia were an item?"

"I sure didn't," he said, "until it came out after she died. I'm disappointed, too. I'd have figured she had better taste than that."

"You don't like him?"

His tone became more businesslike. "I don't have much to do with him one way or the other. General sales managers don't have much truck with the drones down in the trenches."

"Mr. Lemmons," I said, "was Ginger working on anything that might have been considered hot?"

"I wouldn't know," he said. "If it's hard news we usually don't get our assignments until the night before, or even that day if the story's breaking. It's only the puff pieces, the Home Show and the Auto Show and things like that, that we know about way in advance."

"Would Ray Aylmer know?"

"The assignment editors usually take care of things like that, but if Ginger had anything hot, Death Ray probably knew about it."

"Death Ray?"

"No one calls him that to his face," Lemmons said with a sour grin. "You'll understand why when you meet him."

And a few minutes later, back up on the top floor and down the hall from Nicky Scandalios's office, I did.

Ray Aylmer was a cadaverous six foot six, couldn't have weighed a hundred and seventy pounds, and had thinning red hair that he wore too long so he could comb it over his bald spots. Being slightly frizzy, it tended to fly around his head when he moved. His was the long, sad face of a little boy whose parents forgot to pick him up from summer camp at the end of the week. His office was unpretentious, cluttered, and smelled stale and musty. An unremarkable overcoat hung on a hook, and on the hook above, a black wool hat that might have been worn by a Russian commissar. Aylmer was about forty-five but moved as slowly as someone twice his age, and he was slow to smile, too, as if it might cost him money.

Death Ray.

"I've already been over all this with the police," he said with the arrogance of one who's been given a certain amount of authority even if he doesn't run the whole circus. "I can't imagine what more I can tell you that I haven't told them." He spoke without looking at me, riffling his long fingers through a box of file cards.

He had a cigarette voice and his hands shook slightly, as if he were taking several different kinds of medication. "Nicky told me I had to talk to you," he said, "but even Nicky can't change the fact that we go on the air in precisely two hours and twenty-three minutes. So of necessity this will have to be brief."

"I'll get right to the point, then. First, was Virginia Carville on the trail of a particularly sensitive story before she died? Any local scandal that someone might not have wanted made public?"

"Not that I know of."

"Wouldn't you know everything she was working on?"

"Not necessarily. Ginger could be a cowboy sometimes, going off on her own, sometimes even on her own time, when she smelled a story. She'd massage it and tweak it and develop it to the point where she could bring it to the assignment editor; he'd bring it to me and I'd decide whether I wanted her to go after it or not."

"She was a good reporter, then."

"She was getting to be one, yeah. She had a way of turning up stories nobody else could."

"How'd she manage that?"

"Like every other reporter, she had a network of snitches and stringers all over town. The difference was, Ginger's sources were usually more reliable than anybody else's. Don't ask me why."

"Every good cop has snitches, but they're all druggies and petty crooks. What kind did she have?"

He shook his head. "Journalists don't give up their sources or they wouldn't have them very long. But Ginger's were people who worked in hospitals, law offices, at city hall, even in the county lockup. I don't know how she did it, but she was a master at developing them and keeping them."

"She paid them for information?"

"I didn't ask her," he said. "I didn't want to know. All I knew was that she had them and they were goddamn good."

"She was a pretty valuable commodity to a news department then, huh?"

He considered that for a while, and his eventual nod was almost tentative. "Eventually she would've been. As it was, she was too much of a hot shot, but she was young. They teach 'em that in J-school these days; kids with not much more than a blow-dryer and a makeup case have visions of winding up on *Sixty Minutes*."

"You sound as if you disapprove."

He took a videocassette from a shelf and tossed it on his desk. "Sometimes I did. There's such a thing as jumping the gun. Every story has its own time."

"Like wine?"

Taking a drag on the cigarette that had been sending up smoke signals from the oversize ashtray on his desk, he got up and went to a metal file cabinet across the room. "This is a tough town, Cleveland. You don't want to blow any whistles until you're sure there's really a train coming."

"You're talking about stories that might be politically sensitive?"

Aylmer turned and stared at me. "If you're implying that this news department succumbs to any outside political pressure or influence, I take that as a grievous insult."

"I wasn't implying anything," I said, trying to remember if I'd ever before heard someone actually use *grievous* in conversation.

"Damn good thing or you'd be out of here on your ass."

"But if a reporter came up with something potentially embarrassing to the mayor or a judge or a councilman, you'd think twice about using it, wouldn't you?"

He sighed. "We can't do our jobs here unless we have access to the people who make the news. Piss them off, and they start calling the other guys first—as punishment—and we're left looking like idiots. It's a business, and you don't want to alienate the people you do business with unless you absolutely have to."

He jerked open the top drawer of the filing cabinet with a bit more force than was required and pawed through it. "Let's say, for instance—and this is strictly hypothetical—that one of our people hears a rumor going around that a teacher at a local private school is under suspicion of some kind of sexual misconduct with a student."

"That's pretty ugly."

"It happens. And that's exactly my point. We poke around a little to see if there's anything to the rumor, but we don't run the story until actual charges are brought. That kind of thing could ruin a reputation, even if it isn't true. We believe in the public's right to know, and that it's our job to inform them, but there's a responsibility that comes with that."

"And Ginger wasn't always responsible?"

"That's why I'm here—to make sure my reporters *are* responsible."

"She was working on a story about sexual misconduct?"

"No," he said. "I told you it was hypothetical." He extracted a folder from the drawer and slammed it shut. "Ginger was young, full of piss and vinegar and drive. Sometimes in her eagerness to make a splash she'd go off half-cocked." He squeezed his eyes shut for a minute, then opened them again. "She was learning, though."

"But there was nothing like that in the hopper when she was killed?"

"Not to my knowledge." He sat on the edge of his desk, took another drag on his cigarette, and crushed it out.

"So Carville was basically good on the job?"

"Or she would've been gone," he assured me.

"I thought she was Vivian Truscott's special project. And Nicky's, too."

He went around behind his desk and sat down, his mouth twisting into a grimace. I wondered if he suffered from chronic back pain. "I run this department," he said. "Not Nicky, and sure as hell not Vivian."

"Just trying to cover all the bases."

"I know. You're working for Steve Cirini, and I wouldn't want to see him or anyone else locked up for something he didn't do. But I have to be honest, I don't like him much."

"Because he's a suit?"

His mouth didn't smile but his eyes did. "I'm a suit myself," he said. "Now. I *was* a journalist. I guess I still am. But in this business they punish you when you're good. They kick you up-stairs, double your salary, and make you wear ties." He took another cigarette from a half-empty pack on the desk and stuck it in the corner of his mouth without lighting it. "No, I don't like Cirini because he's an arrogant, empty-headed prick. I'd be very surprised if he killed her, though."

"Why?"

He shook his head. "Cirini's interested in two things: money, so he can have his toys—his sports car and his sound system and his expensive house—and women. That's what floats his boat."

"And what floats your boat, Mr. Aylmer?"

"I didn't kill Ginger Carville, if that's what you're suggest-ing. And I sure as hell didn't have sex with her first. She wasn't my type."

"Oh?"

"I could have taken a shower with her without anything hap-pening."

"That's pretty strong," I said.

"Believe it or don't, I couldn't care less. If I'd wanted a shot at Ginger, I could've had it."

I just raised my eyebrows.

"She was an ambitious gal. Driven, you might say. And she let me know early on she wasn't exactly opposed to sleeping with the boss to advance her career."

"But you weren't interested?"

"No," he said levelly. "I'm a happily married man, but even

if I weren't, I don't want anyone in bed with me for any other reason than they want to be there. This isn't my own personal pussy farm. I'm running a television news operation." He looked at his wristwatch. "Speaking of which, Mr. Jacovich, you're outta here."

Chapter Eight

Everybody in Cleveland, whether a regular Channel 12 viewer or not, knows Vivian Truscott. She's as close to royalty as this town can boast. Tall and stately, and beautiful as only a mature and self-possessed woman can be, over time she's gained acceptance with a viewership that generally wants its TV news personalities to prove themselves first. She arrived in town more than ten years ago, and she's helped make Channel 12 number-one in the ratings. Along with her husband, a world-famous cardiologist, she serves on the boards of several arts organizations and is visible and active in most of the good-works causes that keep local high society hopping from one benefit to another.

I know more about Vivian than people who only watch her on the news do. In an investigation several years ago involving an advertising scam that had turned into a triple murder, I'd unearthed the fact that before her career as a TV anchorwoman in Cleveland got started, Vivian Truscott had been a high-priced call girl working out of Caesar's Palace in Las Vegas. She doesn't know I know, and of course I hadn't told anyone else about it.

I wonder if former hookers who have buried their secret pasts like that ever worry about running into a former john and having their carefully constructed cover blown, but when Vivian Truscott greeted me with, "Hello there, Milan. It's nice to see you again. We *have* met before, haven't we?" I didn't think that particular concern crossed her mind. With my off-the-rack suit and a too-wide necktie I'd acquired somewhere around 1983, I hardly looked like anyone who could ever have afforded the pleasure.

We were in her private office–sitting room on the third floor of the Channel 12 building, which looked almost like the negative of Nicky Scandalios's office—walls, carpets, furniture, the telephone console were all various shades of white. The lady herself was dressed in a white linen suit with gray piping on the lapels, white stockings, and white low-heeled pumps that minimized her impressive height. All the white made me think of Lana Turner's outfits in the old movie *The Postman Always Rings Twice*, except Vivian Truscott is taller, slimmer, and even more attractive.

She was already made up for the afternoon newscast. Little peaks of lipstick on her upper lip made her mouth a kind of Betty Boop cupid's bow. She was sipping an Evian water with lime, sitting at one end of her oversize white-leather sofa. I was at the other, praying I wouldn't somehow leave a smudge.

"This has been such a terrible week for us," she was saying, her perfect brows knitting into a frown. "We're supposed to report the news, not *be* it." She closed her eyes and then opened them again. "Nothing I've ever covered has hit so close to home. The news has always been abstract—terrible things happening to strangers."

"Film at eleven," I suggested.

"Exactly. I feel such a genuine sense of personal loss." She put her right hand upon her bosom as if she were about to pledge allegiance. "I was instrumental in getting Ginger hired here, you know."

"So I've been told."

"She was very special. I spotted it right away, when she was just a kid."

"Her talent?"

"Her tenacity. I knew the kind of drive she had—I had it myself at her age. I figured I could either harness and use it or it was going to roll right over me. So I made her a special project of mine. I managed to snag her as a personal assistant, and then when other, better jobs opened up, I went to bat for her."

"You were close, then?"

"As close as we could be, given the generational differences," she said primly. "And once Ginger sank her teeth into being a reporter, we didn't see a lot of her around the station except during the news."

"Why was that?"

"Because she was always out in the field. Sniffing out good stories."

"Do you know whether she was sniffing out anything in particular recently?"

Vivian Truscott touched her chin thoughtfully. "No. At least nothing she told me about."

"Did she usually tell you about what she was working on?"

She laughed. "Journalists don't even share a corned beef sandwich with other journalists. I never knew what she was working on until she filed the story," she said. "I write my own copy, so that's when I generally find out what's going on. I'm an anchor, Milan—what they used to call a "newsreader" until it became a glamor job and had to have a glamor title. I sit at the desk and read people the news. I don't run around investigating things." She smiled prettily. "The way you do."

"Did you spend much time with Ginger socially?"

"As I said, our schedules were different. And our lifestyles."

"Your lifestyles?"

"I have a husband," she explained. "Ginger was a young single woman. We had different friends."

"When's the last time you had lunch with her, for instance?"

She waved a hand vaguely. "I can't even remember. Last fall, probably."

"Long time."

"Busy time," she said.

"Did she ever talk about anybody she was dating?"

Truscott wrinkled her nose; when she did it, it was charming. "Oh, no. We hardly ever got that personal."

"There wasn't any—animosity between you, was there, Ms. Truscott?"

The professional smile lost several watts. "Certainly not! I've said we were friends." Then she recovered and added, "And please call me Vivian."

I tried to look apologetic. "I had to ask."

"I've been very fortunate," she said with a grace that took any hubris out of it. "For the last ten years, the ratings have been such that I don't need to look over my shoulder at anybody new coming up behind me. Especially . . . well, I never viewed Ginger as any sort of a threat, or a competitor. We were friends and professional colleagues. Period."

"Okay," I said.

She took a final sip of the Evian water. "I'm afraid I'm due on the set for the five o'clock, Milan, so if there's nothing else . . ."

"There's a lot, Ms. Trus—Vivian. Maybe we can talk again another time."

"If you really think it's necessary." She put her head back and looked down her long patrician nose at me. "Surely you don't believe I had anything to do with . . ."

"Not for a minute," I assured her. "But evidently somebody had a reason not to like Virginia Carville very much."

"Everyone has enemies," she said, "especially those of us who are so visible in the community. We make bigger targets. Perhaps it's simple jealousy, perhaps someone doesn't like the way we wear our hair or becomes resentful at some ad-lib. Or it could have something to do with the work itself, with a story." She looked sad. "There are a lot of very disturbed people out there."

"Did Ginger do the kind of stories that might get some of those disturbed people mad at her?"

"That was her job."

"Anything recent?"

She laughed; she had a breathy, girlish giggle that was at odds with her reserved image. "Well, I don't think she was terribly popular at city hall these days, especially around the council."

I wrote down *City Cncl* in my notebook.

Her eyes widened; she seemed suddenly worried that she might have said something indiscreet. "But neither is any good reporter, really," she hastened to say. "I hardly think—"

"I don't either." I got to my feet, struggling out of the sofa cushions. "Thanks very much for your time."

She stood up too, extending a cool and gracious hand. "Are you going to talk to anyone else here at the station now?"

"Not today," I told her. "Right now I'm going home so I can watch your newscast. I try not to miss it—and if I do, I always catch you at night before I turn in."

Her smile became radiant. "What a gallant thing to say, Milan. I wish everyone were that loyal."

She was still smiling when I left. It doesn't take a whole lot to make some people happy.

I did turn Vivian Truscott's newscast on, but I didn't pay much attention to it. I was busy eating the chicken left over from the aborted dinner with Nicole the night before, augmented with thick slices of warm, buttered Orlando Ciabatta bread, and reading the Rosemary Kelley historical romance I'd bought at the drugstore.

I report that with great reluctance. There are certain things you simply can't get most people to admit: that they are not perfectly competent to drive home after a party. That they occasionally have sexual fantasies that exceed the boundaries of what's considered decent. That they pad their expense accounts, cheat on their taxes, or that they not only went to see *Dumb and Dumber* but actually enjoyed it.

And that they read romance novels.

After forty-odd years of existence on the planet, this was my very first experience, and I can't say I found it particularly uplifting. Or enlightening.

Full of clumsily constructed sentences and cardboard cutout characters, *Desire With a Stranger* was not exactly *The Great Gatsby*. It wasn't even *The Valley of the Dolls*. Rosemary Kelley wrote with her feet.

The characters of both genders were uniformly described as gorgeous and sexy. They exchanged several teasing kisses and a few deep ones that led to love scenes that, while fairly explicit, still managed to maintain a loopy kind of delicacy. Certain female body parts were invariably referred to euphemistically as "heat," certain male ones as "manhood." The word *urgency* popped up quite often.

I only read about a third of the novel. There was a monotonous predictability to it, and I figured I knew how it was going to end anyway. After three hundred pages of misunderstanding, the devastatingly handsome hero and the impossibly beautiful heroine would realize they were indeed meant for each other, and ride off into the sunset after a final steamy clinch.

At the front of the book was a page listing other works by the author; I counted twenty-three, all with *desire, lust, love, flirtation,* or *affair* in the title. Rosemary Kelley had worked hard for her preeminence in Cleveland's world of letters.

I devoured the rest of the chicken, washed it all down with a Stroh's, and slipped a worn black-corduroy sports jacket with suede elbow patches over my gray turtleneck. If I was going to talk to a writer, I figured I might as well try to look like one. Then I went downstairs, climbed into my four-year-old Pontiac Sunbird, and headed across the Cuyahoga River to the west side to keep an appointment I'd made with Rosemary Kelley.

Edgewater Drive hugs the bluff above the lake and affords a breathtaking view of downtown at night. It begins where Edgewater Park ends, running by gracious homes just a hair short of mansions, and extends all the way out into Lakewood through what Clevelanders call the Gold Coast: the lakefront lined with brightly lit modern apartment and condo high-rises. They resemble nothing so much as the more garish Miami Beach luxury hotels that draw the snowbirds down to the white sand and the sunshine in the wintertime.

Most of the large homes at the Cleveland end of Edgewater Drive look as if they were built sometime during the twenties. Occasionally there is a newer one, a fifties' ranch-style affair, conspicuous as a pygmy in the land of giants. It might seem elegant in most other locations, but it looks sadly middle class on Edgewater Drive.

Ginger Carville's house was like that, a split-level Y-shaped structure of sandy brick, with what appeared to be an added-on second floor. It had a sloping tile roof and a crescent blacktop driveway that would have been more impressive had it been paved with crushed oyster shells. The yellow crime-scene tape strung across the doors and drive looked shockingly obscene in this neighborhood of fine homes and well-tended lawns; it was as if someone had defaced a painting.

I parked in front of the Carville house and stared at it for a long moment. The windows were dark, and there was virtually no residual daylight left, so I couldn't see much of anything.

Rosemary Kelley's house was directly to the east of Carville's, a stately Tudor two or three stories high, depending on where you looked. The front was floodlit like a foreign embassy, and through the large leaded-glass windows I could see lights on in almost every room downstairs. The house was set farther back from the street and closer to the lake bluff than Ginger's, so the driveway was a lot longer. It was guarded on either side by two stone carvings of what the Chinese call "lion dogs."

I got out of my car, walked up the curving drive to the front door, rang the bell, and waited. A stiff wind from off the water about a hundred yards away cut through my car coat and the corduroy jacket as if they were made of chiffon. I couldn't see the lake from where I stood, but I knew it was still frozen, the coastal ice probably extending five miles beyond what the un-aided human eye could see. If you looked straight out and ig-nored the downtown skyline to your right, you might think you were stranded somewhere in Antarctica, scanning the horizon for a rescue ship.

When Rosemary Kelley opened the door, her appearance took me by surprise. I'd always assumed that most romance fic-tion was written by plump, middle-aged midwestern house-wives with their hair in buns and whole wardrobes of polyester pantsuits. But Rosemary Kelley might have been the model for one of the romantic characters in her books. She was tall and voluptuous, with translucent skin the color of skim milk, and a mane of flame-red hair, which was set off by a blouse that matched the impossible emerald green of her eyes. She must have been wearing green-tinted contact lenses; eyes like that simply don't occur in nature. The two swells of flesh asserting themselves at the V neck of the blouse were lightly dusted with tiny freckles. I estimated her age to be a well-preserved forty-five. Despite the clinging, revealing clothing, there was some-thing very asexual about her, as if she were one-dimensional, like the façade of an old-time movie set.

"You must be Mr. Jacovich," she purred, and stood aside so I could come in. She was holding a foot-high crystal goblet half-filled with white wine, and there was something not quite fo-cused in her eyes, leading me to assume it wasn't her first drink of the evening. A large cat with a flat, haughty face and long hair almost the color of its mistress's curled in and out be-tween Rosemary Kelley's ankles, looking up at me with the kind of withering resentment a cat can convey to someone who isn't particularly fond of cats.

Directly ahead of me a curving mahogany staircase swept up to the second floor. Along its left wall had been mounted an ascending row of framed book jackets, all featuring women in period costumes who looked vaguely like a younger version of Rosemary Kelley, although most of them were blonds or brunettes.

The living room was two stories high with a cathedral ceiling and was furnished in almost masculine taste with mahogany and dark-green and burgundy leathers. Over the fireplace, wide and deep enough for an ox roast, was a three-quarter-length portrait of the house's owner in a sapphire-blue evening gown. From hidden speakers somewhere came the kind of soft New Age music whose natural habitat is elevators and doctors' waiting rooms and whose relentless blandness makes Muzak sound like Dizzy Gillespie. Wide windows of leaded glass looked out onto the lake, invisible now in the dark, and there was a startling view of the lit towers of downtown Cleveland rising out of the blackness.

I handed her my business card. "Thanks for seeing me on such short notice, Ms. Kelley."

She tucked it into the breast pocket of her blouse. "It's kind of you to visit me. I live here and work here, Mr. Jacovich, and sometimes I go for days without seeing another human being, so it's my pleasure." She put a red-nailed hand on my bicep and squeezed gently. "Please, have a glass of wine with me. Drinking alone is so dreary."

"Sure, thank you," I said, and watched her cross the room to a walnut serving cart to pour, her lush body rippling beneath the green silk that clung to it.

"As I mentioned when you called this afternoon, there's nothing I can tell you that I haven't already told that disagreeable young woman from the police." She raised her eyes toward the heavens, or rather toward the ceiling, which was almost as high. "Ad infinitum."

"Well, the police and I have slightly different agendas, Ms. Kelley, so if you'll indulge me, I'll try not to take up too much of your time."

"Ro," she said, gliding back to hand me my wine. "Please call me Ro. Everyone does. I'll be happy to indulge you." As she came close to me I could smell her perfume—spicy, subtle, and probably very expensive. She herself was not very subtle, but probably the other two adjectives fit.

We sat in matching leather wing chairs on either side of the hearth and listened to the fire crackle and pop for a moment. Then she said, "I don't mind telling you that I'm scared to death, living here all by myself when something that gruesome went on right next door. The wind gusts off the lake and rattles a window and I jump out of my skin. I'm thinking seriously of getting a Rottweiler." She cocked her head archly. "But I'm not exactly the Rottweiler type."

I had to agree with her; she was more the matching-brace-of-borzois type. "A good security system would be better than a dog," I said. "And it would never pee on the carpet."

Her laugh was ice cubes tinkling in a goblet of the finest crystal. She took my card from her breast pocket and examined it. "Milan Security. Are you here to sell me a burglar alarm?"

I sipped my wine. It was a Chardonnay, dry as dust but no doubt costing considerably more. "No. As I told you on the phone, I'm trying to get a line on what might have happened next door on Thursday night."

She shivered. "That poor girl," she said. "I still can't believe it. It isn't real to me yet. I've had nightmares ever since."

"You knew her pretty well?"

"As well as any of us know our neighbors in this impersonal age," she lamented. "When she moved in three years ago I went over with a Bundt cake I'd baked as a kind of welcoming gift, and I gave her the names of my gardener and the snowplow guy who clears the driveways. After that we said hello on the rare occasions we saw one another out back, and when one of us was out of town the other one would pick up her mail. And we had keys to each other's house, in case of emergency."

She put a hand to her mouth. "My God," she said, "what if the—whoever—what if he took the key I gave her? He could just walk in here and . . ."

"You should mention that to the police so they can check Carville's house and see if they can find that key," I said. "But in any case, it might be a good idea to change your lock."

She got up and hurried to a spindly antique table against the wall to pull a notepad and a pen from the single drawer. "I definitely will," she said. "I'll make a note of it right now." Her red hair tumbled around her face as she bent over the table, and she tossed it back. Rita Hayworth singing "Put the Blame on Mame" in *Gilda.* "You have to forgive me; writers make notes about virtually everything."

"You didn't happen to make any notes about who Virginia Carville was dating?"

She straightened and turned to face me, somewhat flushed. "We weren't quite that good friends."

"I thought perhaps she might have mentioned someone."

"She was an attractive single lady, and a local celebrity to boot. I imagine she saw a lot of different people."

"No one in particular that you knew about?"

"No."

"Or anyone you might have seen who was over a lot?"

"Mr. Jacovich," she said, crossing slowly back to her chair, "I write three full-length novels a year. That means I spend ten hours a day or more in my sunroom up on the second floor, pounding away at my word processor. I wouldn't have known if Ginger was dating Godzilla, unless they happened to do their frolicking on the back lawn." She sat down in queenly fashion, and the cat jumped up into her lap, giving me a smug glare because it was allowed to do that and I wasn't.

"The police report says you went to bed early Thursday night and didn't see or hear anything."

"I'm not a very sound sleeper," she said. "I get my best ideas in the middle of the night. But the houses are pretty far apart here, as you might have noticed, so I'm not sure I would have heard anything even if I'd been awake." She rubbed her upper arms. "After what happened to Virginia, I might never sleep again."

"It must have been a terrible shock."

She ran a hand through her thick red hair, her fingers tangling in the curls at the ends. "Especially living in such a big house all alone. Almost makes me sorry I divorced my husband. Ex-councilman Frank Kelley; he's a partner with Rachmil, Prots, Kelley, and Davison, in the Leader Building. When he left the council he rejoined his former law firm. He's a wonderful man. Do you know him?"

"Not personally," I said. "I know of him, of course."

"When he heard about what happened next door, he offered to hire a full-time security guard for me until things quieted down. He's a love, really," she said, smiling fondly. "So caring and considerate."

"If you don't mind my asking, if he's such a love, why did you divorce him?"

She looked at me coolly, her green eyes deep and unfathomable. "Because he never read my books."

I suppose I must have blinked at that one. "A writer works from the gut, Mr. Jacovich," she went on, "from that secret place where he or she lives. And when you share a bed and a life with someone who simply doesn't give enough of a damn to take two or three hours out of their schedule to find out something about that secret place, the situation becomes unbearable."

She pushed her hair away from her face, grasping the thick coil of it and lifting it away from her neck before letting it fall. "Otherwise, he's a perfectly lovely man. He's going to be governor some day, you mark my words." Her expression turned serious, somber. "But I don't suppose my life story is helping you find out who killed poor Ginger."

"Everything helps," I said.

"Your glass is almost empty. More wine?"

"I really have to be going. But I thank you for taking time from your work to talk to me."

"I finished working hours ago." She laughed the tinkly laugh again, and waved her wineglass at me. "I never drink while I'm writing. Not even a little teeny one. I can't understand serious writers who do. William Faulkner may have been a major drunk, but being a drunk doesn't make you William Faulkner."

Having sampled her latest effort, I thought the comparison was pretty farfetched, drunk or sober. I stood up, and she went with me to the door.

"I hope you'll let me know the minute you find out anything," she said, putting her hand on my upper arm again. "Even with a security system I'd be uneasy alone here now."

I started to promise that I would when the doorbell rang. I jumped at the sound so close to my ear, and she looked startled and puzzled for a moment, glancing at her watch. It was almost nine o'clock.

"I can't imagine who . . ." she said, and swung the heavy door open. Gasping her surprise, she staggered backward a few steps, one hand going to her breast.

The man who stood there was in his middle thirties, not quite six feet tall, ruddy-complexioned and beefy. The knot of his plain red wool tie peeped out from the neckline of a maroon pullover sweater, over which was a windowpane sports jacket, and he wore black pleated slacks cinched tightly over his thick middle. Brown tassel loafers completed the ensemble. His hair was gummed up into a country western singer's pompadour with some kind of mousse, and he brimmed with the kind of raw and desperate confidence that makes a guy choose to become the State Farm Insurance agent in a small town in Tennessee. Over his shoulder I saw a white van parked in the driveway with zzz CARPET CLEANERS painted on the side panel.

"Hiya, babe," he said, leading me to conclude that he wasn't there to clean her rugs.

The color drained from Rosemary Kelley's face, leaving two bright spots of rouge in vivid relief against her cheeks. Her fingers fluttered almost helplessly, and she clasped her hands together in front of her to stop them. "What in the hell . . . ?" If her voice had been pitched one note higher only dogs could have heard it. "What are you *doing* here?"

"I was in the neighborhood," he said, "so I thought . . ." His eyes flicked to me and his brow furrowed. He didn't look hurt, exactly. But almost. "I didn't know you had company. I thought maybe—"

"How *dare* you just drop in here like this!" she fumed, blinking convulsively.

"I couldn't exactly call first, now could I?" he said, a slight smirk making his mouth crooked and unattractive. "I don't know your phone number."

I made a move to get past him and out the door. "Look, I was just leaving," I said, but not quickly enough. Rosemary Kelley moved forward like the advance guard of a panzer division.

"You get out of here," she told the visitor in a quavering voice. "And don't ever come back! Forget this address, forget you ever met me."

The smirk became more pronounced. "Hey, come on, now," he said, "don't get mad."

"Don't you tell me what to do! Now get the hell away from here, get off this property. At *once,* do you understand? And don't ever come back!" She sounded dangerously close to hysteria.

The man's little brown eyes glittered with a defensive kind of nastiness, and he wiped the corner of his mouth with his thumb the way Humphrey Bogart used to. "Kind of changing your tune all of a sudden, aren't you, bitch?"

I sighed, suddenly weary. Being in the wrong place at the wrong time was my kismet, it seemed, my karma. "You'd better change yours, my friend," I told him in my most authoritative voice—no, let's be honest, the tone was bullying. "You've been asked to leave."

His head swiveled toward me like an antiaircraft cannon, and his large hands knotted into fists. "Who the fuck are you, anyway?"

"Somebody who's a lot bigger than you are. And watch your mouth in front of a lady."

"Lady!" he sneered, and he stretched his thick neck, as if he was trying to make himself taller, but there was uncertainty in his eyes, and a little fear, and he baby-stepped backward off the front stoop, almost losing his balance.

"This isn't over," he stammered, the false bravado somehow pathetic.

"It is for now," I told him, "and that's what's important."

His chest heaved, and he huffed and he puffed, but he didn't blow the house down. He simply tramped away and got back into his van, slamming the door so hard they could have heard it way out west in Bay Village. Then he backed down the driveway with a screech of rubber that made my teeth hurt.

Rosemary Kelley closed the front door and leaned against it as though she would fall down if she didn't. A fine film of perspiration had appeared across her forehead and her full upper lip, and her chest rose and fell as if breathing was almost too great an effort. "I'm so sorry," she said. "I'm sorry you had to see that. I am truly, *truly* embarrassed."

"Don't worry about it."

"I do. I get so damned lonely sometimes—and I guess when I do I have execrable taste in men." She brought both hands up to cover her face for a moment, then dropped them. "It's—humiliating."

I tried to sound gentle and reassuring. "I've forgotten about it already. Really."

"You're very kind." She attempted a smile but it faltered and faded away.

"I'll be in touch," I said, but she made no move to let me by.

"Mr. Jacovich?" she said urgently.

I waited.

"I—I don't suppose I could persuade you to stay for a little while? In case that dreadful man comes back."

"He won't be back. Not tonight, anyway. I scared him away too easily. He's not the tough-guy type."

She ran her eyes slowly over me. "You are, though, aren't you?"

"I just look tough because I'm big," I said. "Inside, I'm a pussycat."

"I believe that. I believe that you are a deeply romantic man." She moistened her lips with her tongue and put both hands behind her, thrusting her breasts seductively forward and lifting her chin. But the invitation that seemed tacit in the pose I somehow felt wasn't genuine. She didn't look vulnerable or romantic at all. She looked like the prow of the ship that hunted down Moby Dick.

"I think," she said with a sly wink, "I'm going to put you in my next book." She took a couple of steps toward me. "As an outlaw, I think. A daring, dashing highwayman."

"It's your career," I said.

Brushing by her, I opened the door and went outside, aware that she kept the door open for about thirty seconds before finally getting the idea I was leaving. I looked up and down the street before I got into my car, but there was no sign of ZZZ Carpet Cleaners; my assessment of him had evidently been right on the money. I thought things over for a while, and then I pulled out my notebook and recorded the conversation between Rosemary Kelley and her unexpected visitor as best I could remember it.

I made a U-turn on Edgewater, jumped onto the Shoreway, and took it all the way to East Fifty-fifth Street where, on a whim, I got off and dropped into Vuk's Tavern, just a few blocks from where I'd been born and had grown up. Vuk—

Louis Vukovich to his mother but Vuk to everyone else—had served me my first legal drink of alcohol more than twenty years earlier, and I go to his place now when I want to wash the taste of the rest of the world out of my mouth. We shot the breeze for a while—quite a while, I guess, because I wound up having four or five beers before heading home to Cedar Hill and an empty apartment.

CHAPTER NINE

Mr. Scandalios," I said, "I'd like permission to look through Ginger Carville's office."

Nicky Scandalios was racketing down the hallway on the second floor of Channel 12—on his "morning rounds," he said, something he'd probably heard on one of the hour-long medical dramas his station aired. Despite my greater height and longer legs, I was scurrying to keep up with him and not much liking the obsequious way it was making me feel.

He rolled his eyes in exasperation, studying the ceiling as though Michelangelo had painted the Creation up there. He was wearing a blue suit today, with tiny red threads running through the dark fabric, and a white shirt and a pink tie with little blue squiggles that looked something like spermatozoa. "I'm afraid that's out of the question," he said.

"Why?"

"The police have already been through it, for starters. It would be extremely disruptive to the newsroom, as I explained to you yesterday. And I don't like the idea of strangers pawing through Ginger's things."

"Pawing through her things? It's an office, not a boudoir."

Ice came out of his eyes as he turned his head to glare at me without breaking his stride. "That's hardly what I meant. However, the principle remains the same. There may be material in there that's . . . sensitive."

He barged ahead, and I found myself looking at the pinkish

scalp beneath the thinning white hair on the crown of his head, which grew a bit redder as we walked. "When one of your employees has been murdered and another is about to be arrested for it, somebody's sensitivity doesn't seem so important, does it?" I offered.

He stopped suddenly, and my momentum took me several feet past him. I turned around, embarrassed.

"We've gone the limit with you, Mr. Jacovich, because we want whoever killed Ginger Carville caught as badly as you do. We answered all your questions yesterday, and we allowed you to question some of our people—against our judgment, I might add. And we were right. The five o'clock news sucked! Did you see it? Everybody's timing was off, especially Vivian's."

I didn't say anything. I was damned if I'd give him the satisfaction.

"I don't like doing shoddy work," he went on. "So for the sake of the station, and for the sake of the people who make their living working here, we're going to have to draw the line. Life goes on, you know."

"Not for Ginger Carville, it doesn't."

Now his face was almost purple. He wasn't the affable, good-humored big shot that viewers recognized from the public service announcements, and that his well-heeled buddies knew from the benefit circuit; he was a man in a state of high fury.

"Have you ever heard of journalistic ethics?" he roared at me like some road-company Jehovah.

"I have a master's degree, Mr. Scandalios. Don't patronize me."

"Then don't be such a dolt!" he said through clenched teeth. "Don't you understand the importance of keeping confidential sources confidential? Suppose there's something in Ginger's office, in her notes or something, that would seriously compromise someone she'd been talking to."

"Suppose there is."

"Well," he said, holding these truths to be self-evident, "we've given that person—or Ginger did—a promise of discretion, of protection, whether tacit or stated." He went through his peculiarly narcissistic ritual of stroking his own chest. "We've given our word."

"That's more important than someone's life?"

He put his fists on his hips and glared at me. "To a journalist? You're goddamn tootin'!"

"I doubt the police would feel that way."

"The police searched her office the day they found her. I told you that!"

"They might have missed something."

"Let them get a warrant, then," he said, walking away. "You get one, too. Otherwise get the hell out of my station or I'll have security *show* you out."

"I thought you were going to cooperate."

"Pound salt, Mr. Jacovich," he tossed over his shoulder, picking up speed.

I watched him charge down the hallway. Everything in me wanted to go and grab him by the collar and bounce him off the walls a few times, just to get his attention. But one doesn't try to muscle Nicky Scandalios in Cleveland. He is one of the town's major players, with all sorts of friends in very high places, and he has the arrogance to go with it.

I turned the corner into the corridor where the sales office is and went through the glass door behind which I'd first seen Mary so many years ago. She was there, a phone pressed to her left ear, a pencil in her right hand. A gold earring was on the desk in front of her. She looked up quizzically and put her hand over the mouthpiece while I mimed that I wanted to talk to her right away.

"Uh-huh. Uh-huh. Excuse me just one second, Nina," she said into the phone, and pushed the hold button. "What's wrong?" she asked me.

"Meet me at Cotton's in fifteen minutes," I said, referring to a little barroom diagonally across Euclid Avenue from Channel 12.

"Cotton's? It's ten o'clock in the morning."

"I have to talk to you. Only take a few minutes."

"I'll be through with this call—"

"Not here."

She frowned. "Okay, I guess," she said, and reengaged her caller. "Sorry, Nina," she said. "Now we're going to need the copy over here by five o'clock this afternoon. . . ."

I came out of the station into a fine drizzle and was almost run down by a handcart on which several large potted palms and ferns and broad-leafed rubber trees seemed to sprout, which was being pushed entirely too fast by a man dressed in work clothes. He was probably delivering them to one of the nearby office buildings, but cruising down Euclid Avenue like that, almost all of him obscured by the tall plants, he looked like a fugitive from a high school production of *Macbeth*, Birnam Wood coming to Dunsinane. You never know what you're going to see on Euclid Avenue.

I waited for a slight break in traffic and crossed the street in mid block, heading for Cotton's. It's a no-frills little bar, convenient to Channel 12 for a quick lunch or a quicker drink. I sat there nursing a cup of coffee until Mary came in and sat down on the barstool next to me. The bartender drifted over for her order but she shook her head.

Two people sitting at the bar and he was going to sell one cup of coffee. He seemed to take it pretty philosophically; he went back to the far end of the bar, where he was watching Regis and Kathie Lee.

"Steve hasn't come back to work?"

She shook her head. "Under the circumstances he'd probably do more harm than good if he came in now. The whole station would be talking about it—about him being questioned by the police last week, I mean. They are anyway, but with him sitting there it'd be worse. Really uncomfortable. For everybody." She examined her nail polish. "For me, especially."

"I need you to do something for me," I said. "For Steve, rather. I want you to search Ginger Carville's office."

She blinked. "For what?"

"I don't know," I said. "Notes. A date book. A confidential file, or a computer disk of some sort. Anything that has writing on it."

She chewed her lower lip nervously. "Milan, I can't do that."

"Sure you can."

"No!" She took a deep breath. "I can't. I'm not a spy, or a detective. That's your job. I'm just not very good at that sort of thing."

"I'm running into blank walls, Mary."

"Everyone has an alibi?"

"No—but nobody seems to have a motive."

"You think I'll find one in Ginger's office?"

"I don't know."

Her forehead was creased with worry. "What if I get caught?"

"There's less chance of that than of my getting caught; you work here. Nicky blew his cool at me just now and pretty much banned me from the premises."

"Why would he do that?"

"Good question. He said it was because of journalistic ethics. What his real reasons are, I don't know. But he went up like a skyrocket when I asked if I could see Ginger's office. That makes me wonder."

She glanced over at the bartender to make sure he wasn't eavesdropping, but he was engrossed in watching Kathie Lee interviewing Elle McPherson, and like most bartenders everywhere, he probably wouldn't have given a damn anyway. "How can I just walk in there and toss the place?"

"Toss the place? Where'd you learn that?"

She smiled a little. "I used to hang around with a hard-boiled detective, remember?"

I ignored the knife quartering my heart. "Do it at night, then. Nobody would question your being at the station late."

"They'd question my being in Ginger's office," she said. "The newsroom is occupied twenty-four hours a day. I don't see how I can, Milan." She traced something with her finger in some moisture on the bar, writing something I couldn't make out. "They'd can me in a flash," she said. "Nicky would. If I was caught."

I looked away from her, embarrassed. I didn't say the things I wanted to about making hard choices, because even as the words formed in my head they sounded fatuous and pre-sumptuous. Imposing my own values on Mary was one of the reasons I'd lost her in the first place.

Finally she said, "Is it that important?"

"We won't know till we look. It might be to Steve."

I watched the flush crawl across her cheeks, spreading outward from her nose; Mary's blush was one of the qualities I'd always found most endearing about her.

She didn't answer for a moment. Then she rubbed out whatever she'd written in the condensation. "I have to get back now," she said, sliding off her stool. Although we'd been together for a long time, I didn't recognize her expression as one I'd ever seen before. She rolled her head around as though she'd awakened with a crick in her neck. "All right, Milan. I'll try. Maybe tonight during the eleven o'clock news, when everyone is in the studio."

I just nodded a little encouragement.

"I don't know what I'm looking for, is that right? And if I find anything, then what? Should I bring it by your apartment afterward?"

"No," I said, a little too quickly. "Drop it off at my office, first thing in the morning."

My hand rested on the bar, and she covered it with her own, bringing her mouth close to my ear. Her perfume was Opium, and I wondered if it had come from the same bottle I'd bought her for her birthday several years ago. Her tone was almost teasing. "Why? Are you afraid of me, Milan?"

I swiveled around to face her, pulling my hand away. "Scared to death."

She looked at me as if for the first time. Then her mouth and jaw turned rigid and her voice got chilly. "Whatever you want," she said, and walked out, her heels clicking on the dingy linoleum floor.

I watched her go, a physical pain in my chest, and gulped down what was left of my coffee, now cold. The last thing in the world I wanted was for Mary to turn up at my apartment after the eleven o'clock news.

I got off the 422 freeway spur about an hour later. Bainbridge Township is in Geauga County, east of the city in the middle of what most TV weathermen call "the Snow Belt." It's one of those small, Connecticut-esque municipalities in northeast Ohio that in the wintertime look like an old-fashioned Christmas card. There are trees almost everywhere, buckeye and maple and oak, a few scattered birches, and several varieties of pine, interrupted only by the occasional shopping center or strip mall, and two or three nice family-type restaurants. The rest of Bainbridge is all well-kept middle-class homes; a classic bedroom community, with some retirees who saved their money thrown into the mix just to make it interesting.

Winfield and Evelyn Carville lived in one of the older homes on Chagrin Road. Neat and compact, it was nearly invisible behind a thick stand of pine and maple trees that were probably a hundred years old. As I turned into the curving driveway, the crunch of my tires on about an inch of yesterday's snow disturbed several cardinals, blue jays, and grackles, who flittered skyward from a tall redwood feeder, screeching their outrage.

I got out of the car and trudged across the driveway to the small covered front porch.

Evelyn Carville opened the door before I had a chance to ring the bell. I'd seen her on the home videos Channel 12 had shown, but in person her resemblance to her daughter was startling, except for the white hair and faint cobweb wrinkles around the large, almost startled-looking brown eyes, and I thought that Ginger would probably have looked just like that had she lived to be seventy.

"You must be Mr. Jacovich," she said kindly. She tried to smile, but I figured there weren't too many of them left in her, and I felt a wrench of sympathy, at odds with the professional distance I try to maintain when I'm working on a case. We somehow expect that our one inalienable right is that our children will outlive us; when they don't, the loss is often insupportable.

"I'm very grateful you allowed me to come, Mrs. Carville," I said, and she inclined her head. I stamped the snow off my shoes and wiped them clean on the raffia mat as best I could before going past her into the house.

Inside, the house was warm and cozy, with an eclectic mix of modern and period furniture, all of good quality while not ostentatious, and an old mahogany-stained Gulbransen spinet against the wall. Photographs of Ginger were on nearly every flat surface—snapshots of her as a baby, and as a laughing little girl on a sled, her high school yearbook picture, and several others of more recent vintage. The woodsmoke of grief hung in the air.

Through the picture window I could see another bird feeder in back, and a small pond, frozen and lightly dusted with snow. I wondered if, as a child, Ginger had skated on that pond. Fallen. Banged her knee and bruised her dignity. Cried.

"This is my husband, Winfield," Mrs. Carville said, and the dark-haired man in the easy chair leaned forward with a grunt, his Irish cable-knit sweater stretching across broad shoulders.

"Forgive me for not getting up," Winfield Carville said. "Old bones."

I shook his outstretched hand. His grip was strong and his eyes bright and alert, but several of his finger joints were swollen and misshapen with arthritis, and I was careful not to squeeze his hand too hard. "I'm very sorry for your loss," I said, looking from one to the other of them.

"Thank you. Please sit down, Mr. Jacovich," Evelyn Carville said, pointing to a sofa. "May I get you something? Tea? I made Toll House cookies for the—. All our friends came over here yesterday after the cemetery."

"I don't want to disturb you at what I know must be a stressful time. I won't be more than a few minutes."

She lifted her shoulders in resignation and then perched nervously near her husband on a chair upholstered in needlepoint, her toes just touching the floor, her knees pressed tightly together. I think that, like my late Auntie Branka, she was the type of woman who becomes uncomfortable if a guest in her home is neither eating nor drinking.

"The police have already been here, of course," Winfield Carville said, clearing emotion out of his throat with a sharp cough. "We're naturally willing to help any way we can, but you can imagine how difficult . . . "

"Ginger was our only child," Evelyn said in a lost voice.

And now, I thought, there would be no grandbabies laughing delightedly and skipping stones across the pond. There would be no family gatherings, no singing carols around the piano on Christmas or lighting sparklers out back on the Fourth of July. The insane, obscene act that had snuffed out a young woman's life had trampled down a lot of other dreams at the same time.

I felt foreign here, out of place, too large and awkward for the small room.

I took out my notebook and pen. "Did you see her quite often?"

"Every three weeks or so." The old man shook the large head that time and recent suffering had bowed low. "She had a tight schedule. She was under a lot of pressure. Television . . . "

"It's a very competitive business," his wife finished for him.

"I was a civil engineer until I retired," he said. "I don't know the first thing about television. But I guess there's a lot of rushing to meet deadlines, a lot of pressure. She had very little time to call her own."

"But we talked on the phone almost every day," Evelyn put in quickly, her eyes darting from me to her husband. She looked painfully alert, her movements birdlike. "We were very close."

"When you talked recently," I said, "did she seem worried about anything? Did she mention anything to you about what she was working on?"

"She never did that—talked about her work. She said if we wanted to know what she was doing we could just watch the news program. It was a way of keeping in touch. . . . " Her voice fluttered with the sorrow of all the things she and her daughter never talked about and now never would.

"Did she keep in contact with the people she grew up with out here? Her school friends?"

"I surely don't know." Her hands, which must once have been small and delicate, were now as gnarled at the joints as her husband's, and she rubbed them as if they might be causing her pain. "I think she called Jeannie Shaftoe once in a while. They were roommates at Kent."

"Jeannie Shaftoe?"

"She's a lawyer now, in Chagrin Falls."

I wrote down the name and *Chgn Fls.*

"But most of her friends were people she'd met after she moved to the city, I believe," she continued. "People she knew through work." She crinkled her nose a little. "West-siders, a lot of them. I didn't mind her moving to be closer to her work, but when she crossed the river . . . " She gave a little breathless chuckle. "Well, you know how people on the east side feel about the west side." She put a hand up to her mouth, suddenly embarrassed and concerned. "I didn't mean to offend you, Mr. Jacovich. You're not a west-sider are you?"

"No, ma'am," I said. "I grew up in the St. Clair–Superior corridor. Around East Sixty-seventh Street."

"That's good," she said.

"Mrs. Carville, did Ginger ever mention the name Steve Cirini to you?"

"What is that, Italian? No, I don't believe she did. Is that someone she worked with?"

"He's the general sales manager at Channel Twelve."

"Oh," she said. "No, I don't recall that name. She'd often mention that nice black man, Andrew, though. He was very helpful to her, she told me. And of course there was Vivian Truscott. Not so much lately, as I recall, but Ginger used to talk about Vivian a lot." She looked over at her husband. "Someone we've been watching on the TV for so many years, haven't we, Win? And then to think our daughter became her friend!"

"Ginger could have taken her place on the news one day," Winfield Carville said.

"It's hard to believe," his wife added.

She turned and looked at the photo of Ginger on top of the spinet, which had probably been taken more than ten years earlier, and her eyes reddened and filled with tears that threatened to fall but never quite made it. She fiercely rubbed the end of her nose.

"What about men friends?" I said. "Did she mention whether she was dating anybody?"

Winsfield Carville jerked upright, suddenly defensive. "Ginger didn't have time for any of that nonsense!" The words almost exploded from his lips. "Why, she worked every night until midnight and then got up early the next morning to go chasing after a story! She always was a hard worker. When she was in high school she took a part-time job with a dry cleaner, and she still kept her grades up. She was the most conscientious . . . " He stopped, his breath coming with difficulty, and his wife cast a concerned, almost frightened look at him. "She never had time for boys. Men. She wasn't that kind of a girl," he said, and put a hand over his eyes as if to shield them from an unbearably bright light.

That certainly wasn't the impression I'd gotten from Steve Cirini. But some parents, especially older ones, choose to keep their eyes averted from the realities of modern life when it comes to their children. Winfield Carville didn't strike me as a stupid man, so he was either lying to me or else he was deep in denial.

Of course there was still a chance it was Steve Cirini who lied. Or Mary.

Evelyn Carville rose and hovered over her husband, arms outstretched to protect him from whatever ugliness he chose not to face, and her glare at me was wounded and resentful; evidently I'd crossed an invisible line, violated a boundary.

"This wasn't a good idea," she said. "Your coming here today, I mean. It's too soon."

I stood up. "I didn't mean to upset you. I just thought you might be able to give me some insight as to what your daughter's life was like when she wasn't at work."

Winfield Carville had crumpled like a ten-day-old helium balloon. The skin around his mouth and eyes sagged, and all at once he seemed broken. "You don't ever get to know your children, Mr. Jacovich," he said, eyes fastened on the carpet. "Not really. You raise them in your home and your heart for twenty years or so, and then they move away and they become different people. Strangers." With effort he raised his head and fixed his gaze on me. The pain that ravaged his eyes under their shaggy dark brows was almost too terrible to look at. "And you're suddenly on the outside of their lives."

I wanted to say I was sorry again, but there didn't seem to be much point. Instead I simply ducked my head at him and allowed his wife to lead me out. She came out onto the porch with me, shutting the door behind her.

"This has been terrible for both of us," she said, hunching her shoulders and pulling her white sweater closed at the neck, "but especially for my husband. Ginger was everything to him. He was just so proud of her." She shuddered, and it wasn't from the cold. "Her . . . what happened to her has just about taken the heart out of him."

A couple of aggressive jays, more daring than the others, had staked out their territory at the feeder again, chattering noisily, and she glanced over at them. "I know she was very ambitious; a lot of that had to do with wanting to please her father, to make him proud of her. He's an old-fashioned man, Mr. Jacovich, from a simpler time, and he has the values to match. He doesn't understand what happened to Ginger, and he doesn't understand what's happened to the world, either."

"I'm not sure any of us understand, Mrs. Carville," I said gently. "Will it be all right if I need to contact you again?"

She hesitated.

"After all, we want the same thing," I told her. "We want to find out who was responsible for what happened to your daughter."

She cocked her head at a funny angle, and once more I was struck by her resemblance to a bright-eyed, inquisitive bird. "I don't think that's what I want, Mr. Jacovich. What I want is not to have to think about it. I want it never to have happened."

Turning, she put a liver-spotted hand on the knob, almost caressing it with the tips of her fingers. Her smile was sad and kind. "But I've lived a long time now. Long enough to realize that so very often we just don't get what we want."

She went inside, closing the door with a quiet, firm click, leaving me standing there on the porch. From the bird feeder the arrogant blue jays jeered at me, mocking the sorrow that hung over the pretty pondside cottage like a Lake Erie storm cloud.

CHAPTER TEN

Late afternoon found me leaning on a railing and watching the cascade of the Chagrin River over the sheer rock face above me, which had given the village of Chagrin Falls its name. I was munching from a bag of popcorn I'd bought from the little shop at the top of the falls, waiting for five o'clock to roll around so I could keep my appointment with Jeannie Shaftoe, whose law offices were in the neoclassical building across the street. With my car coat buttoned up to the neck and my scarf pulled up against the cold, it was pleasant to enjoy the falling water. The steady roar almost drove from my mind the grief I'd witnessed in the home of Winfield and Evelyn Carville.

Which is what waterfalls are supposed to do, I guess. I think the love of water, or at least a fascination with it, with rivers and lakes and oceans, is visceral, basic. I'd never thought much about it; I'd grown up only a few blocks from Lake Erie but because there is little access to the shore on the east side, I'd never really connected with it in any sort of emotional way. But now that my office is on the Cuyahoga riverfront I find myself entranced by the sluggishly moving current and the passage of the huge, lumbering ore boats and sleek pleasure craft.

The Chagrin River is a different kind of river: peaceful, rustic, and in most places shallow enough to be virtually unnavigable except in the smallest rowboat or canoe, the kind of lazy river Hoagy Carmichael must have had in mind when he wrote the song.

But it's not without its terrors, at that. Years before, I'd watched the police pull a corpse out of the half-frozen Chagrin, the body of Mary Soderberg's former lover.

And some time after that I'd met Nicole Archer because one of her old boyfriends had been murdered too.

Was there a pattern there? If so, it was a pretty morbid one. I tried to put the thought out of my mind, concentrating instead on the flashes of silver and the foam that boiled up as the water tumbled over the rocks. I couldn't hear the busy quacking of the ducks who lived above the falls, but I knew they were there. They're always there, winter or summer. Few things are constant and dependable in life, but the aggressive mallard ducks of Chagrin Falls are forever.

By four fifty-five there wasn't much left of the light. I wadded up my empty popcorn bag and put it in the trash bin, wiped the residual salt from my mouth, and climbed the steep flight of wooden steps to street level.

Jeannie Shaftoe's law office was a small, cozy, two-room suite above a bank. Any secretary, receptionist, or law clerk there might be had gone home for the day. On the door gilt lettering read: JEANNE SHAFTOE, ATTORNEY-AT-LAW.

Shaftoe was a pleasant-looking, squarely-built young woman in her late twenties. She wore glasses and was dressed in a boxy gray suit that seemed to call attention to the chunkiness of her figure rather than disguising it. Her manner was just as abrupt in person as it had been over the phone when I'd called to make the appointment, but the brusqueness seemed almost forced, as if she thought lawyers were expected to be tough and was acting accordingly. I couldn't help noticing that her fingernails were bitten nearly to the quick.

"I don't mind telling you that what happened to Ginger shocked the hell out of me," she said when I'd seated myself across the desk from her. "At school we used to wear each other's clothes. Of course that's when I was closer to her size than I am now." She shook her head. "You never really believe anything like that is going to hit so close to home, do you?"

"You were roommates at Kent?"

"For the last three years of undergraduate school."

"Good friends?"

She took a five-count before answering. "I'm not sure I'd characterize our relationship that way. We had different interests, different habits. We didn't really hang out together, if that's what you mean. I think that made the living arrangements easier."

"How so?"

"We didn't get in each other's way. I was a grind. The social aspect of college was less important to me than getting a good education. I always had my nose in a book. Ginger was more the party girl." She raised a cautionary hand. "Not that Kent State is a party school."

"I know. I'm a Kent graduate myself."

That seemed to loosen her up a bit, and she even allowed herself the luxury of a smile. "A jock?"

"Got me," I admitted. "A partial football scholarship."

"Ever try to go pro?"

I shook my head. "I'm not big enough to be a lineman or fast enough to be anything else. Or tough enough, for that matter."

"So what made you decide to be an investigator?"

It was my turn to smile. I liked it that she hadn't said "private detective" or "private eye," the way most people do. "It's a long story."

"Sorry," she said. "I'm used to asking questions, not answering them. It comes with the law degree. You want to know about Ginger."

"That's right."

"Why?"

"My client is a suspect in her murder," I said. "I'm looking for some reason she would be killed. If I find one, it might clear him."

"A reason?" She snorted. "There's no logical reason such a horrible thing should happen to anyone."

"I didn't say a logical reason, Counselor."

"I guess you didn't, at that. So how do I know this client of yours isn't guilty?"

"You don't," I said, "and I don't. But if he is, hiring a private detective to dig through the muck is an act of supreme stupidity."

She chewed on that for a minute and then nodded. "Well, all right, I'll tell you what I can, although I really haven't been close to Ginger since we left school. And even at school, we were more roommates than friends. As I mentioned, she ran with a pretty wild crowd at Kent. The journalism and theater and English-major kids."

I laughed.

"What's funny?"

"I never thought of English majors as being wild. When I was at Kent they spent all their time analyzing *The Mayor of Casterbridge*."

"Oh, you know what I mean. The artistic types, all pipe dreams and moonbeams. Some of them never touched the ground through four years of college."

"Drugs?"

She gave me what might be construed as a dirty look. "Everybody did drugs in school, didn't they?"

"Not everybody," I said.

"Oh, right, you were an athlete." She made it sound like something shameful. "Your body was a temple and you didn't want to abuse it."

"If you say so."

"Well, Ginger wasn't an athlete. At least not outside the bedroom."

My stomach fluttered. "You mean she was promiscuous?"

Her nostrils flared. "Why is that always the word used to describe sexually active women in a pejorative way? You never hear anyone call a man promiscuous."

"We can get into the sociological rhetoric some other time, Ms. Shaftoe. Right now we happen to be talking about a woman. And you were the one who said she was a bedroom athlete, not me. I'm asking why you did."

She made a steeple of her fingers. "Maybe because that's the way it seemed to me. I was a virgin until I was twenty-one, Mr. Jacovich. By the time Ginger was that age she was well into double figures."

"Not that unusual in the late eighties, was it?"

"I guess not. But Ginger went at it with a vengeance. It seemed very important to her that she be popular." A wry smile. "It didn't seem to matter much why."

"Sounds like low self-esteem."

"I'm a lawyer, not a shrink. But she used every bit of her new freedom. Her parents were pretty straight arrows."

"I met them this afternoon."

"Right, so you know. Well, Kent was the first time Ginger had ever lived away from home, and I think she looked at college as a chance to kick up her heels a little bit. Not that she didn't take her studies seriously, because she did. She knew just where she wanted to go, career-wise. She was very ambitious, even back then—driven, even. In everything she did. Grades, career, social life."

"And you weren't?"

She shrugged. "Two out of three isn't bad."

"You lived in the same room with her. Would you say she had a drug problem?"

"It wasn't a problem at all. A little weed, a little coke. Nothing serious. It was the thing to do in her crowd, so she did it. She certainly wasn't hooked or anything. She wasn't really hooked on sex either, I don't believe. It was a means to an end."

"Which was?"

She held out her hands palms upward like a waitress balancing twin trays. "Take your pick. Popularity with men, certainly. Visibility, being at all the right frat parties, the right campus events. It gave her a chance to meet everybody who was worth knowing. It was a brand-new term then, but it was almost as if she was always around for photo ops. And then there was that apprenticeship at Channel Twelve. God, there were an awful lot of people in the journalism department after that one. And Ginger was the one that got it." She rolled her eyes. "Any way she could."

I scribbled some notes. "Are you saying she slept her way into that apprenticeship?"

"No. I couldn't accuse her of something like that without being sure of my facts," she said, the sharp courtroom mind once more at work.

"Did you disapprove of her, Ms. Shaftoe?"

"In school?" She slid down in her chair, resting all her weight on the base of her spine. "Yeah, I guess I did. So what?"

"Were you jealous of her?"

She hesitated for just a second, then, "Of course I was jealous," she said, almost with exasperation. "Ginger stole a boyfriend right out from under me, the first guy I'd ever seriously dated. He dumped me for her because she was willing to sleep with him and I wasn't." She crossed her arms across her chest in the classic pose of defense. "You think I killed her because I was jealous of her ten years ago?"

"I didn't mean to imply that. But stranger things have happened."

Pursing her mouth, she stared over my shoulder at a spot on the wall that seemed to be her window to the past. "Dickie Partos was his name," she said with a kind of wonder. "Zorba the Greek, we called him, even though he didn't look much like

Anthony Quinn. More like Anthony Hopkins, when you get right down to it." She cocked her head. "Wow! I haven't thought about him in years."

"Where is he now?"

"I don't know and I don't care. I think I heard he was living in Atlanta, working in middle management with Coca-Cola. He was a business major."

"A business major," I said. "No moonbeams."

"No, he wasn't the moonbeam type. Or at least he wasn't until Miss Ginger got her claws into him. It didn't last very long, as I recall. Just long enough to wreck whatever he and I had together. But then nobody lasted very long with Ginger." She was deep into bitter remembrance for a moment, then her eyes refocused on me. "I can't really blame him, the big stupid slob. Look at me, and then think of her."

"You're a very nice-looking woman," I said. "And I understood that when Ginger was younger she used to run around with no makeup, wearing scruffy jeans and baggy sweatshirts."

"Yeah, but underneath them she had that great body. Look, what the hell's the difference, anyway? That's all ancient history."

"What about recent history?"

She sat up, and her right hand played an imaginary piano on the top of her desk. The rhythm seemed to correspond to "Doe, a deer, a female deer." She thought for a moment. "I can't really tell you much about that. She didn't confide in me. She wasn't a confiding kind of person." She stopped drumming her fingers and inserted one beneath the lens of her glasses and rubbed her eye. It was red when she took her finger away. "Most women are more open than that, especially with their other women friends. About feelings, I mean. But if Ginger ever let it all hang out, it certainly wasn't with me."

"Her mother said that she called you frequently. That you were just about the only friend from college she kept in touch with."

Jeannie Shaftoe nodded. "But that's only recently."

"How recently?"

"Within the past year or so. And it wasn't personal. I mean, she wasn't rekindling an old friendship. I doubt if that meant anything at all to her. She called to ask me if I'd do some legal work for her."

"Is the nature of that work confidential?"

"Not really. I helped her make out her will."

"Who was the beneficiary?"

She looked down her nose at me, highly trained lawyer to not-too-bright layman. "Until the will clears probate, that *is* confidential."

I made another notation. "Isn't it unusual for someone so young to be thinking about making out a will?"

"Unusual but smart," she said with more than a hint of pedantry. "Not enough people think about things like that until it's too late. For instance, I'll bet you don't have a will, do you?"

"As a matter of fact, I do. But I didn't when I was twenty-nine."

She gave me a supercilious smile, as if she'd scored some sort of coup. "Then let's just say that Ginger Carville got smart younger than you did."

"That's right," I said. "She got dead younger, too."

It was as blunt and shocking as I'd intended, and I watched the color drain from her cheeks with a supercilious little victory smile of my own.

As I drove back west on South Woodland Avenue I couldn't help thinking that the mental picture of Ginger Carville coming together in my mind was very much like the blind men's elephant. People's perceptions of her seemed to depend completely on what part of her they'd laid their hands on. Her father thought she was a career-obsessed saint. Andrew Lemmons knew her as a friend and a thoroughgoing professional.

To Steve Cirini she was little more than a hot, willing, and readily available bed partner. To her next-door neighbor, Rosemary Kelley, she was an enigma. Her immediate supervisor, Ray Aylmer, thought she was a hard-nosed and overly ambitious journalist; her boss, Nicky Scandalios, had feelings about her that were downright avuncular, and her colleague, Vivian Truscott, viewed her as a subtle but very tangible threat.

And Jeanne Shaftoe, her college roommate, had pegged her many years earlier as an amoral user.

Put them all in a blender and throw the switch, I thought, and I still wouldn't have the real Ginger Carville.

When I got home I picked up the mail from my box in the vestibule and sorted through it as I climbed the stairs to my apartment. Ever since I moved my business to the Flats I never get mail at home anymore that isn't either an ad or a bill. The art of writing personal letters is disappearing faster than the spotted owl, and I wondered if fifty years from now my sons or grandchildren would be enjoying a volume of the collected e-mail of some famous philosopher or statesman.

As soon as I got inside I turned on the news. There was no mention of Carville's death. It had occurred six days earlier and was already an old story. There were new murders and rapes and automobile fatalities and suburban political scandals that took precedent.

When the telecast was over I scrubbed a potato, punctured it in several places with a fork, and threw it into the oven. Then I microwaved a couple of frozen pork chops, set them sizzling in a cast iron skillet, and built myself a salad out of romaine and leftover croutons and peppercorn dressing. I opened a can of Stroh's and decanted it into a pilsner glass; I normally swig it right from the can but tonight for some reason I wanted to make myself feel special. Switching on *Fresh Air* on National Public Radio, I sat down to my solitary feast at the kitchen table.

Listening to the interviewing technique of the skillful, perceptive Terry Gross, I wondered if Ginger Carville might ever have gotten that good had she lived. Local news personalities have often used Cleveland as a way station to national recognition, and one thing on which everyone seemed to agree was that she had drive and ambition.

But now Ginger Carville slept forever in a cemetery in Bainbridge Township, so the point was moot.

After I washed up the dinner dishes I went into my little den, kicked off my shoes, and dug into the trials of Jay Gatsby and his unrealistic dreams, coming to the inevitable end of the novel a few minutes before midnight.

I'd been asleep for almost an hour when the telephone on my nightstand jangled.

"Milan? It's Mary. Did I wake you?"

"That's okay," I said, struggling to a sitting position. I forced my eyes wide open, and it took a couple moments before I could dredge up the memory of why she was calling. "Are you all right?" I asked, nerve endings out there, exposed.

"I guess so. I didn't get caught, anyway." The hollow quality of the reception and the slight crackling noise told me she was calling from her car phone. Then she said, "I think I might have something."

"Not over the phone. Meet me tomorrow at the office. Early."

"Seven o'clock?"

I looked at the luminescent face of my wristwatch. It was nearly one A.M.

"Not that early," I said.

CHAPTER ELEVEN

Even though it was only eight o'clock, the parking lot at my office was already half full; my industrious tenants on Collision Bend habitually start their workdays earlier than I do, and through the downstairs windows I could see workers moving around, going through their daily paces. The blue flame of an acetylene torch flickered, throwing grotesque shadows on the wall. Gulls screamed, wheeling overhead in casual formation, and the cold wind that swept down from Lake Erie brought the not unpleasant smell of fish. Of course nobody but a gull would eat a fish caught out of the Cuyahoga River; although the powers-that-be have done a remarkable job of cleaning up the waterway in the many years since it caught fire and forever blackened the city's eye, it's still a long way from being a crystal mountain stream.

Down the road three shabby men huddled around the remains of a trash can fire in the parking lot of a machine tool manufacturing concern. They knew that the morning's light would bring someone out to chase them off. Cleveland in February is a cold place to be homeless.

I went upstairs, my still unread morning newspaper under one arm. The office smelled stale and smoky, and despite the low temperature I opened one of the windows to air things out; the breeze rustled the pages of the Sierra Club calendar I'd hung on the wall. I booted up my computer before setting about making a pot of coffee. I was working on the second cup, having finished reading Ed Stahl's daily broadside, the same old news about Congress on the front page, Joe Dirck's column, and the sports news, when Mary Soderberg arrived.

"Milan," she said. Her face seemed pinched. I stood up and helped her take off her coat, which I laid across the second client chair. "Sit down, Mary," I told her. "Relax."

"Easy for you to say," she said, but she sat down anyway. She was wearing a dark green jacket over a cream-colored blouse and charcoal slacks, one of her many business uniforms. She probably had several sales calls to make later in the day.

I went to close the window, but she said, "That's all right, you can leave it open. It feels kind of good."

I sat down on the corner of my desk. "Did you have any trouble last night?" I asked her.

She put one hand out flat, palm down, and waggled it a little. "Yes and no. I mean, nobody seemed to think it was strange that I was at the station at eleven o'clock at night. But I had to wait until the news was on until I could sneak into the newsroom and into Ginger's office." She brushed back a wisp of blond hair that had escaped from one of the barrettes on either side of her head. "No one saw me because they were all in the studio."

"That's good."

"It wasn't so good when they all came back right after the show and I was stuck in Ginger's office for about forty-five minutes until the coast was clear and I could sneak out." She inhaled raggedly. "It was the longest forty-five minutes of my life." Her gaze turned inward, hard and bitter. "All to help a man who's been a total shit to me."

I couldn't disagree with her. "There's plenty of time to sort that out afterward. First things first. You said on the phone you had something."

"I don't know if I do or not," she said. "The police had already picked over her things pretty carefully. There was no address book, no Rolodex, hardly anything personal of hers in there at all. And I could tell they'd gone through her files."

"How?"

"Ginger was very organized, almost compulsive about her office. She was known for it around the station. But the folders in her file cabinet were a mess. Out of order, some of them stuffed only partway back in, some even backwards. That's not like Ginger."

I nodded.

"I went through her computer disks, too. The blank ones were all together in one place, looking like they'd never been touched, and the full ones were all alphabetized and carefully marked." She fumbled with the clasp of her purse and fished out a diskette. "Except this one. It was in with the full ones, but it's not labeled or anything. I thought that was kind of peculiar."

"What's on the disk?"

Her voice rose along with her color. "I don't know! I was scared to death of getting caught. You think I took the time to boot up her computer and look at it?"

I took the disk from her hand. "Maybe we should do that now," I said. "Except I don't think I know how."

She smiled, shaking her head. "Mr. High-Tech. We use Windows at the station. Even you can do that, Milan."

"Why don't you call it up for me, just to be on the safe side?"

She shook her head so hard that the errant wisp of hair escaped again, along with several others; this time she didn't bother tucking them back where they belonged. "I'm not sure I want to see what's on it."

The small disk felt like a dinner plate in my hand, heavy and portentous, and I put it down on the desk. "You know, don't you, Mary, that if I find something on this diskette that incriminates Steve Cirini in Ginger Carville's death, I'm bound by law to give it to the police?"

The nod was nearly imperceptible.

"Even though he's my client?"

"I know," she said.

"Then don't you think you ought to be here while I look at it? If it's something about Steve, something bad, I'd rather not have to tell you about it over the telephone."

She looked up at the clock on the wall. "I should be getting to the office."

"Mary, you haven't gotten to the office before nine thirty since I've known you."

She put her hands on either side of her head, pressing on her temples. "Jesus, what if it's Virginia's secret sex diary or something lurid like that, something about Steve?" she said with a lot more force than necessary. "You think I could stand that? I don't think I could be here in the same room with you reading something like that." Her lower lip quivered, and she dropped both hands into her lap and concentrated on picking at the polish on her thumbnail. "I just don't want to get hurt anymore. I've been hurt enough, okay?"

I stood up. "However you want it."

Her blue eyes reddened with inner pain and about-to-be-shed tears, and she got to her feet quickly, with less than her usual grace. "Don't even call to tell me what's on that disk. I don't want to know. I don't have the right to know, anyway; I'm not your client, Steve is."

"He wouldn't be my client if you hadn't asked me," I reminded her.

"Well, I've done my share and I'm out of it now. I got him his own detective and I swiped a computer disk for him at the risk of my job, and now I'm finished." She snatched her coat up and headed for the door. "Don't ask me to do anything else like this, because I won't. I feel like a thief." She turned, one hand on the doorframe. "I *am* a thief."

I didn't have time to disabuse her of the notion before she was out of the office. I could hear the hurried clatter of her heels as she went down the stairs.

I went to the open window and lit a Winston, blowing the

smoke outside, where the wind caught and dissipated it. Boat traffic is fairly rare in February because of the ice, although the river looked navigable this morning, so I watched the gulls and counted cars and buses as they whizzed past Tower City and the Ritz-Carlton Hotel on Huron Road across the water.

When I'd finally puffed the cigarette down to the filter, I closed the window, went and stubbed out the butt in the ashtray on my desk, and brought the disk over to my computer.

There was a chance the damn thing might be blank and Carville had just stuck it in the wrong pile, but I knew immediately that I had something, because a document title popped up on the menu. I don't know what I would have done if there had been some sort of password necessary to access the file. Not really being computer-literate, I would probably have had to call somebody who was. But Ginger Carville must have had a sense of humor; the only document on the disk was entitled The X File, apparently after the very popular scifi TV show I've never seen.

I punched the keys that opened the file and waited for Enlightenment.

There wasn't much on it, only random word and sentence fragments which made absolutely no sense to me:

> VIOLET GRBA
> PRNTS TRK RD
> FK INC SPNG-SMMR 83
> POL REP? FOLOUP?
> CNT DR FLYGENRING
> REP MRY?
> PMNT MADE?
> STAT LIM???

I stared at the screen long enough for my eyes to get tired. Then I punched another button and my printer clacked and whirred for about five seconds until I was able to tear off the hard copy. I'm still more comfortable with a readable piece of paper in my hand than with electronics.

It appeared that Virginia Carville had not only deliberately left this diskette unmarked amongst a slew of others that had been carefully labeled, but that she'd gone to great pains to keep her notes virtually incomprehensible in case anyone like me came across them. The only words she had fully spelled out were *violet, made,* and *stat.*

I stared at the printout for a few minutes, trying to make some sense of it. For me, a math moron, it was like trying to puzzle out a problem in advanced algebra.

But if you look at something long enough, eventually something jumps out at you. After too long a time I discerned that SPNG-SMR 83 might be spring-summer 1983, and I drew a circle around it, feeling fairly confident that was one puzzle piece I'd nailed.

But what in hell was a flygenring?

Could PRNTS be "prints"? TRK RD? Truck Road? Turkey Raid? Trick Rod?

Was FK INC a company doing business in the Cleveland area? Who was Violet, and what could it mean? Or did it signify a grba, whatever that might be, that was violet? Maybe the letters G-R-B-A stood for something.

Grand Railroad Boxcar Advocate.

Grim Reaper Benevolent Association.

Great round blubber ass.

Virginia Carville had needed to buy a vowel or two.

I hauled out my dictionary and tried in vain to find *grba.*

Then I checked the business section of the Ameritech white pages for the metropolitan area under F, hoping I'd discover a corporation called something like Food King or Frost King or Floral King, but I came up empty.

It was nearly nine o'clock, and I was pretty sure Marko would be in his office, so I dialed the direct number of the homicide division, knowing from long experience that it's always best to bypass the desk and call the division directly, because the guy on the desk doesn't want to take the report because it means paperwork.

"I was just getting ready to call you," Marko said when he came on the line. "I got a complaint about you yesterday. You've been naughty."

"You mean I forgot to separate my trash into recyclables and nonrecyclables again?"

"You forgot to make nice with Nicky Scandalios. He's not happy with you. As a matter of fact, you're out of his will."

"Why?"

"He said you were a nuisance." I heard him gulping his coffee. "Translated, that means you're a pain in the ass."

"And?"

"And I agree with him. Stay away from Channel Twelve, Milan. He's got a real woodie for you."

"Tough. I'll put alum on my thumb to keep from sucking it in my sleep. Anything happening with the Carville murder on your end?"

"We're beating the bushes, but we haven't flushed out so much as a quail. I'm starting to like your guy for it a lot."

"If you mean Cirini," I said, "he isn't my guy."

"Touchy. Have you got anything?"

I looked at the printout on the desk in front of me. If I told him about it, I'd have to tell him how I got it, and that would land both Mary and me in all sorts of trouble, legally and professionally. "No," I lied. "But except for her parents, nobody thought Carville was the Virgin Mother exactly."

"So a good-looking woman in her late twenties liked to screw," he said. "I've got a big oil painting of me taking *that* to the county prosecutor."

"You get anything from the next-door neighbor?"

The sound of papers shuffling came through the receiver. "Um, Rosemary Kelley? No, but after Detective Farmer interviewed her she was so impressed she ran out and bought every book Kelley ever wrote, and now we can't get her nose out of 'em. Why?"

"I don't know," I admitted. "When I talked to her she just seemed a little hinky."

"Oh, right. *She* had sex with Carville and then strangled her."

"Probably not. So what's the deal on Cirini, Marko?"

"Let's see," he said. "It's Thursday morning. If we don't get anything else by the end of business on Monday, we're going to bring him down to headquarters Tuesday morning and slam a window shut on his dick."

"That's only five lousy days."

"God created the whole world in six."

"Yeah, and look what happened," I said. "He put Steve Cirini in it."

Five days. Five days to keep my client out of jail, five days to find someone else at whom the police could point a finger.

Five days and then my dealings with Mary would be finished, and how would I feel about that?

After I hung up I studied the printout some more. Except for spring-summer 1983, all I had were the answers to a crossword puzzle in some alternate universe.

I turned on the boom box on the shelf behind me. On MAJIC 105, John Lanigan, John Webster, Jimmy Malone, and Tony Rizzo were arguing. No big surprise there, they argue every morning, usually about social politics; it's why everyone listens. This morning's topics seemed to be about backups, number-two people who stand around and wait for a lucky break—the U.S. vice president, the Miss America runner-up who'll serve if the real winner can't, and backup quarterbacks in the National Football League, which seemed to draw the largest number of listener call-ins. I set the volume as low as I could get it, hoping they'd soon announce the name of the song that was to be the Cash Bribe Oldie of the Day so I could call in and win a hundred and five dollars.

STAT LIM, the inscrutable printout read. In my head I ran through some possibilities.

Stationary limousine.

Statistical Limburger.

Or perhaps an unusual name for a Chinese restaurant.

And what of POL REP? Political representative? That would be a peculiar way to put it. And would that mean a member of Congress, an Ohio state legislator, a city councilperson or county commissioner?

Political reputation?

Polish repast—like kielbasi and pierogies?

Polar something-with-an-*R*?

After a few more minutes of brainstorming, something at least reasonable occurred to me: police report. Was Carville wondering if a police report had been filed in the spring or summer of 1983?

Once that fell into place it wasn't too hard to figure out that FOLOUP was probably *follow-up*: If a report had been made to the police, had there been a follow-up investigation?

But of what, or whom? FK INC? I made a note to check whether anyone had filed a complaint about a corporation in the Cleveland area whose name might fit, in the spring or summer of 1983.

But filed a complaint with whom? The Cleveland police? Or one of the twenty-eight suburban police agencies in the metropolitan area? Or somewhere out of town? The whole thing was becoming more and more daunting.

I moved on down the list: PMNT MADE? Payment made? *Yes!* I wrote that down, wondering why Carville hadn't bothered to disguise it better. And what kind of payment, and from whom to whom?

That still left me with a lot of gibberish on the page, but it was at least a start.

REP MRY: was MRY Mary? It's hardly an uncommon name,

especially in very Catholic Cleveland, but if it was a reference to Mary Soderberg, what was Mary's name doing in Virginia Carville's X File? Even thinking about that made me nervous.

And what about REP? Did it mean *report* her as well? Report Mary? Repeat Mary? Represent Mary?

Repeat Murray, I thought. Trying to decipher this nonsense was getting me nowhere; except for PAYMENT MADE? and POLICE REPORT, I hadn't a single frame of reference.

I ran my eyes up and down the page, waiting for lightning to strike. CNT DR FLYGENRING. Could CNT be *count?* County? Maybe the police report, if that's what it was, had been made to the county, to the sheriff's office?

Did DR mean Drive? County Drive? I didn't think there was one. County Road, yes, but no County Drive, at least not that I'd heard of. I made a note to look in my trusty red book of county streets and roads.

Doctor, perhaps. If Ginger Carville had been stingy with the vowels on her cryptic little page, she'd been downright niggardly with punctuation, and perhaps the simplest and most obvious explanation for DR was the right one. If I put a period after it, it looked right.

I hauled out the phone book and turned to the impossibly long section listing physicians. The health care industry is Greater Cleveland's leading employer, so there were plenty of doctors from which to choose. I looked under F—and there, unbelievably, was Oscar J. Flygenring, M.D. In a high-rise building downtown on East Ninth Street.

I wrote his address and phone number on the printout. CNT Dr. Flygenring. Count Dr. Flygenring? Control Dr. Flygenring? Perhaps CNT had been Carville's shorthand for *contact.*

I'd soon find out, I thought, and tapped out his number.

The woman who answered the phone, who seemed terribly put out that I didn't have an appointment with Doctor and that I hadn't been referred by anyone to Doctor, informed me haughtily that Doctor pronounced his name FLIG-en-ring. I begged and cajoled a little more until I finally got to talk to Doctor himself.

He spoke with a very slight accent that led me to conclude his last name might be Norwegian. He sounded both middle-aged and not too pleased to be talking with a private investigator. I asked him if he had known Virginia Carville.

"From the television only," he said. "Of course I read of her unfortunate death in the newspaper. But I've no idea why my name should be in her files. To the best of my memory, we had never met, nor spoken on the telephone."

"Had you been in contact with anyone else at Channel Twelve News, Doctor? I mean recently?"

He cleared his throat. "I hardly ever watch the news programs on television. I have too much to do, and I hear enough tragic news right here in my office. I certainly have never had a reason to speak with anyone in the television news business." I heard him smack his lips. "Or with a private investigator, for that matter."

"Does spring or summer of 1983 have any particular significance to you, Doctor?" The question sounded stupid even as I asked it.

"I have no time for riddles, sir," he said, his voice turning frosty. "I have a patient due at any moment, and I'm afraid I really have nothing more to discuss with you."

The click on the other end of the line was definite and terminal. I replaced my own receiver.

I should have known better. When it comes to protecting themselves and their own, doctors have a stricter code of silence, of *omerta,* than the Mafia. Of course Flygenring wouldn't have told me if he'd been treating Ginger Carville as a patient; that would have been an ethical violation. But the first thing out of his mouth was a denial that he'd ever had any contact with her, despite the fact that his name appeared in her "secret" diskette. I doubted gravely that there could be two people in the metropolitan area called "Dr. Flygenring." Or even two people in the world. Maybe the doctor with the strange last name was hiding something. Or maybe he was telling the truth and his arrogant manner was only the natural outgrowth of being a snotnose.

Were the payments made to him? I underlined CNT DR FLYGENRING on the printout—several times.

Ed Stahl could give me the skinny on Flygenring, I knew. Ed, with a mind like a file cabinet, could come up with deep background on damn near anyone worth talking about in the Greater Cleveland area. I called him on his direct line, and he answered as he always does, by firing his last name at the caller as if he were launching a torpedo.

"Stahl!" he barked.

"Ed, it's Milan. I need to run a name by you," I said, holding the cordless phone with my shoulder so I could pour yet another cup of coffee.

"Is that why you called? Not to tell me how wonderful my column was this morning?"

"Your column was terrific."

"Not to congratulate me on my insight and on the guts it took to criticize the governor?"

"I marvel at your guts and insight."

"Not to praise my elegant yet forceful prose?"

"That your prose is elegant yet forceful goes without saying, Ed."

"See, that's the trouble, Milan. Everything goes without saying. That's why there's no courtesy left in the world, no grace and dignity." He sighed into the receiver, and it sounded like a tidal wave. "All right. Who've you got on the griddle this time?"

"A Dr. Oscar Flygenring." I spelled it for him.

"Hmm," he said. "That sounds familiar. Of course it's the kind of name you hear once and never forget."

"You mean you don't know it off the top of your head?"

"It may shock you, but no, I don't. However, I'll know it off the top of the medical editor's head as soon as he decides to bring his sorry ass into the office."

"When do you think that might be?"

Ed laughed. "God only knows. Every time he writes a piece on a specific disease, he gets the symptoms. You should have seen him after his column on PMS."

"Flygenring is a psychiatrist, Ed."

"And a psychiatrist," he explained pompously, "is an M.D. Ergo, the medical editor."

I thanked him and hung up, my nerves and my teeth on edge. Waiting is one of the frustrations of my profession, and now I was stalled until the hypochondriac medical editor decided to show up for work. I tapped another Winston out of the package and lit it, turning up the radio to join in the fun and perhaps clear my head.

Listening didn't help much, funny as the Lanigan crew is. I realized that even if I managed to decipher all the code on the diskette, it might not have a damn thing to do with Ginger's death, and I would have spent precious hours chasing wild geese that fly with the moon on their wings.

But then again, Virginia Carville had gone to a great deal of trouble to disguise her notes in her own particular shorthand and then had put them on an unmarked diskette, which she'd made difficult to find. And that meant that whatever and whoever the notes referred to, the story had to be pretty hot—if it was a news story at all and not something that was going on in Virginia Carville's personal life.

Hot enough to get her killed?

Could be.

CHAPTER TWELVE

I'm telling you, I never even heard of Oscar Flygenring! I can barely say it, for God's sake!" Steve Cirini, in a black cashmere sportcoat worn over a gray sweater and gray twill slacks, paced the floor of my office like a captive panther, shoulders slightly hunched, head forward. In my mind's eye I could almost see his tail lashing.

When I'd called him and said I wanted to meet with him that afternoon, he'd suggested I come out to his home in Mayfield Village, but I'd vetoed that, insisting he drive down to the Flats instead. It was game-playing, I knew, and I don't play games very often. Maybe I don't do it nearly enough. In any event, I'd decided I'd be more comfortable on my own turf, conducting my business with him on my terms.

Screw what made *him* more comfortable.

The sky had been getting more gray and oppressive since the morning, and Cirini's presence in my office was pretty oppressive in its own way. He somehow made the air seem heavier. I hoped very much I could clear up this business soon and be done with him; every time I looked at him, it made me think about things I'd much rather forget.

"Was Ginger seeing a psychiatrist?" I said.

The question surprised him; at least it brought his pacing to an abrupt halt. "Is that what Flygenring is? A psychiatrist?"

"That's right."

"No, I doubt it," he said. "I doubt she'd ever feel she needed one. She was a pretty self-possessed chick. But if she had been, she probably wouldn't have told me."

"Why not?"

He flapped his arms. "We didn't confide in each other like that. It wasn't that kind of relationship."

"Strictly ba-da-bing, is that it?"

His eyes glittered. He'd finally reached the point with me where he knew when he was being zinged. "Right. Ba-da-bing! You have a problem with that?" His voice was low and angry, almost mean.

"I have a problem with you in general," I said. "But this isn't about my problems—it's about yours. And if the police come after you Tuesday, you've got a big one."

He backed up a few steps; I was pleased to see that I'd cowed him. "Where'd you hear about this Dr. Flygenring, anyway?" he mumbled.

"I found his name in some of Ginger's notes."

"How'd you get hold of them?" he asked, suddenly wary.

"None of your business."

"Hey, I'm paying for this information!"

"You're paying for me to take the heat off you, and that's all."

He pouted. It wasn't nearly as cute as when Shirley Temple used to do it. "Anything in those notes about me?"

"Do you want there to be?"

He pushed back the tails of his jacket and plunged his hands into his pockets, a self-conscious pose right out of an L.L. Bean catalogue. "I just don't want my private business spread all over town, that's all."

"If I were you, I wouldn't either. But no, there wasn't anything about you."

He visibly relaxed, some of the tension going out of his shoulders and neck.

"Did Ginger ever mention anything to you about 1983?" I asked him. "The spring or summer of 1983?"

"No. What is that, 1983? Is that supposed to mean something?"

"You tell me."

"I didn't even know her then." He stopped, doing the calculations in his head. "She was sixteen years old in 1983."

"Uh-huh."

"So something happened to her when she was sixteen?"

"I don't know. The reason I wanted to see you is that I thought maybe you knew."

"I don't know a goddamn thing!" he declared. "That's what I'm paying *you* for—to find out. I'm going under for the third time here."

I put the printout of Ginger Carville's file on the desk and turned it around so he could read it. "Take a look at this. Is anything here familiar to you?"

He leaned over the desk, peering at the page, and the scent of the spicy men's cologne he wore too much of rose from him. He smelled like a French whore.

"It looks like gibberish," he said, shaking his head. "Except for Dr. Flygenring, and that doesn't count."

"Look again," I said. "Free associate. Take guesses. That's what I've been doing."

"I'm not good at this kind of thing, Milan. Word games." His head moved as he looked up and down the list, brow knit, mouth pursed.

"Statue of limitations," he suddenly announced. He straightened up and pointed triumphantly to the last entry on the list. "STAT LIM? Could mean statue of limitations. Question mark."

If it hadn't been such a great guess I would have felt pretty superior that he'd said "statue" instead of "statute." But I turned the paper around to stare at it again, and all at once I felt the way I do when I've been studying an optical illusion and it suddenly comes clear and begins to make sense so that

I can never look at it the same way again. Now there seemed to be little doubt in my mind. With a frisson of excitement I wrote *Statute of limitations* next to the two cryptic nonwords and then drew a curved line between them and the year 1983. Something had happened to someone, somewhere, in 1983, maybe to Virginia Carville herself, and she was wondering if the statute of limitations had run out.

"That was very good, Mr. Cirini," I said.

He stood taller, almost preening. "I'm surprised you didn't see that."

"Yes, well, let's not take any bows until we know for sure that it's right." I was extremely irked at having been bested at my own game; it was like the time I was playing trivia with a friend of mine from Minneapolis and we were trying to name the films in which there were three best actor or actress Oscar winners, past or future, and I came up with a bunch of obscure ones and totally overlooked Brando, Pacino, and Duvall in *The Godfather*. It made it worse that it was Steve Cirini who'd figured this out.

"Do you have any other blinding flashes of insight up your sleeve?" I asked. "How about FK INC?"

He looked blank. "Fuck Incorporated?"

"Thanks," I said, and put the list in my desk drawer. "I think you ought to go back to work as soon as you can. Tomorrow, if possible. It doesn't look good that you seem to be hiding."

"Nicky doesn't agree with you; it was his idea that I stay out of the office until all this blows over." He began pacing again. "Costing me a goddamn fortune."

"He's docking your pay?"

"I'm a salesman," Cirini said. "I work on commission. I don't work, I don't sell. I don't sell, I don't make a nickel."

"Did Nicky Scandalios forbid you to come back to work?"

He got tough—as tough, I imagine, as he ever got. "Nobody forbids me to do anything," he informed me with a Sylvester Stallone you're-the-disease-I'm-the-cure sneer.

"Lucky you. Then you can go back tomorrow."

Macho flickered, warring with uncertainty. "Maybe," he said weakly. "I'll talk to Nicky."

"Let me ask you something, Mr. Cirini. All the times you were at Ginger Carville's house, did you ever meet her next-door neighbor, Rosemary Kelley?"

He ran a hand through his black curls. "I don't think so. I was almost never there except pretty late at night."

"Ever heard of Rosemary Kelley? She's a famous local author."

"Nah. I don't read much."

"You say that like you're proud of it."

I couldn't tell whether that exasperated him or hurt his feelings. "Why are you always busting my chops, Jacovich?"

"You know damn well why."

"Well for Christ's sake, give it a rest," he said, really angry now, and not whining a bit. "You made your point, all right? When this is over you can call me all the names you want. You can even take a swing at me. But right now I've got enough troubles without having to eat a truckload of shit from you every time we talk."

I picked up a pencil and doodled my empty gallows with a hanging noose. "You're right," I said finally. "And it's lousy. I'm taking your money and I should be on your side. I apologize, okay?"

"Okay. Friends?"

I laughed in his face—I didn't mean to, I just couldn't help it. "Don't push it," I said.

"Lord, it's been a day," Ed Stahl said, leaning round-shouldered over the bar at Vuk's Tavern.

"Nothing to write about?" I said.

"Too damn much to write about. I couldn't seem to settle on a single story, and I'm plumb wore out." He looked at me over his glasses. "Even a journalist uses lousy grammar some-times. It feels good."

"I'm plumb wore out too," I said, and signaled Vuk to bring us another round.

"You remember Red Smith?" Ed said. "Used to write sports for *The New York Times.* "One of the greats, right up there with Lardner and Grantland Rice. He said once that there's nothing to writing—you just sit down at a typewriter and open a vein. Days like today I know what he meant."

Vuk came over and set our drinks on the bar—a Stroh's for me and a Jim Beam with water for Ed.

"Haven't seen you around much, Ed," Vuk remarked, folding his Popeye forearms across his chest, and for him it was a full-blown oration. You don't find many people from outside the neighborhood in Vuk's—they aren't exactly warmly welcomed—but Vuk knows Ed through me and from the unflattering photograph at the top of Ed's daily column, and on the rare occasions that Ed comes into his bar with me, Vuk never fails to speak to him, even though he isn't Slovenian.

"There's just so many places to do your drinking in this town," Ed explained. "I try to spread it around a little."

Vuk grunted and scooped up some money from the pile in front of me, stalking down the bar toward the cash register. It was around six thirty, and the place was full up with the after-work crowd, mostly blue-collar and virtually all Slovenian or Croatian except for Ed. Business would boom until about seven o'clock, when everyone went home, and then there would be a lull until the evening drinkers came out after ten o'clock.

"I did more than bang out sixteen column inches today," Ed said after taking a healthy sip of his drink. "I got a little information on your Dr. Whosie-face."

"Dr. Flygenring."

He looked at me, twisting his mouth up in an effort to pronounce it and then giving up. "What you said. The medical editor breezed into the newsroom at about three o'clock, and I managed to catch him before his Prozac kicked in. He didn't know much—which is why he's a medical editor—but here's what I got."

Fumbling in his inside jacket pocket, he brought out a black leather-covered notebook, the kind used by many veteran cops. The leather was dull, cracked and creased from many years of service, but I noticed Ed had put a fresh pad of paper in it.

He pushed his glasses up on his nose and paged through the notebook until he found the entry he was looking for. "Dr. Oscar . . ."

"Flygenring," I said again, pronouncing it carefully.

"He's a downtown shrink."

"I know."

"With a psychiatric specialty." He lovingly caressed the sides of his glass but didn't drink. "Everybody specializes. Football players, lawyers, psychiatrists. Next thing you know, Vuk here will only serve Stroh's beer, and if you want a Bud or a Heineken you'll have to go to another bar where they specialize in that."

"In your dreams," I said.

Ed looked back down at his notes. "Have you ever heard of 'repressed memory syndrome'?"

"I've read about it. It's when a person has had some really traumatic experience—like being physically or sexually abused as a child—and has completely blocked out the memory until many years later, right?"

"Right," Ed said. "It's usually brought out again in therapy of some sort, mostly under hypnosis. So lately we've been faced with a lot of cases where a grown woman who's been going along minding her own business suddenly remembers after all these years that her father used to mess with her when she was ten, at which point she either confronts him with it or files a lawsuit. The situations have turned pretty ugly most of the time." He struck a wooden match on the edge of the bar and stuck the flame into the bowl of his pipe. There aren't too many public places left in the world where one can light up without getting dirty looks—in Vuk's they look at you funny if you *don't* smoke.

"Now the thing to keep in mind here," he went on, making a disgusting sucking sound through his pipe, "is that there are two distinct schools of thought about this particular phenomenon. The first, adhered to by a lot of mental-health professionals and women's groups, is that this is on the up-and-up, that repressed memory happens more often than we think and that even many years later a real memory can be triggered, and when it is, action needs to be taken against the alleged molester or whoever, both as a recovery process for the victim and as a way of healing one of society's more pernicious ills."

"Sounds right."

"Okay. Now the other camp, and there are lots of respected doctors and psychologists in it, believe that nine out of ten of these cases are pure baloney, that it's either a new way for unscrupulous shrinks to milk some more money out of their patients, or else a new kind of sledgehammer to bash the poor middle-class male, and that it's used to get revenge against guys that weren't such terrific fathers or to pry some big bucks out of the old man to keep it out of the newspapers." He puffed on his pipe twice, sending gray smoke climbing toward the ceiling exhaust fan, where it was quickly caught and whisked away. "As you might imagine, no one ever quite recovers from that kind of an accusation when it becomes public, whether or not it's proven."

"I can also imagine that no kid ever quite recovers from that kind of abuse."

"Goes without saying. The question here seems to be whether the repressed memory syndrome is valid or if it's simply the politically correct flavor of the month. But a lot of shrinks have gotten famous and a lot of lawyers have gotten rich trying to prove it's the real stuff."

"I know, Ed. So is it? The real stuff?"

"Depends on who you talk to. Your Doctor Flyg—sorry, I can't quite seem to get it."

"Flygenring."

"Yeah. He seems to think it is. He's gotten his name in the paper and his mug on the six o'clock news several times with it, too. Remember that business tycoon out in Lorain whose daughter accused him? That suburban police chief who was forced to resign before anything was ever proved in court?"

"Sort of," I said.

"Milan, you've got to start reading more of the newspaper than the sports page. Anyway, in both cases that was your doctor, giving very grave and very well-constructed twenty-second sound bites on the Channel Twelve news, and not incidentally collecting himself a raft of new patients."

"You sound like you're in the camp of the nonbelievers."

"I don't believe anything anymore, one way or the other. But I tend to view things like this with a healthy dose of cynicism."

"That seems to be a requirement in your profession."

"Sure it is," he said. "Otherwise I'd be rushing off to do a column on every kookaburra bird who calls me and tells me a tale of woe, at least half of whom are scam artists."

"You think Flygenring is running a game?"

He shrugged and puffed on his pipe some more, frowning when he discovered it had gone out on him. "Damn!" he said, and fished out another match. "I don't know. The medical editor didn't seem to know, either."

I reached into my own jacket pocket for the printout from Ginger Carville's unmarked diskette and spread it out on the bar top. My searching finger found REP MRY. Repressed memory. It fit, and I wrote it down.

"What the hell's that?" Ed said, peering at the paper. "An acrostic?"

"Something like that," I said, refolding it and putting it back in my pocket. "But I've only got it half solved."

"Is there a story in it for me?"

"There's a story for you in what the mayor had for breakfast if you want to write it, Ed. But at the moment it's mostly hieroglyphics."

He struck the match and puffed. "Maybe I should give it to our archeology editor."

"The PD has an archeology editor?"

"I don't know. Probably. Be a pretty easy job for someone, if they do."

"Kind of like being chief of protocol for a bowling league."

He downed the rest of his drink. "I'll be interested to see what happens with this Dr. Whojie," he said, rattling his ice cubes.

"Flygenring."

"Yeah. This repressed memory business is a real hot potato in the courts right now." Ed shook his head. "It can be murder."

"That's what I'm afraid of," I told him.

The apartment seemed particularly empty when I got home later that evening. Maybe the three beers I'd drunk with Ed had rendered me morose. I changed into sweats, put some Charles Ives on the CD player, and sat for a while, smoking and thinking. Once or twice I picked up the phone with the intention of dialing Nicole's number, but I changed my mind at the last minute—or lost my nerve, if you want the truth of it.

I'd finished *The Great Gatsby*, and nothing else on my shelf really beckoned to me. I probably couldn't concentrate on reading anyway—too many wild conjectures were bouncing around inside my head.

Nicole. Mary. Steve Cirini. Ginger Carville. Ginger's cryptic list.

VIOLET GRBA and FK INC and PRNTS TRK RD.

Too much.

I tried to put everything out of my mind and to that end

started thinking about other things. My kids. My job for the plumbing people. Sports, and what that morning's callers had been talking about on the Lanigan, Webster and Malone show on the radio, to wit: the value of a good back-up quarterback.

I've been a dedicated Cleveland Browns fan ever since I could talk. But when Art Modell, the majority owner, stuck a shiv in the backs of Clevelanders and spirited his team out of town to Baltimore, there to become the Baltimore Ravens, whose expectations of ever winning a Super Bowl under the current ownership are "nevermore," the heart kind of went out of me. I don't even pay much attention to pro football anymore.

But the morning's discussion had gotten me thinking, anyway. It's impossible for a team to hope for a really successful season without a number-two quarterback who can really bring it. This is especially true what with the rash of NFL quarterback injuries in recent years. Jeff Hostetler stepped up for the New York Giants, replacing the injured Phil Sims, and won a Super Bowl. Steve Young apprenticed for years, backing up the great Joe Montana in San Francisco and is now one of the greats himself. And if anything happened to him now, the Forty-Niners had Elvis Grbac. . . .

I sat bolt upright in my chair.

Maybe GRBA wasn't shorthand for anything—maybe Violet Grba was somebody's name. Slovenian or Croatian, perhaps. I mentally kicked myself for not having thought of it before; I am not, after all, unfamiliar with Slavic names.

I scrambled up and went into the kitchen to open the cabinet where I keep my telephone directories.

I looked through the residential pages. There was no Violet Grba listed, but sure enough there were two other Grbas in Greater Cleveland. One of them was out on Lake Shore Boulevard in Euclid, not too far from Tetka Branka's old house. The other, a Bosko Grba, lived on Track Road in Cleveland.

VIOLET GRBA. PRNTS TRK RD.

Violet Grba. Parents, Track Road.

CHAPTER THIRTEEN

Track Road isn't the wrong side of the tracks; it *is* the tracks, a bewildering network of them used by Conrail for switching and unloading freight cars. The houses fronting on Track Road, across the street from the train tracks, are small, square, and colorfully painted, set close together and at odd angles because of the funny angle of the street. Close to the Slavic melting-pot area near Broadway and East Fifty-fifth Streets, Track Road has a personality all its own.

Oversize truck tires share tiny backyards with bicycles and swing sets. Many of the homes have neatly tended gardens; some are vegetable patches but most are flower gardens with decorative colored rocks and lawn ornaments and here and there a plaster statue of the Blessed Mother. Bright winter sunshine reflected off the side of the huge black oil tank car parked on a rail spur scant feet from where flower-faced babies in multicolored parkas laughed and sometimes cried, toddling to explore the little world of the February backyards. Romping neighborhood dogs, black and yellow and lots of other shades that beggar description tumbled on the track beds in a playful pack. A smart breeze snapped the clean laundry that hung on the lines.

The names on the mailboxes evoke the nations of Eastern Europe that tourists seldom visit, Slovenia and Croatia and Lithuania and Ukraine and Poland. They also evoke America—the America that smelted the steel and loaded the trucks and laid the tracks and worked the railroads. Generations of sweat got them here, these children of immigrants, who fly the stars and stripes and wear patriotic tattoos, who have made this small slice of Cleveland and of the American Dream pie their own.

It was a little past ten on Friday morning when I parked the Sunbird in front of a white house with dark red trim. The building could have fit neatly inside my office, with room to run around the perimeter. A small American flag fluttered on a slender staff outside the front door. Not much grass grew in the tiny yard at the side of the house, but there was a vegetable patch, with stakes for the tomatoes. To a Slav, the soil is connected to the soul, and the soul is the image of God. There is a great reverence for that which produces.

I'm no mechanic but I recognized the pieces of machinery strewn around the yard as parts of an automobile engine. In the driveway on the other side of the house, which had clearly been constructed in an era when cars were smaller and narrower, was last year's model Cadillac DeVille in candy-apple red. From the oil leak on the pavement behind it, another car must frequently be parked there.

I opened the gate in the chain-link fence and started up the uneven, cracked-asphalt walkway. When I was about halfway to the house the door opened, and a man peered at me through the screen. He waited until I was at the bottom of the steps, and then he came out on the small porch.

He was about sixty-five, and with a head as big and round as a pumpkin, atop which he wore a lavender knit stocking cap that made him look like an incongruously huge elf. The way his ears stuck out might almost have been comical, but somehow there was nothing about him that was in the least mirth-provoking. His belly seemed to begin where his pendulous jowls left off, sloping down to watermelon proportions and protruding over the waistband of his khaki trousers, which were held up with white suspenders. His plaid flannel shirt was half unbuttoned over a dark gray T-shirt. He was almost as tall as I am but must have outweighed me by seventy-five pounds. His face was pale and his hands were big, gnarled with arthritis and perhaps old injury, and I imagined that in his younger days he had been awesomely powerful.

"Are you Mr. Grba?" I said.

He blinked in what might have been confirmation, but he didn't answer. Under brows that swept wildly upward like the wings of an owl, his small blue eyes narrowed in suspicion.

"I know you?" he demanded. His voice was rough, like the crunch of a boot heel on ice-encrusted snow.

"No, sir. My name's Milan Jacovich." I thought my own Slavic name might buy me some goodwill, but apparently none was available.

"Whatchew wan'?"

"Actually I'm looking for a Violet Grba."

His eyes got even smaller, almost vanishing; he might have been squinting into the morning sky, but I didn't think so. He rocked forward on his toes, redistributing his weight in the manner of someone who has has been in more than one situation he'd had to batter his way out of with his fists. "She's not here."

"Does she live here?"

"Not no more."

"Could you tell me how I can get in touch with her?"

His face was a mask. "Whatchew wan' wit her?"

"Just to talk," I said. "I'm a private investigator."

I pulled a business card from my pocket and extended it to him, but he made no move to take it. He kept his eyes glued on my face for a long moment and then glanced in the direction of the Cadillac. "She don' wan' talk to nobody," he said.

"Look, she's not in any sort of trouble or anything. I just want to ask her—"

"Don' matter a goddamn whatchew wan'." He sucked in a lungful of air, seeming to get bigger before my eyes.

We stood there looking at each other, he towering over me from two steps above. We were still as a mural for about twenty seconds.

"It's really very important that I talk with her," I finally said. "Maybe you could give me a phone number where I could reach her?"

Silently he moved his head from side to side twice, maybe only three quarters of an inch in either direction, but it was as forceful and effective as if he'd roared "No!" at the top of his lungs.

Maybe a different approach was called for, I thought, and I pulled a twenty-dollar bill from my pants pocket. "Look, if you could see your way clear to telling me where I might find Violet, I'd be more than happy to—"

He came down the two concrete steps quickly, so quickly that I almost lost my balance as I stepped back. We were nose to nose; three spiky gray hairs, half an inch long, bristled from the bulb of his.

"Put you goddamn money away!" he said without raising his voice very much. "You want me t'break you back? I c'd break you fucking back."

He probably couldn't have, but I could think of a hundred men half his age I'd rather be tangling with. I backed up another few paces.

"Let's not get excited," I said. "No offense meant."

"Get out," he said. "Get off my proppity. An' don' come back no more! Hear me?"

I heard him.

I retreated down the walk. When I opened the gate I threw a last look back at him, but he hadn't seemed to change his mind. He stood at the foot of the steps, solid, intractable, guarding his home and his privacy and whatever else he was guarding. I closed the gate and got back into my car.

As I pulled slowly away from the curb three of the dogs romping on the track bed galloped over, leaping at the car windows and barking. But there seemed to be no malice in it, only canine curiosity and playful bravado. I had a lot less to fear from the wild dogs, I thought, than I did from Bosko Grba.

Driving back toward town, I took the time to review some of the pieces that had fallen together in the Virginia Carville case.

Dr. Flygenring, a psychiatrist who specialized in repressed memory syndrome, was mentioned in Carville's secret file. That probably meant somebody had been abused sometime in the past, possibly in the spring or summer of 1983. Carville had wanted to know if a police report had been made, and if so, was there a follow-up. Had the statute of limitations for prosecuting the abuse run out? Was a payment made by someone to someone else, and for what? And where did Violet Grba, whose parents lived down on Track Road, fit into this equation?

To say nothing of FK INC.

I was back at Third District Police Headquarters on Payne Avenue in fifteen minutes. Marko had been generous with his information, and I felt I owed it to him to be the same.

But he was barging down the steps as I was coming up, followed by a plainclothes officer I didn't know.

"No time to talk to you, Milan," he barked, brushing past me.

"Five minutes," I protested.

"I don't have five seconds."

"I might have something for you on the Carville case," I said.

He broke stride, not stopping but slowing down a little. "Hell. All right, then, come on," he said, "ride along with us," and hustled around the side of the building to the official police parking lot.

I trotted after him dutifully.

Once we were all in the unmarked police car the other officer, hurriedly introduced by Marko as Bob Matusen, slapped the flashing bubble light onto the roof and hit the siren. As we sliced through lunch-hour traffic, the cars pulling off to the right to let us go by, I was taken back to my own days in uniform, the heady adrenaline rush brought on by the piercing shriek of the siren, the sense of power and invincibility as everyone else got out of our way.

"Quick," Marko said over his shoulder from the front seat. "Give it to me quick, without the bullshit."

I leaned forward to talk into his ear so he could hear me over the noise. "Carville was working on a story involving repressed memory syndrome. Know what that is?"

"Yeah," he growled. "Woman decides thirty years later that her Uncle Julius molested her. So?"

"So it was pretty hush-hush. Carville had all her notes in a secret file."

"What do you mean, secret?"

"They were kind of hidden."

"How'd you get them?"

"Never mind," I said, which earned me a hard-eyed glare from the front seat. "The point is that several years ago there might have been some kind of sexual abuse of an underage child, and somebody somewhere got paid off to keep their mouth shut."

"Why would Carville give a shit about that after all these years?"

"A story."

"A pretty stale one." The car careened around a corner onto Superior Avenue, and I had to hold on to keep from getting thrown against the door. "This sounds like it's for sex crimes, not homicide. And if you sashay in there with some moonglow about some kind of sexual abuse, somebody somewhere sometime, they'll throw you right out on your ass."

We turned another corner on two wheels. All along the street the residents, mostly African American, moved off the sidewalks and porches into buildings and alleyways as the police car zoomed through.

"Ghetto deer," Matusen observed, years of cynicism sharpening his tone. "They all scatter when the hunters go by."

"Wouldn't you?" I said.

He hit the brakes hard and we jolted to a stop in front of a battered frame house on East Thirty-ninth Street. There were already three black-and-whites on the scene, as well as a police ambulance. Several of the neighbors stood in clumps on the sidewalks and tree lawns looking grim and frightened.

Marko was out of the car in a second. "Come on," he said. "As long as you're here."

We went up the steps to a wooden porch bowed in the middle like the back of an old dray horse, and through the open front door into the living room. The cloying smell hit me with almost physical force. I knew what it was. Once you've smelled death, you never forget it.

All three of us, Marko, Matusen, and myself, pulled out handkerchiefs and put them over our noses and mouths. "Hey, Lou," one of the uniformed officers called out, and Marko gave him a curt wave and glanced around at the neat, old-fashioned living room with its lace doilies and antimacassars and silver-framed photographs of children and young adults and a larger print of Jesus at Gethsemane before leading us upstairs to the second floor. Through an archway I could see that the kitchen had been ransacked.

There were three more officers in the hallway upstairs, one of whom was young and looked a little green around the gills. The oldest one pointed us into the bedroom at the rear of the house, where a plainclothes officer bent over a corpse. The coppery smell of blood was strongest in here.

"Two shots, Lieutenant," the suit said to Marko, straightening up with an audible pop of his hip joint and firing off a half-hearted salute. "Close range, right through the ticker."

The dead man lying on his back at the foot of the neatly made bed was elderly, probably about seventy, with a fringe of curly white hair around an otherwise bald head. He was wearing shiny gabardine pants and a light-blue shirt, the front of which was ragged and bloody.

A nightstand next to the bed stood with its drawer half hanging out. Atop it were a clock radio and a bottle of Tums, and a well-thumbed copy of *Up From Slavery* left lying facedown. On the floor as if dropped there was a Holy Bible covered in supple pebble-grain leather, also looking well used.

I looked away, out the window into the backyard, where the uneven ground was littered with clumps of dirty snow. Along the side of the garage was a long narrow flower bed bordered with bricks and planted with what looked like crocuses; the green spear-shaped leaves were there already, bravely beckoning the spring. The man who lay dead behind me had probably planted them; he would never see them bloom.

I coughed into my handkerchief and turned back to Marko and the other two cops.

"Any sign of forced entry?" Marko said, taking notes.

The plainclothes cop shook his head. "He probably knew them," he said. "Like always."

"Them? More than one?"

The cop shrugged. "I'm guessing," he said. "Anybody who'd kill an old man like this would have to be pretty gutless—probably needed somebody with him to give him the balls."

I stood off to one side to let the policemen work, and wondered how much balls it required to shoot an old man in the heart. I've killed people—in the army, where they gave me medals for it, and a few times as a cop and a private investigator. It didn't take any sort of intestinal fortitude that I could remember. Only a terrifying deadening of the mind and nervous system and a willful abandonment of everything moral and decent and right you'd learned at your mother's knee.

"Probably neighborhood punks looking for pocket change to buy rock," Bob Matusen observed. "Or maybe they just shot him for the fun of it."

"When did life get so cheap?" I said.

Marko looked at me. "When drugs got so expensive."

When the crime-lab technicians arrived, Marko and Matusen took their leave; it was, after all, the plainclothes cop's squeal. We went back downstairs and out to the curb. The neighbors were still clustered around, the adults stern-faced and sad, the wide-eyed children clinging to their parents' legs, scared silent.

"Who'd want to do a thing like this?" an elderly black woman was saying to nobody in particular. "He never hurt nobody. Always polite, say hello in the street whether he knew you or not. Halloween he used to dress up and have fun with the kids when they came 'round for candy. Dress up like a ghost most years." She pushed her steel-framed glasses up on her nose. "Who'd do a thing like this?"

We got back into the car and left the scene without speaking.

Marko leaned back against the headrest and closed his eyes. "You get a wild hair about a case, Milan," he said after several minutes, "and carry on as though if we don't help you out it'll be the end of civilization as we know it. But we have to deal with shit like this practically every day. And it doesn't get any easier."

"That's your job, Marko," I said. "Carville—or Steve Cirini—is mine."

Matusen kept his eyes on the road but turned his head slightly so I could hear him. "From what little I hear," he said, "you ought to be giving the father a hard look."

"What father?"

"You said an underage kid was sexually abused—that usually happens inside the home. Sick, but true. Check out the father."

"I still want to know how you got hold of notes and things," Marko said. "You didn't go and violate a crime scene, did you?"

"That I can tell you: no. But there's a psychiatrist downtown who specializes in repressed memory whose name was in Carville's notes, and he probably knows all about it."

"Knows and won't tell," Matusen said.

"Doesn't have to," Marko pointed out. "Patient-doctor privilege."

"You want to go talk to him anyway? Dr. Oscar Flygenring."

He looked at me and laughed. "Dr. *what*?"

"Flygenring. Really." I jotted the name down on a clean page of my notebook along with that of Violet Grba and ripped it out. "If you have time, check back through the sex crimes reports from the spring of 1983 through the present and see if a complaint was made regarding Violet Grba," I said, pointing to it.

"If I have the time, huh?" He took the page from me, jerking his head backward, toward the site of the old man's murder. "I look like I have the time?" He studied it. "You're kidding me with these names, right?"

"Like Meglich and Jacovich," I said. "Grba's parents live down on Track Road."

"Track Road." He scratched his head vigorously. "God, I haven't been down there in years."

"It hasn't changed any," I said. "That's its charm."

He folded the piece of paper and slipped it into his own notebook. "Well, I can't go talk to Dr. Ring-a-ding because I have absolutely no reason to, and because he probably won't talk to me anyway. And since you won't tell me how you got his name, I'm up the well-known creek. But I gotta tell you, Milan, I think this is a big waste of your time. Ginger Carville was working on a lot of stories that would likely give somebody grief—we found some of those notes ourselves. Why is this one so important?"

"Because she was keeping a secret file on it."

He thought about it for a while. "Thin," he said. "A lot thinner than her secret boyfriend—your client—getting cheesed at her because she wanted to break it off and wrapping her pantyhose around her neck."

We were back on Payne Avenue now, heading toward the

Old Central at a much more leisurely pace than when we'd left it. The huge silhouette of the Society Tower loomed ahead of us against the gray sky.

"You've got your mind made up about Cirini," I said.

"You haven't given me anything to make me change it. And how do I know these notes of Carville's are even genuine?"

For a moment I considered not telling him. "They came from her office, from an unmarked diskette."

"And how did that happen to come into your possession?"

I didn't answer him.

He turned around in the front seat and looked at me. It was Marko's patented, hard-cop glare, one I'd seen before, more times than I care to count.

"Damn you, Milan," he said. "What the hell you want from me?"

CHAPTER FOURTEEN

Two freight cars were coupling noisily on a siding not ninety feet from Bosko Grba's gate. A group of kids, getting in their last few minutes of playtime on the berm of the track bed before having to come in for dinner, skipped nimbly out of the way of danger as the railroad workers shouted and shook their fists at them. Trains were business as usual for the children of Track Road.

The street looked different in the twilight; more of its working parents were home, and the older kids and teenagers sat on the steps of the tiny porches, speaking in low tones so as not to be overheard by their parents inside, occasionally puffing arrogant cigarettes, and watching the younger ones play. Through the windows of the houses I could see the flickering blue ghostlight of television sets; from what I could hear of them, most were tuned to the nightly news. Traffic was heavier as workers came back from the mills or the freight yards. Now there were one or two cars in every driveway. In Bosko Grba's, a 1981 Capri that hadn't quite survived a $99.95 repainting job was parked over the oil leak on the pavement, and I could make out a collection of brooms, dry mops, buckets, and cleaning supplies in the back seat. There was no sign of the Cadillac DeVille.

Opening the gate, I approached the house carefully. I knew I wasn't Bosko Grba's favorite visitor, and I didn't want him to come out swinging—or shooting. But what Detective Matusen had said that afternoon in the car made a lot of sense. In cases of sexual abuse of children, the father is often the likeliest suspect. It's inconceivable to me, as it is to most people, but it happens to be a sad truth.

This time I got all the way up to the top step. Looking through the glass in the door I could see directly into the kitchen. A tired-looking sixtyish woman wearing a coarse white linen dress stood at an ancient four-burner range, stirring something in a battered aluminum saucepan. She was stout, with legs like tree trunks encased in thick lisle support stockings; the knuckles of her hands were large and chapped, and her lank graying hair was pinned up into a careless bun. A lifetime of hard work had etched deep lines into her sallow face.

Beyond the kitchen, through an archway, a big-console TV was tuned to Vivian Truscott and the Channel 12 news in the living room.

I was going to knock but I changed my mind. It was her husband I wanted to see, if this indeed was Mrs. Grba, and if she did answer the door I didn't know what I'd say to her. I turned and went back down the steps. Just as I got to the gate the big red Cadillac DeVille came down the street and turned into the narrow driveway.

The door opened, and with an effort Bosko Grba swung his legs from beneath the wheel. When he looked up and saw me, he lurched from the driver's seat like an avenging angel, his furrowed brow dark-clouded, and came pounding toward me with his huge fists knotted. He was wearing a wool fingertip-length jacket with a red-and-white checkerboard pattern over the clothes he'd had on that morning.

"Sorry, but I have to talk to you, Mr. Grba," I said in my most authoritative voice, and the sheer force of it slowed him down a little.

"Tol' you not to come back arount here," he rumbled as he approached the fence.

"I'm afraid I have to. Someone has been killed, Mr. Grba. Murdered."

He lifted his enormous head like a grizzly sniffing the air. "Kilt?"

"Virginia Carville," I said. "You probably heard about it on the news."

"Dat woman from the television?" He swatted the air with a huge hand. "She don' got not'ing to do wit me."

"Your daughter Violet's name was in Virginia Carville's files."

His entire body shuddered. He was breathing heavily, his chest and belly rising with every inhalation.

"That's why I wanted to talk to her," I said.

"Violet don' know no TV woman."

"Maybe she doesn't. But Ms. Carville knew her, or knew about her."

"What about her?" Grba's voice was low and dangerous, his small eyes glittering.

"Something that happened in 1983."

He glanced nervously at the kitchen door, and my gaze followed his. The woman inside had left the stove and was standing behind the closed door, looking at us through the glass, her forehead creased with a deep frown.

"Not'ing happened," he said.

"Are you sure, Mr. Grba?"

"I said."

"Maybe it's something you wouldn't want me to know. Look, I'm trying to help you."

He took a belligerent step forward. "Go away. Leave us alone. Me an' Violet. That's how you help me."

"If Virginia Carville found out about it, someone else will, too. Look, there are places you can go to get help."

"You the one gonna need help in a minute," he threatened.

"Mr. Grba, answer me one question and then I'll go away."

He waited. The breath whistled through his nose.

"I'm not accusing you of anything, please understand that." I took a deep breath. "Was your daughter Violet sexually abused in nineteen eighty-three?"

I should have seen it coming but I didn't, not until his fist landed on the side of my head. The sucker punch knocked me sideways, into the fence, and when I hit it he was all over me, punching and kicking and kneeing. Each time he connected he grunted something that sounded like "Bastard!" I could smell the beer on his breath.

Dizzy and seeing stars from the first blow, I tried to fend him off, but he not only outbulked me, he was terribly strong. He was more than twenty years my senior and I didn't want to hit him, but in the end that's the only way I could save myself a further beating.

It was one punch, and it didn't travel more than six inches, but my hand sank almost up to the wrist in his large gut. The wind whooshed out of him and he sagged, gasping, to his knees and then fell forward, supporting himself with his fists on the ground in front of him like a gorilla.

The woman came running down the walkway screaming for me to stop, but I had no intention of carrying the fight any further.

"Come on, now, Mr. Grba," I said. "Let me help you up."

He coughed from deep inside his massive chest.

"Git away from him, git away from him!" his wife screamed, and pushed me out of the way. She knelt down next to him, put an arm across his back and patted him ineffectually, murmuring something soothing to him while she looked daggers up at me.

He coughed again violently, retched, and spit up a gobbet of phlegm and dark blood.

"I'm sorry," I said, and it sounded lame. "I'm really sorry I had to do that."

The woman chopped a sidehand karate blow at me that

missed by at least a foot. "What's wrong witchew, bastard?" she demanded. "Hit a ol' man like that, an' him wit cancer!"

The ugly, almost unspeakable word hung there in the evening air, and it took me a few seconds to process it. Suddenly I was feeling sick myself.

"Git away from him now!" she ordered. "Git away from us. Why you wanna hit a sick ol' man for?"

Telling her that he hit me first was so relentlessly kindergarten that I couldn't bring myself to say it. "I didn't mean to hurt him," I said. "Really. I'm looking for your daughter."

"She ain't here no more, so you git!"

"Where can I find her?" I said. "Tell me and I promise you I'll never come back."

The old man was still on his fists and knees, coughing. He let out a strangled roar; something that sounded like "Anna!"

"She live in Garfiel' Heights now. You go see her, lee my husban' alone!"

"N-no-o-o!" Bosko Grba choked.

"You git out an' let us be," Mrs. Grba said. "Big guy like you hit a ol' man—shame to you! Big bully."

I watched as he clutched at the fence to haul his huge bulk to his feet, and the chain link buckled slightly beneath his weight. His face was the color of fireplace ashes and slick with sweat. He leaned heavily on his wife's shoulder, almost crushing her. The two of them stood there looking defiance at me, the kind of heartfelt contempt that cuts clean through to the bone.

"Mr. Grba?" I said. "I'm really sorry I hurt you. I didn't want to."

His lips were trembling, but his eyes were pig-mean and hard.

I tried to smile. "Twenty years ago and you would've probably killed me," I offered.

He blinked. "Fi' years ago," he gasped. His chest spasmed again, and he spit another bloody chunk of phlegm between my feet, then turned away, and the two of them went up the walk and up the steps into the house.

I went out through the gate and got into my car, slamming the door hard. The side of my head hurt where he'd first punched me and my ear was ringing, and there was a deep-seated muscle ache in my thigh where he'd kicked me. But the guilt pain inside my chest was worse than any of it. There have been some terrible moments in my life that I wish I could take back; the one in which I'd hit Bosko Grba certainly made the top ten.

It was almost nine o'clock before I got home. I'd gone out of my way heading back to Cleveland Heights, a trip which should take no more than twenty minutes, and stopped off at Vuk's for a beer. Then I'd had two more. I felt down-to-the-bone lousy—not only physically, but in every possible way.

The answering machine was blinking, indicating that I'd had three calls. I have a beeper, but now that I've moved my business down to the Flats, it works off my office number, not my home phone. When I hit the playback button I discovered the calls were all hang-ups. Probably, I reasoned, made by members of that voracious horde of dinnertime telemarketers selling lawn service, aluminum siding, basement waterproofing, credit card protection, and burial plots, who prey on all the poor souls indiscreet enough to list their numbers in the phone book.

I kicked the heat up to about seventy, changed into sneakers, jeans, and an old sweater, put a Dave Grusin-plays-Gershwin CD in the player, and sat in the dark smoking cigarettes for a while by the bay window in my living room. I stared at the cars heading down Cedar Hill to the blues and jazz clubs at University Circle, the dance clubs downtown and in the Flats, and whatever other places people go for a good time on a Friday night that I don't know about. If I craned my neck a little I could see the lighted pinnacle of the Society

Tower through the crisp, cold air; the dancing red taillights of the westbound traffic seemed to terminate at its feet.

Bosko Grba was stuck in my head like a golden oldie, half forgotten but insistent.

He might be old enough to be retired, but men like him work until they drop. Perhaps because of his illness he was on disability, which is why I'd found him at home that morning. From the household cleaning materials I'd seen in the back seat of the old Capri in his driveway, I guessed his wife worked as a cleaning woman. They grew their own tomatoes and lived in a house smaller than a one-bedroom apartment. The image didn't quite jibe with the candy-apple red Cadillac.

When I'd approached him the first time, he'd been hostile and mean. Having suffered so much perfidy and betrayal, Slavic people are often suspicious by nature, but they are also hospitable and welcoming; Grba threatened to break my back. When I'd asked him if his daughter Violet had ever been molested, he tried to carry out the threat. And I'd hit him. In the stomach. I hadn't meant to, but at the time it seemed like the thing to do. Shame to me was Mrs. Grba's parting curse, and it nipped at my heels like the bloodhounds that chased Eliza across the ice. I know the cliché that nobody can make you feel guilty except you, and to tell you the truth, this time I didn't need anybody else.

Grba was hiding something; I was sure of it. I suppose if I had molested a child I'd try to hide it too. But there was something amiss, and I couldn't figure out what it was.

Maybe when I went out to Garfield Heights and talked to Violet Grba, I'd find out. Or maybe she was as hostile and secretive as her father. In any case I'd have to wait until Monday.

One of the things I hate about weekends is that most people are impossible to reach. One of the many.

I went into the kitchen for a cold Stroh's. The side of my head was still hurting where Grba had popped me, and the three beers I'd had at Vuk's hadn't helped. They'd only left me halfway between sobriety and a nice buzz. Not enough to make me fall asleep at such an early hour, but I couldn't think of a single reason to stay awake, either, with Bosko Grba and Ginger Carville and Steve Cirini and Mary and FK INC. chasing one another in my head. The weekend was already beginning on a low note. I switched on the reading lamp beside my chair and thumbed through a *Newsweek,* but I got few laughs from their "Conventional Wisdom" column, which I usually enjoy. I couldn't seem to concentrate on the words.

The Grusin CD ended but I wasn't motivated to get up and put another one on. I looked at my watch and found it was ten twenty. I supposed I'd sit there until eleven, watch the news, and then go to bed, but the ringing of my doorbell changed my mind.

"Hi, Milan," Nicole Archer said when I opened the door. Life was really full of surprises these days.

"Hello." I was too taken aback to think of anything else. Maybe I should hire someone witty and clever to write my dialogue.

"I was at a lecture at Case, and I was driving back up the hill and saw your light, so I took a chance and came on up." She glanced quickly over my shoulder into the living room. "I hope I'm not disturbing you. Is this a bad time?"

"No," I said thickly. "Uh, come on in."

She walked past me into the apartment. Under her metallic-green trench coat she wore a black peasant blouse and a black flared skirt with red roses on it. She looked very pretty, very young, very fresh. Her subtle perfume drifted into the air as she went by; she smelled good, too.

I closed the door behind her. "Kind of a surprise."

"It shouldn't be," she said as she took off her coat. Draping it on a chair near the door, she moved easily across the living room and settled onto the sofa, her skirt swirling around her. She didn't seem to be wearing a bra beneath the blouse.

If I'd known she was coming over I'd have opened a window to get rid of the smell of stale cigarette smoke, or at least squirted room deodorizer around.

"I sort of thought you'd have called me by now," she said, her tone conversationally neutral.

"My impression was that you didn't want me to."

"I guess I didn't at that. But it would have been nice if you'd tried."

"Want a glass of wine?"

She shook her head, her bright hair moving like a model's in a shampoo commercial. "I was hoping we could talk a little."

I sat down on the other end of the sofa. "Okay."

"How've you been?"

"I've had better days, but I'm all right, I guess."

"How's your case coming?"

"It's tough."

Her look was level and direct. "And how's Mary?"

"I've barely seen her," I said.

"Barely."

"That's right."

"And how was it?"

"What do you mean, how was it? We just talked. About the case."

She leaned toward me. "I meant how did you feel? Seeing her again."

"Fine," I said.

"That's a little unresponsive, isn't it?"

"Nicole, remember *why* Mary came to me in the first place. It was to get her lover off the hook."

"That still doesn't answer the question."

"Why don't you just ask me what you want to ask?"

"All right." She took a deep breath and shifted on the sofa to face me squarely. "Did she inspire any . . . lust in you?"

I had to laugh. "I'm a normal male," I said. "I go across the street to Russo's to pick up a head of lettuce and I see five women who inspire lust in me—but I don't do anything about it. What the hell kind of question is that?"

"Milan, I need to know whether you still have any of the old feelings for Mary."

"Old feelings is exactly what they are. Not new ones, not current ones. Old feelings." I stood up. "I'm going to get a beer. You sure you don't want anything?"

Nicole smiled and shook her head. I went into the kitchen and took another Stroh's from the refrigerator, thinking hard. I came back out and sat down again.

"There are none of the old feelings, Nicole," I said. "At least not the ones you mean."

"Which ones, then?"

I searched for words. "Anger, I guess. Resentment, sadness, a sense of loss. All those, from when we broke up." I opened the beer. "And some lust, too, I suppose."

"Thanks for being honest."

"That's me all over. When Diogenes got one look at me, he blew out his lantern and went home." I sucked at the beer with a savagery I tried hard not to let her see; I was so tired of women telling me what a stalwart, upstanding, honest guy I am and then dumping me.

"Can I be honest, too?" she said.

I sat down. "When you cross this threshold you can't be anything else. It's the Jacovich curse."

She chewed on the inside of her cheek for a moment. Finally she took a deep breath and began.

"When you started seeing Mary again—"

"I never 'started seeing Mary again.' She brought me a client, and that's the way it's been."

"Strictly business?"

"Right."

"No romantic dinners with candlelight and wine?"

"Just a really unromantic cup of coffee in a Euclid Avenue bar at ten o'clock in the morning."

Nicole digested that. "Nevertheless. It bothered me. A lot. More than I thought it would, frankly."

"It shouldn't have. I told you I wasn't in love with her anymore."

"This isn't about you," she said heatedly, and then smiled a little to soften it.

I shrugged and gulped down more Stroh's.

She took a few seconds to get her thoughts back on track. "Anyway, it really scared me that your getting involved with your ex-girlfriend bothered me so much. I don't like being vulnerable." With a finger she traced the outline of one of the roses on her skirt. "All day I work with little tiny babies, some of them weighing only a pound or two. And they're so helpless, so vulnerable, so . . . "

"So dependent?" I suggested.

"That's it, Milan. That's the thing. I don't want to be dependent. On you or on anybody else. It goes against everything I stand for as a woman, in my life and in my work." She glared at me. "And don't roll your eyes that way. I hate it when you do that!"

"I'm sorry, Nicole, but why is this becoming a gender issue? I haven't done a goddamn thing wrong, and—"

"You're making this about you again."

"From where I stand" I told her, "it is about me, because it's my life. It's my feelings, too. You're assuming I don't have any just because I happen to have come with exterior plumbing. That kind of narrow-minded stereotyping makes me tired."

"Well, from where *I* stand, I got scared because I was caring too much, and that's why I had to back away a little."

I didn't say anything.

"You don't understand, do you?" she said.

"Whether I do or not won't make any difference, Nicole.

You're going to feel the way you're going to feel, no matter what."

"What I feel is that I've missed you."

"I've missed you too," I said, and tried not to make it sound petulant and grudging.

"What are we going to do about it?"

"I don't seem to be calling those shots right now. You're the one who rang my doorbell tonight."

We sat there and looked at each other for almost a minute, and then she got up, came over to my end of the sofa, and sat down on my lap, straddling my thighs and bunching her skirt up around her hips. She was wearing sheer black pantyhose that concealed nothing. Her perfume made me dizzy.

She leaned forward and crushed her soft lips against mine, exploring my mouth with her tongue. I could taste wine in her mouth; she must have stopped off at Nighttown or the Mad Greek before coming upstairs. Maybe she'd needed a little bottled courage.

"Is this all right, Milan?"

"It always has been," I reminded her.

She kissed me again, and when we came up for air she pulled the elastic neck of her blouse down, letting it catch below her bare breasts. I kissed each of them in turn, lingeringly, feeling the pink nipples harden under my tongue. She made a pleasureful little noise deep in her throat, grabbed two fistfuls of my hair, and ground her crotch against mine. Her eyes closed dreamily, and I seemed to feel the heat radiating from between her legs.

Although I'd never give the son of a bitch the satisfaction of admitting it to his face, I have to agree with Steve Cirini: there's something extra-sensual about making love partially clothed. Leaving the light on doesn't hurt either.

It was about one o'clock in the morning, and I'd somehow wound up in the green-and-yellow-striped terrycloth bathrobe my son Stephen had given me for Christmas several years before; I sat on the sofa, emotionally and physically wrung out, and watched Nicole get dressed. She usually doesn't wear much makeup, and what little she'd had on was mostly gone from the evening's exertions. She looked young and pretty and flushed as she pulled her pantyhose up under her skirt.

"You don't generally put your underwear back on if you're planning to spend the night," I observed.

That got a smile out of her. "You're such a good detective."

"Any reason you're not staying?"

She hesitated, one shoe in her hand. "I . . . just don't think it's a good idea."

"I see," I lied.

She steadied herself against the back of a chair while she slipped the shoe on. "It was wonderful, Milan. Don't get me wrong."

"But?"

"I just think we have to put our relationship on a different basis."

"What basis is that?"

"Not quite so hot and heavy."

"I thought hot and heavy was pretty terrific this evening."

"I mean less—intense."

Padding out to the kitchen, I got another beer, noting that it was my last one. When I came back into the living room Nicole had her other shoe on. Ready to go, I thought. Ready to escape.

"Less structured," she continued. "More casual, I guess." She gestured at the sofa, with two of its pillows on the floor, and at the coffee table, accidentally knocked crooked. "Like tonight."

I waited.

"That was fun, wasn't it?" she said.

"So is scratching off an instant lottery ticket, but it's not quite the same thing."

She looked around, up at the ceiling, into the corners, as if she'd find some sort of explanation there, some way to make me understand. "I was feeling hemmed in. Smothered. It isn't your fault, really. I didn't realize it until this business with Mary came up, but Mary really has nothing to do with it. She was just a catalyst."

"*Now* I *don't* see."

She folded her arms across her chest and spoke patiently, as if to a child. "When you said you were involved with Mary—"

"I'm not involved!"

"That she was back in your life," she corrected herself. "On whatever basis. Anyway, I was mad at first. You know that. I was mad because I love being with you, I love making love with you, and I was afraid I was going to lose you to an old love. And then, this past week, I realized that I wasn't mad anymore but I'd gotten to thinking. And I realized that, as much as I care for you, I don't want us to be so . . . such a couple, I suppose."

"You don't want us to be a couple," I repeated dully. The King of the Zombies. I pulled at the tab on the beer can and got a satisfying, answering hiss.

"I care a lot about you, Milan, and I still want us to see each other. Just not a five-times-a-week, regular thing."

"You think I was starting to take you for granted?"

"No, not at all." She shook her hair back from her face. "Call it commitment-phobia if you want. I just want it to be not so . . ." She gestured helplessly.

"You just want that whenever you feel like getting laid, you drive by and see if my light is on."

She flushed. "That isn't fair."

"You're damn right it isn't." I put the beer down; all at once I didn't feel like drinking it anymore. "I'm sorry, Nicole, but that just doesn't fly. I guess I'm just an intense kind of guy."

"You mean you don't want to see me anymore?"

"Not on the basis you're talking about. There are plenty of women I could see if that's all I wanted. There are men you can see, too. But if I'm with somebody, I'm with them. I need to know I can count on them." I sighed. "I guess you don't need that. Okay, so now we know, and we don't have to waste each other's time anymore."

Her brown eyes grew wide. "I can't believe you're just going to dump me like this."

"Excuse me," I said, "but as far as I can see, I'm the dump-ee."

She stared at me for a minute. "I'm sorry that's as far as you can see, Milan," she finally said, and went and picked her coat up from the chair by the door. She shrugged into it, turning to look at me. "I wish you well," she said. And left.

I took one gulp of beer and then went and poured the rest into the sink. Then I stood under a hot shower, as hot as I could stand it, and scrubbed every trace of her from my body until my skin glowed pink.

I dried myself off and took her good wishes to an empty bed.

CHAPTER FIFTEEN

I suppose that if I had a better understanding of the female sex, I'd have more successful and lasting relationships, but each time I think I have women figured out they go and change the rules on me.

I do know that men and women are different, even though that observation, obvious though it is, might irritate a lot of people. It isn't that one gender is better than the other—they're just different, that's all.

And the differences aren't all physical differences, either. It's in the thinking.

Men, for instance, have great powers of concentration, almost a tunnel vision, that allows them to laser in on one spot; they are imminently suited to microsurgery, to rebuilding the transmission of a 1956 Thunderbird, and to many types of engineering. Women, on the other hand, make wonderful executives because they are able to do several things at once, efficiently and well, and have remarkable peripheral awareness, something that is lacking in most males. A woman president would probably do a hell of a job—better than many of the men we've had in the White House.

That's of course a generalization. There are many gifted women surgeons, and we've had a couple of pretty good male presidents, but these are my own personal observations, based on a lot of years of keeping my eyes and ears open. If someone else thinks something else, fine.

Conversely, I've always felt that men tend to take a more universal view of the world, that they put everything that happens to them into a larger context. I guess you could say they are more philosophical. Most of the women I've known are individual nurturers; they want to know where it hurts *you* and to take care of that immediate problem right away. It's why they are for the most part better at parenting, and better at sustaining loving relationships.

Yet here's Nicole, whose very career is devoted to nurturing, and she says she cares about me as a person, enjoys my company and loves to go to bed with me, but she's decided she doesn't want to be a couple anymore. She wants to keep it casual.

I don't operate that way, and I couldn't accept it.

So I woke up slightly hung over on a Saturday morning to find the sky pewter-colored and cold, a misty rain falling, and myself once more alone.

It had been eight days since Andrew Lemmons found Virginia Carville's body, and all I had were some vague encoded words on a computer disk that might or might not have anything to do with her death.

I carved a couple of slices off the end of a loaf of Orlando Ciabatta bread and stuck them in the toaster and brewed a pot of strong coffee, which I drank in the time it took me to read the paper. Then I called Steve Cirini.

"How's it going?" he said.

"I'm making a little progress, but not enough to matter yet. I've got a couple more questions."

"You should be asking questions of other people, not me. I'm the innocent one."

"So you say. Does the name Violet Grba mean anything to you? Did you ever hear Ginger mention her?"

I heard him swallowing something, probably his own morning coffee. "It's someone's name? Wasn't that on that list you showed me?"

"You have a good memory."

"Yeah. Well, it didn't mean anything to me then, and it doesn't now. I told you before, Ginger and I weren't much for small talk."

"Did you go in to work yesterday?"

Another hesitation. "Yes, I did. For a little while, anyway."

"How did that go?"

He laughed nastily. "Nicky Scandalios would barely talk to me—and that's not like him; usually when Nicky stops talking, everybody says a little prayer of thanksgiving. And nobody else came within fifteen feet of me all day. It was like I was the invisible man."

"Claude Rains," I said.

"Who?"

"Never mind. So you left the office early?"

"Yeah," he said. "I cleaned up some paperwork on my desk and then came home right after lunch. It was really uncomfortable."

"It'll get better," I said. "People forget."

"People don't forget when you're accused of murder."

"They do if you're found innocent. Done any thinking about who else it might have been that Ginger was involved with?"

"It's not something she was likely to tell me, now, was it?"

"But she knew you were seeing Mary."

"That's different," he said.

"Why?"

"Because I got the idea that her other boyfriend was married."

That was something to ponder. I switched the receiver to my other ear and began playing with a pencil. "What makes you think so?"

"Just a feeling. The rare times she mentioned him, she always called him 'my friend.' 'I was telling my friend the other night . . .' 'My friend and I went to Chicago for the weekend.'

Never a name. Like she didn't want anyone to know who he was."

"Why didn't you tell me that before? About her maybe having a married boyfriend?"

"I don't know—I didn't think of it."

I tried to keep the exasperation from my voice, but when I was talking to Steve Cirini it seemed to bubble up from some natural wellspring. "I'm not looking at a murder rap, you are. So you better start thinking of things like that if you expect me to do you any good."

He didn't answer for a moment or two. Then, "Yeah. Right. I'm sorry," he said.

I doodled an empty gallows on the cover of a *Newsweek* lying face-up on the table beside me. "I've talked to the police. If nothing better turns up, they're probably coming after you on Tuesday."

There was a sharp intake of breath. "They have enough for an arrest, you think?"

"I don't know. But one way or the other they're going to bring you in and lean on you some more. And make sure you put on your deodorant Tuesday morning, Mr. Cirini, because you're going to sweat."

After I hung up, I spent a pleasant few moments imagining that very thing. Unworthy of me, I knew. I tried to remember the last time I'd had a client I really liked in a criminal case. Nothing came instantly to mind. But there had been none I disliked quite as much as Steve Cirini.

Of course that was personal. And I had no business allowing my personal feelings to get in the way of my work. Or in the way of justice, either, as abstract a concept as that has become in our society. As much as I thought he was a smarmy slimeball, I couldn't picture Steve Cirini wrapping a pair of pantyhose around a woman's neck and pulling until she stopped breathing.

And I thought it might be nice to nail whoever had killed Ginger Carville. Because I'd punched a terminally ill old man in the stomach to find out. Because I'd always enjoyed her work on the Channel 12 news. Because the sadness in her father's eyes had stayed with me. And because nobody deserves a violent death, not Carville, and not the elderly black man in the upstairs bedroom on East Thirty-ninth Street.

He was Marko's problem, not mine. Cleveland isn't Metropolis or Gotham City, and I'm not a caped superhero out to right wrongs. But I could do something about Carville, because I'd been asked to.

That's why I do what I do for a living. Every once in a while I do get the chance to make wrong things right.

With any luck.

From what I'd learned of Ginger Carville from Cirini and Ray Aylmer and Jeannie Shaftoe, it didn't surprise me that she might have a married boyfriend. And that suggested a lot of other possibilities to me as to who might have had reason to kill her.

I called Marko at the Third District, but they told me Saturday was his day off. He might get pretty snarky if I bothered him at home with business stuff, especially if I interrupted a dalliance with Brittany or one of her clones. But he was the one who'd imposed the Tuesday-morning deadline on Steve Cirini, and I reminded him of it when he answered the phone and I asked him for a favor.

"A favor," he said. "No kidding! What a surprise, Milan. You *never* ask for favors."

I let it go. When you're asking for a favor you sometimes have to bite your tongue.

"Look," Marko said, "I've got a lunch date at noon—"

"It'll take five minutes."

"That means an hour."

"Whatever. Call the Bureau of Motor Vehicles for me and

see if you can get an unlisted number and address for Violet Grba in Garfield Heights."

"Isn't that the name you gave me with that doctor's? The repressed-memory shrink business."

"Right."

"I had them run her through the CID computer already, Milan, and got zippo in terms of any police report. You have no real reason to suppose she had anything to do with Carville getting killed, do you?"

"It's like arthritis," I said. "I feel it in my bones."

"Suppose I tell you you're just chasing your own tail?"

"It's my tail."

"It's your client's ass, though."

"It's all I've got."

"And you won't give it to me, either. Secret files." He said the last two words like a malediction.

"I'll give you something else, though. Carville was probably seeing a married man."

"Where'd you get that?"

"From Cirini."

"Sure," he said. "He'd probably tell you she was boffing the Archbishop of Chicago just to get you to go looking somewhere else."

"Maybe," I said. "But I don't think so. Will you get me Grba's address? If it pans out, it's yours. I promise."

"How do I know you'll keep that promise, Milan?"

"What am I going to do with it? Sell it to CBS for a movie-of-the-week?"

He thought about it for a minute. "Not a bad idea at that," he said. "Do I get to play me?"

It wasn't five minutes later, but it was more like forty than the hour he'd estimated, when he called back with an address and telephone number for Violet Grba, telling me the information would cost me good seats to a Cavs game at the Gund Arena. I assured him it was a deal; it was not only a fine excuse to spend some leisure time with my oldest friend, but I could charge the tickets to Steve Cirini.

I dialed Violet Grba's number, but no one picked up the phone and there was no answering machine. It was Saturday morning, and she was probably doing the kinds of errands there never seems to be enough time for during the work week.

I wasn't in much of a mood to take a long drive that might turn out to be for nothing, but I didn't have much else to do. So I took my time getting dressed—slacks, shirt, tie, and tweed sports jacket. Then I checked my *Official Street Atlas of Cleveland and Cuyahoga County* to make sure I knew where I was going. Garfield Heights is outside my usual theater of operations, and I hadn't been there in years. But my recollections were good; it was pretty much south of downtown, in the area of Valley View and Maple Heights. All blue-collar neighborhoods, or what in the dear dead days when everyone didn't wear their sensitivities on their sleeves used to be called lower middle class. I descended Cedar Hill to Carnegie Avenue, turned down East Fifty-fifth Street, slicing through the middle of the east-side inner city, and headed south toward Garfield Heights.

I found myself on Turney Road, Garfield Heights' main drag, a few minutes past noon. I drove by a stretch of commercial buildings, schools, and malls, and a civic center that looked like that of half a million other so-called bedroom communities in middle America. The side streets were slightly hilly, lined with tall white frame houses, many with second-floor balconies, and squat red-brick ones.

The address the Bureau of Motor Vehicles had given Marko was that of a two-story apartment building with a veranda running all the way across the front of the second floor. The red bricks had been carelessly painted white, which made it look somewhat as if the building had been picked up in Las Cruces, New Mexico, and dropped into the middle of northeastern Ohio.

Along the side were numbered spaces for the residents and several others marked VISITOR. I parked in one of those and got out of the car. Marko had told me Violet Grba lived in apartment 14; in the space with the corresponding number was a new beige Toyota Camry. I touched the hood as I walked by; it was warm. Evidently I'd been right about Violet Grba running her Saturday-morning errands.

Climbing the exterior stairway, I walked along the veranda until I found the apartment. From inside, too-loud music was playing—or what passes for music these days, the kind of stuff that all sounds the same to anyone over thirty.

I pushed the doorbell, producing a faint electronic *bing-bong*, and although I couldn't really hear anything happening inside, I sort of sensed someone coming to the door.

Violet Grba was somewhere around twenty-five, I thought, although she had the kind of face that ages early. Her hair was dark brown and straight, cut in bangs and falling just below her shoulders. She had a weak chin and high flat cheekbones, and there was a tracery of wrinkles at the corners of her pale blue eyes, probably brought about by her hanging her cigarettes out of the side of her mouth, the way she was doing when she opened the door. Under jeans and an aqua Northern Lights sweatshirt her figure was lumpy, to put the kindest interpretation on it. I could see where she might resemble her father when she grew older. That was something to think about.

There was a wariness about her; she seemed tightly coiled, and at the same time she had a sort of seen-it-all, nothing-would-surprise-me world-weariness. If she was only twenty-five, it was twenty-five the hard way.

"Yuh?" she said, and the cigarette bobbed.

"Ms. Grba? Violet Grba?"

She took the cigarette out of her mouth and waved the

smoke from in front of her face with the same hand. "I know you?" I figured it was the Grba-family way of welcoming strangers.

"My name is Milan Jacovich," I said, and produced a business card. "I'm a private investigator."

Her neck seemed to stiffen, and her eyes narrowed in a sort of recognition. "You the one been bothering my old man, huh?"

So they'd called her. "I was trying to locate you," I said.

Her chest rose and fell with a deep breath. "Whadja hafta hit him for? Doncha know he's sick?"

"As a matter of fact, I didn't know. He started the fight. I feel really terrible about it."

"Yuh, well, fuck you, okay?" She stepped back and started to close the door.

I stuck my foot in, like a door-to-door salesman in a cartoon, and it whacked me on the ankle. I felt the pain clear up to my hipbone. "Please, Violet. Let me talk to you for five minutes. That's all."

She stuck the cigarette back between her lips, freeing her hands for whatever might come next. Her eyes were crafty, calculating. "You want me t'call the cops?"

"Do you know who Virginia Carville was?"

Some of the truculence went out of her, replaced by a curiosity she could neither deny nor hide. "TV lady who got killed?" She ducked her head in assent. "What's she got to do with me?"

"Your name was in her files," I said.

"My name?" She blinked twice, either from surprise or the smoke that was rising into her eye. "I don't know nothin' about her."

"Then are you familiar with a Dr. Oscar Flygenring?"

Almost as though someone had snipped the ligaments that held her vertebrae together her body slumped, and she reached out a hand to the doorjamb to steady herself. "Oh, shit," she murmured, and took the cigarette out of her mouth, letting her head fall forward.

"You'd better let me come in, Violet. We need to talk. You don't have to—I'm not a policeman. But I don't mean you any harm." I put on my most beseeching manner. "A woman has been killed, Violet. You don't want whoever did it to get away with it, do you?"

"I don't care."

"Sure you do. We all care when somebody gets killed like that."

Her chin had sunk so low onto her chest that I almost couldn't hear her say, "You gonna get me in a lot a trouble."

"I promise I won't."

She stared at the floor, shaking her head sadly. Then she turned and went back into the apartment. I noticed as she walked away from me that the jeans stretched tightly across her broad buttocks bore a pricey designer label.

The paint on the carelessly plastered walls in Violet Grba's apartment was patchy and uneven, and the furniture was strictly Value City, all inexpensive fabrics and cheap veneered wood, but it looked fairly new. I wondered how long she'd lived there. Against the far wall was an entertainment center, a big-screen TV and a complicated-looking audio system, which she went to turn off, and through an archway I could see a tiny kitchen. On the blond-wood coffee table was a CD case, and from it I was able to identify the music that had been playing as something by a band called Prick; I thought I remembered hearing they were a local group that made good, but I wasn't sure and probably never would be. "I'm sorry to bother you on a Saturday like this," I said.

"It's my day off," she said, crossing her arms over her chest, what was left of the cigarette held between the second and third fingers of her right hand. "I'm an apprentice welder. Look, whaddaya want from me? I don't know nothin' about that lady on the television that got killed. I never seen her in my whole life."

"I know."

"So then . . . ?"

"But you know Dr. Flygenring."

Taking a last drag on the cigarette, she stubbed it out viciously in an overflowing square glass ashtray on the coffee table, refusing to look at me.

"Are you one of his patients, Violet?"

Her eyes closed, and they stayed that way. "This don't mean nothin' but trouble," she said glumly.

I was standing in the middle of the small living room, and I felt as if my bulk was filling it up. Without being invited to, I sat down in an uncomfortable chair covered in an ugly nubby gray fabric overprinted with big blue flowers; the kind of chair you might see in the waiting room of a neighborhood free medical clinic. On the small table beside it were a *People* magazine and an open can of diet root beer with a bent plastic straw sticking out of it.

Violet didn't seem to notice whether I stood or sat; she was too engrossed in an old tape she was running inside her own head. Finally she said, "Yuh, I use'ta go to Flygenring. Not no more." She spoke as if it required a great effort.

"Why not?"

She looked around almost frantically, fairly lunging at the pack of More Lights on the sofa. She shook one out and put it between her lips, then pried a plastic lighter out of the pocket of the tight jeans.

"Why did you stop seeing Dr. Flygenring, Violet?" I prodded gently.

"Cuz we finished," she said, lighting the cigarette and taking a deep drag. "It's over with, okay? It's a done deal."

Curious choice of words, I thought, and then chalked it up to the woman's general inarticulateness. "Why do you suppose

Virginia Carville had your name and Dr. Flygenring's together in her file?"

"How do I know?" She dropped gracelessly onto the sofa; she seemed to do everything with a minimum of grace and a maximum of apathy. "I tol' you I never heard of her except from the TV."

"You think Dr. Flygenring talked to her?"

She snorted her derision, blowing twin jets of smoke through her nose. The air in the room was a blue haze, and I didn't figure she'd mind if I added to it, so I lit a Winston. I figured I was about to venture out onto the thinnest ice, and I'd have to be very careful where I stepped.

"Violet, some of Dr. Flygenring's patients are people who were—abused when they were younger. Sexually abused."

Violet crossed her arms again, hunching her shoulders against some inner cold. What little light there was behind her eyes seemed to have been switched off.

"Did that happen to you?" I said softly.

Her body jerked.

"It's important, Violet. Just say yes or no, okay?"

She looked away, letting about twenty seconds tick by. "I'm not s'posta talk about that."

"Not supposed to? Who said you couldn't? Dr. Flygenring?"

She shook her head, still without looking at me.

"Is it a secret?"

A nod this time.

"Can you tell me who it was that did that to you, Violet?"

Her averted eyes filled up with wetness, and she blinked rapidly to contain it.

"It wasn't your father, was it?"

That made her snap her head around to glare at me. "Hey!" she said. "The ol' man wouldn' do nothin' like that!" She puffed on her cigarette, right out of *Now Voyager*. "He isn't much of a father, but he's no perv."

"Was it another relative, then?"

She jerked again. "I can't tell you, okay?"

It was time to play my only ace. "Violet, I understand this is painful for you to talk about, and I don't want to cause you any trouble. But I think that Virginia Carville found out about what happened to you, and somebody killed her to keep her from telling."

Violet Grba didn't have much color in her face to begin with, but what was there quickly fled. "Howd'ya know that?"

"I don't. But if you talk to me, maybe I can find out. Save anyone else from getting hurt."

The muscles at the hinges of her jaw bulged as she gritted her teeth.

"Save it from happening to some other little girl," I said.

The tears that had been shimmering in her eyes finally broke free, falling in two thick rivulets down her cheeks. She brushed angrily at them with the back of her hand and stuck out her lower lip in an aggressive display of petulance.

I waited for a moment, but I knew when I was licked. I'd lost her. I crushed my Winston in the brimming ashtray and stood up. "Well, thanks for your time anyway. I'm sorry I bothered you."

She didn't move. I forced a good-bye smile and went to the door. Her mumbled "Okay" was so soft I almost missed it.

I turned around. "Okay what?"

"Okay, siddown," she said.

I saddown.

Sticking her cigarette in the corner of her mouth, she got to her feet, jammed her hands into the back pockets of her jeans—a tight fit—and began pacing back and forth in front of me, gathering her thoughts, searching for the courage to speak. After about a minute later, she stopped and turned squarely to face me.

"Okay. 'Bout a year ago I was havin' trouble sleepin', y'know? I was nervous alla time, drinkin' a lot, fallin' asleep on the job. That's dangerous for a welder t'do. I coulda hurt myself." Her right eye started tearing, and she removed the butt from her mouth. "So I went t' the nurse's office at work. We talked a couple a times an' then she sent me t'the shrink."

"Dr. Flygenring?"

"Nuh-uh, not him. The guy from work."

"There's a psychologist where you work?"

"No, but he kinda takes care of their people when he hasta."

"And he's the one who sent you to Flygenring."

She nodded. "Yuh. After a while."

I waited.

"I went t'him about fi', six times, an' then he—y'know, he hypnotized me," she said, pronouncing the word carefully.

"Once?"

"Lotsa times."

"And what happened?"

She sank down onto the sofa again. "Made me remember a lotta shit I didn' even remember before."

"What kind of shit?"

She pulled her feet up under her on the cushion. "Okay. My ol' lady works as a cleanin' woman, y'know? People's houses an' stuff. Rich people. So there was this time when I was eleven? An' it was summertime—no school."

"Was this in 1983?"

She stopped to think about it, and I could see her fingers twitch as she counted backwards. "Yuh."

"Okay, go ahead."

"So she use'ta work in this big house on the west side, y'-know? Once a week. An' she use'ta take me with her, 'cuz there was no school an' there was nobody home t'take care'a me. The ol' man was workin' then. At the mill?"

I nodded.

"So this guy was always there, y'know? Older guy. I mean, he lived there, but he was home a lot, 'specially in the mornings. An' he was always nice t'me, he'd give me Cokes and stuff. And he'd kinda pat me on the shoulder or the back at first an' tell me what a pretty little girl I was. Nobody ever said that before." She took a bitter drag on her cigarette and sent a jet of smoke toward the ceiling. "Or since then. Anyway, pretty soon he started, like, pattin' lower." She flicked the ash off the end of her cigarette. "Pretty soon he was puttin' his goddamn hand in my pants. In the front, y'know?" She looked away, her mouth scrunched up with past pain. "An' then he was pullin' 'em down. He liked t'look at me there."

I looked away too, and then back at her when she said, "An' then he'd make me do him, y' know? Like this." She made a loose fist and pumped it up and down.

"He made me not tell. He said if I tol', my ol' lady'd get fired, an' we needed the money an' everything. So I never said nothin' t'no one."

"Where was your mother all this time?"

She lifted her shoulders, then let them fall. "She was somewheres else in the house, workin'." She took a final drag on her cigarette and stubbed it out. "I didn' even remember all this stuff till I got hypnotized."

"Did this man have a wife?"

Violet nodded. "She was there too, but she was always upstairs or somethin'." She pronounced it "aw-weez."

"So she didn't know what her husband was doing either?"

"Nuh-uh. I don't think I even seen her no more'n twice or three times."

"And you'd forgotten all of this until you saw Dr. Flygenring?"

She nodded. "I guess."

"What happened then?"

Violet sighed. "So Dr. Flygenring tol' me I should see this lawyer about it. An' I did."

"And?"

She glared at me, suddenly angry, her eyes and nose red. "I can't talk about it no more!"

"Why not?"

"Cuz I promised!"

"Who did you promise, Violet?"

She shook her head resolutely. "No!" she said. "No! I *can't.*"

"And you can't tell me the man's name?"

"I promised," she said again.

"Can you tell me the lawyer's name?"

She shook her head again, exaggerating it the way a three-year-old might.

And I got nothing more out of Violet Grba that Saturday afternoon.

Not even good-bye.

CHAPTER SIXTEEN

Since I was pretty much in the neighborhood anyway, I had lunch at the Czech Inn, a bright, noisy ethnic restaurant on Granger with a too-loud jukebox, leisurely service, and good hearty food. I needed some time to think things over, and I didn't figure I'd meet anyone I knew at the Czech.

What Violet had told me seemed to confirm what I had been surmising, but it didn't give me anything solid to connect with Ginger Carville's murder. It certainly didn't get Steve Cirini off the hook—I only had two days plus to accomplish that feat, which was after all what I'd been hired to do. And only one of those days was a weekday, when people would be at their offices and reachable.

In the course of her visits to Dr. Flygenring, it had been discovered that Violet had been suffering from repressed memory syndrome. Yet she said she had promised she wouldn't talk about the abuse she'd suffered as a child, and that got me wondering. If she was telling me the truth, that her molester had been a wealthy man whose home her mother had cleaned, why would she keep so adamantly silent?

I thought of the printout from Ginger Carville's disk. STAT LIM—had the statute of limitations run out on the sexual abuse that had occurred in 1983? No—from what I knew, the statute of limitations on noncapital crimes was fifteen years.

So why wouldn't Violet name her molester?

Maybe it was that other little item on Carville's printout: PMNT MADE? Had someone paid off Violet Grba to keep her mouth shut?

That would fit. It went a long way toward explaining the designer jeans she wore so gracelessly, the expensive sound system and giant TV it would be difficult to purchase on an apprentice welder's salary, and her new Camry. And there was her father's new Cadillac; it might also account for Bosko Grba's anger when he thought I was digging too deep.

All that, though nice to know, wasn't helping me to find out who had wanted Carville dead. Especially since Violet was not about to tell me anything else.

Well, I thought, if you can't go through and you can't go over, you simply have to go around.

I asked for the bill. My waitress was about forty, pretty, with close-cropped blond hair, a dazzling and vivid smile, and a trim, beautiful figure. And a plain gold wedding band too. Naturally.

I went back to my car, found I-77, and headed north toward downtown. It's quieter and less frantic there on Saturdays than during the week. The closing of the historic old May Company department store several years ago and the steep downtown parking fees have kept a lot of shoppers in the suburban malls on the weekends. Being the kind of guy who always considers the glass half full, though, I was only appreciative that I was able to find a rare parking space on the street just two blocks from the library.

The Cleveland Public Library on Superior Avenue just a half block off Public Square is one of the city's many architectural gems, and the centerpiece of one of the country's finest library systems. I don't get down there as much as I'd like, and even though I didn't relish the search I had ahead of me, I was looking forward to spending some time in its quiet high-ceilinged rooms.

I pored through the last three years of the *Plain Dealer* for several hours, scribbling copious notes as I went. I was look-ing for stories about allegations of child abuse involving re-pressed memory, those that had found their way to the courts.

Like everyone else in these peculiar times, lawyers have de-veloped areas of specialization. According to the newspaper files, there were at least two Cleveland-area attorneys who seemed to spend a lot of time with repressed memory syn-drome cases—at least there were two who regularly managed to get their names in the paper.

I looked them both up in the classified directory. The list-ings for attorneys in the metropolitan area take up seventy pages. The lawyer mentioned in eight different cases was one Gorman Wiltrop, who had his main offices in the upscale west-ern suburb of Rocky River, and branches, no less, in Solon and Parma.

Repressed memory syndrome branch offices. No waiting.

The other attorney, whose name had been connected with six of such cases, was Carole Carr, listed downtown on East Ninth Street.

In the same office building as Dr. Oscar Flygenring.

Coincidence? Perhaps. It's a big building, as I recalled, with many doctors, attorneys, consultants, and a medium-size ad agency. But it was enough that I decided to start with her.

It was going to be difficult to get to Carole Carr on the weekend; generally the only lawyers who come to work on Saturdays are young associates on the partnership track in large corporate law firms.

I found a pay phone off the lobby of the library and called her office anyway, remembering what they always said in the NBA—you can't make the shot you don't take. I got exactly what I expected, a recorded message detailing the regular business hours.

Marko's Tuesday deadline didn't leave me the luxury of waiting until the beginning of the work week. I consulted the residential directory. If Carr was married but had kept her maiden name and her home phone was in her husband's name, I was a dead duck. And in any case I might be in for a long afternoon and evening, calling every Carr in the book.

But the law of compensation kicked in again, this time in my favor. My love life might be falling in pieces around my ears, but by golly, I found Carole Carr. Or at least there was a C. J. Carr listed at an address in Brecksville, a well-to-do suburb south of the city. Once more I counted myself lucky to live in Cleveland; except for media celebrities and sports figures, almost everyone in town has a listed number.

Even, it seems, repressed-memory-syndrome attorneys.

I looked at my watch. It was almost four o'clock. I decided to take a chance.

I walked the few blocks to my car and headed south on East Ninth Street, past the Gund Arena and Jacobs Field and onto the I-77 on-ramp. There wasn't much traffic, and I made it down to Brecksville in about fifteen minutes.

In a metropolitan area noted for its pretty suburbs, Brecksville is one of the most picturesque, with a lot of colonial and Cape Cod–style homes shaded by venerable trees. Carole Carr lived in a newer subdivision, though, one in which the streets were paved but the sidewalks had not yet been put in. The rains and snows of winter had left the place pretty muddy. They'd probably had to cut down a lot of the beautiful old trees to build the tract, and the new ones they had planted as replacements were a sorry substitute.

The subdivision was called Plantagenet Village, an attempt to evoke Merrie Olde England, which only reminded me of the fifth-grade teacher who had resolutely mispronounced the royal house "Plantagennette," causing me a moment of humiliation years later when I'd said it that way in a college class and was jeeringly informed that the accent should be placed on the second syllable.

Carr's house proved to be in the middle of the tract, a dark, looming Tudor on an oval street lined with similar homes, each differently configured but still looking very much the same. I guess no one had told the builders or their marketing people that there was a big difference between the Plantagenets and the Tudors.

A wooden sign that read CARR hung from the Amish-style mailbox mounted on a post at the edge of the lawn. There were leaded-glass windows in the front doors of all the houses on the oval, and Carr's house also had a large circular leaded-glass window in the attic story; the effect was that of a small Methodist church.

I parked at what passed for the curb and made my way through the mud to her front walk; climbing the steps to the front door, I wiped my feet thoroughly on the raffia mat. When I pushed the doorbell I could hear what sounded like a Chinese temple gong going off inside the house.

Plantagenet Village was eclectic, if nothing else.

After about ninety seconds without a response, I figured I'd made the drive for nothing. But I hadn't anyplace to go, anyway, so I got in my car and drove back to the main entrance of the subdivision, where I parked.

I felt pretty conspicuous. City stakeouts are a lot easier because there are always so many cars on the street, no one looks twice at someone sitting in a parked vehicle; it could be the beginnings of a drug deal, a jealous boyfriend staking out his ex-lover's house, or simply someone waiting to take Aunt Edna to the doctor's. Here in the green suburbs a guy hunkered down in a parked car stands out like a Hasidic rabbi on the streets of Amman.

No police or security vehicles cruised by in the first half hour. The few cars that did pass either ignored me, or, in the case of one family of four in a new Mitsubishi Galant, gave me no more than a curious look. Of course for all I knew they were heading to their own brand-new Tudor to call the law.

Eventually I felt uncomfortable enough to move my car, making an awkward U-turn and parking about eighty yards into the tract on the other side of the road. On this main street the houses were farther apart, so I didn't have to park right in front of somebody's door.

After another twenty minutes I noticed a gray Saab sedan still displaying its temporary license stickers approaching in my rearview mirror. As it rolled by me I could see that the driver was a woman. At the corner she turned in the direction of Carr's oval. I counted to fifty-Mississippi and then started my car and followed her.

The Saab was parked in Carr's driveway. It was a good guess on my part; Saab is the car of choice for many of Cleveland's upscale attorneys.

I had to wipe my feet again. I rang the bell, and this time it was answered.

Carole Carr opened the door only partway. She was in her late thirties. Her hair was brown, styled short and curly, and her dark eyebrows unplucked; her dark-brown-almost-black eyes, hard and quick behind oversize round glasses, were set far apart in her salon-tanned face. She was wearing a soft blue sweater, beige slacks, and saddle oxfords and sporting a diamond ring the size of a Concord grape. It was, however, on her right hand.

On the tiled floor of the entry hall behind her were two bulging shopping bags from Saks and one from Kaufmann's.

"Yes?" she said in a surprising baritone voice.

"Carole Carr?"

"That's right."

"The attorney?"

Her shoulders stiffened. "Who are you?"

I told her my name and occupation and handed her a business card and the photostat of my license. She looked at them both, then at me, and the look wasn't friendly. She handed back the photostat and put the card in her pocket.

"I don't do business in my home," she told me. "Or on my days off, either. Call my office Monday for an appointment."

"I'm afraid it can't wait."

"Oh, everything can wait, Mr. Jacovich." She didn't stumble over the name. "You can, too."

"Not this time," I said.

Her eyes crinkled with what might have been amusement. "You're kind of pushy."

"It's important."

"Not to me. Good afternoon."

The leaded-glass panel in the door was heading for my face when I said, "It has to do with Violet Grba."

She pulled the door open again and stared at me open-mouthed, a flush suffusing her cheeks. "My clients . . ." Catching herself, she ran a hand through her curls. "I'm sorry, I have nothing to say to you."

"You might not think so, Ms. Carr, but this is all about murder."

Her throat worked, and she wet her lips with her tongue. "That's pretty heavy."

I nodded. "Yes, ma'am."

Annoyed, she furrowed her brow. "Jesus Christ, don't call me ma'am!" she ordered. "It makes me feel a hundred years old." Still holding the door open, she put her fist on her hip. "I'm not a criminal lawyer, Mr. Jacovich. I don't know anything about murder."

"But you do know something about Violet Grba."

It wasn't a question, and she didn't answer it. She thought for about fifteen seconds and then stepped back, opening the door wider. She raised her left arm to look at her watch, a plain silver Timex with a black leather strap. "You have exactly five minutes."

I walked past her into the entry hall. "We can probably finish in four, Counselor."

Inside the house it was chilly. She led me into the two-story living room, where a picture window looked out at a stand of denuded maple and oak trees on one side, and a balcony overhung the seating area on the other, in the fashion of many of northern Ohio's newer and more expensive tract homes.

"How did you know to come to me?" Carole Carr demanded. She hadn't offered me a seat, so we both remained on our feet.

"I took a chance."

"Smart guy."

"I'm a detective."

"Private."

"Yes."

"That means I don't *have* to talk to you."

"No, you don't," I said. "But 'private' is the operative word. You talk to me and I keep my mouth shut. Talk to the police and it's public record."

"It's nothing of the sort," she snapped. "I'm an attorney, remember?"

"Yes, ma—yes, Ms. Carr."

She supressed a very small smile. "Maybe you'd better tell me what this is all about."

"You heard about the death of Virginia Carville, the Channel Twelve news reporter?"

"I don't live at the bottom of a mine shaft," she said, nodding.

"Well, Violet Grba's name was in her secret files."

She didn't say anything.

"So was Dr. Flygenring's."

"Was mine?"

"No."

"What do I care, then?"

"I think Carville was planning to do a story on repressed memory syndrome."

A pale line appeared around Carr's lips as if drawn there with a white pencil, and she ran her fingers through her hair again. Her nails were clipped blunt and short and were without polish. "And?"

"That seems to be one of your legal specialties."

"I've handled a few cases," she admitted.

"You handled one for Violet Grba."

"I never said that."

"You didn't say you'd never heard of her either, which would have been the logical reaction if it were true. And just because I mentioned her name I'm in here with you instead of standing on the porch with a bloody nose from your slamming the door on it. So there must be some connection, no?"

"I don't go around discussing my clients' business, Mr. Jacovich—it's against the ethics of the legal profession. I'm afraid you're wasting your time."

"It's my time."

"That's right," she said with another glance at her wristwatch, "and you have three minutes of it left."

"I've checked with the police, and there was never any report filed with Cleveland sex crimes regarding any abuse of a minor named Violet Grba."

She regarded me with unreadable onyx eyes.

"So I assume that for some reason no criminal charges were brought."

"Assume your ass off," she said.

"All right, I will. I further assume then that the repressed memory syndrome was somehow faulty in this instance, that Flygenring talked Violet Grba into remembering something that didn't happen."

Her nostrils flared along with her temper, which is what I'd been hoping for. "Repressed memory syndrome is a fact," she said. "Sometimes when children suffer sexual abuse it's so traumatic that they simply block it out, push it way down into the subconscious so they don't even have to acknowledge it or remember it anymore." Her lip curled in disdain. "That's the goddamn trouble! It's so easy, isn't it, for a man to believe that women make those things up."

"Not just women, Counselor. There was a case a few years

back where a young man brought charges of abuse against a Catholic cardinal because of a repressed memory that came to light during therapy and then later withdrew them, saying his memory was flawed and it wasn't true."

She nodded. "That doesn't mean it didn't happen; it could just mean he changed his mind about blowing the whistle. I can't imagine that he wasn't put under considerable pressure, considering the circumstances."

"But Violet Grba didn't change her mind, did she?"

"You're assuming again," she said through gritted teeth.

"That's right, I am. So the matter was somehow settled out of court, where there would be no official record. Dr. Flygenring sent Grba to you, and you went to her alleged molester and negotiated a settlement, didn't you?"

Except for a slight twitch of a muscle at the corner of her left eye, her face might have been chiseled from a block of granite. "I think your five minutes are up. Good-bye, Mr. Jacovich."

"No, I still have two left."

"Sue me," the attorney said.

CHAPTER SEVENTEEN

It was seven thirty when I finally winched myself out of bed on Sunday morning, groggy from lack of sleep. I'd been memorizing the cracks and fissures on the bedroom ceiling most of the night, trying to fit together the puzzle pieces of Virginia Carville's murder.

I was pretty sure the scenario with which I'd challenged Carole Carr was the right one, that under Oscar Flygenring's therapy and hypnosis Violet Grba had recalled some incident of sexual abuse back in 1983, when she'd been a child, and that Carr, acting in her behalf, had confronted the molester, who'd quickly weighed his options and decided that paying hush money was a far preferable alternative to public exposure and criminal prosecution.

I was sure because so far nobody had told me I was wrong. No matter how hard anyone tries to stonewall, if you've gotten things completely cockeyed, they'll be more than happy to point that out to you.

So Violet Grba was getting her own back in the form of cash. And judging from her designer jeans and new car, and the Cadillac DeVille that looked so out of place in her father's humble driveway, the payment must have been a hefty one; probably there were an ongoing series. Maybe that was why she and Bosko Grba were being so uncooperative; they didn't want to violate the terms of an agreement that was keeping them in a thin patch of clover.

Some people would consider it small compensation indeed for such a hideous wrong, of however long ago.

And a lot of other people might just call it blackmail.

I couldn't find it in my heart to blame Violet Grba and her father. A buck is a buck, after all, and the gravy train doesn't often stop at Track Road.

So there was still a black hole in the middle of the Virginia Carville story, and that was the identity of the molester. And I didn't know whether that name was encrypted in the one notation on the secret diskette I hadn't yet been able to decipher: FK INC. Or whether Violet Grba and her legal and psychological problems had nothing whatever to do with what happened to Carville and I was completely wide of the mark, fly-fishing for red herring with the wrong bait.

There was no way of forcing Carole Carr to reveal the abuser's name, because of attorney-client confidentiality. Of course if Steve Cirini were ever brought to trial, Violet Grba could be subpoenaed and forced to testify—*if* I could find a single shred of evidence that the Grba business had anything to do with Carville's murder. And that was looking like a pretty big if at the moment.

Fighting a capital charge could cost Cirini every nickel he had—plus his reputation and most probably his career—even if he were eventually found innocent. That's the big glitch in our judicial system. People have long memories and often firmly believe the old saw that where there's smoke, there's fire.

I didn't hate him *that* much.

It wasn't Cirini's problem that had kept me staring at the ceiling for most of the night, though. Have you ever gone into a room in your house, your kitchen, say, and found you can't remember why, except you know you went in there for *something*? And it drives you crazy until you suddenly realize that you're thirsty and were heading for a soda or a beer.

That's the sort of thing that had stolen my sleep. I knew that some little puzzle piece was right there in front of me, tiptoe-ing around the edge of my consciousness, and I couldn't yet see where it was supposed to fit in the picture. It was going to make me crazy until I was able to drop it in where it belonged.

But if you've ever put a jigsaw puzzle together, you'll know it never really works when you try to force a piece to fit.

Outside, a cold rain peppered the pavement, and even though all my windows were closed and I had the thermostat set at a comfortable sixty-eight degrees, the damp chill snuck into my aging bones. I thought about calling my sons and see-ing if I could talk Lila into letting me have them for the day, but on reflection it wasn't a good idea; they'd probably made their Sunday plans already—plans that didn't include me.

Walking up to the Arabica near Coventry for a coffee and pastry and sitting in their front window to read the Sunday paper seemed like an option, but I remembered that Nicole often frequented Arabica—that's where I'd met her—and it suddenly seemed too much of an effort. Too much, even, of a risk.

Instead I brewed a pot in my kitchen, dumped three en-velopes of instant oatmeal into a bowl, poured boiling water over it, and sprinkled it with brown sugar and a big glob of but-ter. Sugar and fat. Nicole would have disapproved—but Nicole wasn't there.

And wouldn't be.

The phone rang at exactly nine o'clock, after I'd gotten through news, sports, the arts, and the Sunday magazine sec-tion and was starting on The Wizard of Id.

"Hi, Milan," Mary said.

I cleared the long night out of my throat before saying hello; I hadn't spoken a word aloud since early the evening before when I'd said good-bye to Carole Carr, and my voice wasn't working right just yet.

"I hope I'm not calling too early, but I wanted to get you be-fore you went off to pick up the boys."

"I'm not going anywhere, it's not my Sunday to be with them. But don't worry—I'm up and awake. More or less."

"How are things going?"

"At this point, too close to call."

There was silence on the line. Then she said, "Nicky Scandalios called me yesterday afternoon."

"Oh?"

"He wanted your home phone number."

"What for?"

"I don't know. He didn't say."

"Didn't you ask him?"

"Milan, he's my boss," she said. "I can't just question him like that."

I doodled a gallows. "I sort of wish you'd called to tell me last night."

Another heavy silence.

Then, "I couldn't. I'm sorry." I heard her take a deep breath. "I was having dinner with Steve last night. We had a lot to discuss."

I reached for my coffee mug, the one with the big orange Cleveland Browns helmet on it. "You don't owe me any explanations."

She made a little clicking noise with her tongue that I knew signified exasperation. "Do you have to be so cold all the time, Milan?"

"I'm not being cold," I said. "Just factual. It's been a good three years since I had the right to ask you what you were doing on any given evening, and nothing's happened to change that."

"I didn't go to bed with him, in case you were wondering."

The hair on the back of my neck prickled, and I could hear my heart thudding in my ears, and I shook my head to be rid of the sound. "I wasn't wondering. And I didn't ask."

"Do you care?"

"Right now all I care about is keeping him off death row.

* *197* *

What he does—or what you do—just isn't a concern of mine right now."

"You really hate me, don't you?" Her voice was shaky. "For leaving you."

"If I hated you, I wouldn't be working for Steve Cirini."

She sniffled. I don't know whether she was deliberately trying to sound small and vulnerable and adorable or whether her nose was really running. "We have to have a serious talk, Milan."

No! I protested silently. "We'll talk Tuesday," I said.

"What's Tuesday?"

"Tuesday is when your boyfriend is either off the hook or sitting in an interrogation room on Payne Avenue talking to some pretty mean cops. Until then, I'll be kind of busy."

She sighed. "All right, Tuesday then. I guess you know what's best."

I found that observation ironic. One of my problems is that I almost never know what's best.

After I hung up I finished the rest of the coffee and washed the dishes, trying not to think about Mary, about Nicole, about anything that was important to me personally. In my business you don't get Sundays off, especially when people's lives are involved.

Instead, I concentrated on figuring out why Scandalios wanted my home phone number, and what he might have to say to me.

I had to wait until almost noon to find out. That's when he finally got around to calling me. I wondered what had taken him so long.

"Sorry to bother you at home on your day off."

"No problem, Mr. Scandalios. What can I do for you?"

"I think it's a question of what we can do for each other," he said heartily. "Would it be possible for us to get together today?"

"Today?"

"I know it's a Sunday, but it's important."

"Uh-huh." I let him worry about it for a few seconds. "What time did you have in mind?"

"Oh, how about around four o'clock? That way we'll both have the evening free."

"That'll be swell," I said. I had such exciting, elaborate plans for the evening—plans that included Mike Wallace and Ed Bradley and Andy Rooney and a TV movie about an adoptive child's search for her birth parents. "My office?"

"I hate to drag you out in the rain, Mr. Jacovich. I can come to your home if that's convenient."

"It's not," I said. Nicky Scandalios lived in a baronial mansion on the lake in Bay Village; I knew because I'd seen a color-photo spread of it in *Cleveland Magazine*. And while my digs are hardly a slum, if I knew Scandalios's type he'd walk into my humble two-bedroom apartment with a superior, richer-than-thou attitude that would irritate me into rudeness. "My office is in the Flats. On Collision Bend."

"I know where it is," he said. "Four o'clock, then."

For a guy who couldn't get rid of me fast enough two days ago, Scandalios sounded awfully anxious for a heart-to-heart. Usually the only thing that might get him out of Bay Village on a weekend was a fancy benefit where he could work the room and self-promote. I wasn't sure, but I thought I knew what he wanted to talk about.

I took a load of clothes down to the laundry room in the basement and fed the machines all my change. Although my ex-wife Lila had tried for years to sell me on the advantages of separating whites from colors, permanent press from cottons, and towels from T-shirts, I do laundry the way most men do: toss it all in together and wash it in cold water, then tumble-dry warm.

Life is too short to be spent sorting your laundry.

At three o'clock I showered, slipped on black slacks, a gray shirt and a darker gray jacket, and made my way down to the

Flats. On this lousy-weather Sunday the streets were fairly empty. I got there at about ten to four and left the downstairs door unlocked for him.

Incredibly enough, there were two or three pleasure boats out on the river, passing my window as they headed back from the lake in the waning hours of daylight. It made me shiver just to look at them; I could imagine how cold it must have been out on the open water, and I turned up the thermostat from fifty-five degrees, where I usually keep it on the weekends, to seventy. The heat kicked in noisily.

I guess when someone spends all that money for a boat and a place to keep it, they don't really care if they're cold and wet and miserable; they are by God going to enjoy their toy, even on a rainy February Sunday. Not really my idea of a good time, but then I don't suppose spending the weekend trying to connect an almost-fifteen-year-old sexual abuse case to a particularly grisly murder would have been their idea of a good time, either.

At five minutes after four a car door slammed down in the parking lot, and a moment later I heard someone bustling up the stairs. I nudged the switch that turned on the tape recorder with my foot and stood up to greet Nicky Scandalios.

He was wearing a belted gray-cashmere overcoat over a brown-tweed jacket, beige slacks, and a maroon turtleneck; his country-squire-comes-to-town-on-the-weekend ensemble no doubt. When he came through the office door he stopped there for a beat or so, posing. I suppose he was waiting for the usual applause.

"Here you are," he said as if he'd been looking everywhere for me.

"Let me take your coat, Mr. Scandalios," I said, going around the desk.

He shrugged the coat off his shoulders and put it on the second chair, nodding toward the windows.

"Wow! Some view. It's worth whatever rent you pay."

"I own the building," I told him with a little snobbish pride of my own.

"If I had this to look at all day I'd never get any work done."

"You get used to it."

He watched one of the pleasure boats make the turn around Collision Bend. "Crazy people! Going for a sail in weather like this. Doesn't make any sense. We probably won't take our boat out until the middle of May." He turned to look at me. "Do you sail?"

"Only on the days I'm not playing polo," I said, and gestured at the other chair. He checked the seat to make sure it wouldn't get his slacks dirty, and then sat down bravely.

"Well, how is your investigation coming, Milan?"

So we were on a first-name basis all of a sudden. It made me feel warm all over. "It's coming," I said.

"Good, good, good." It was one *good* too many, and I think he realized it because he got a silly, caught-in-the-cookie-jar grin on his face.

"It'd be coming a lot better if someone could tell me what FK Incorporated was."

"FK Incorporated. Hmm."

"Ring any bells?"

He knit his brows, which is the way bad actors indicate they're thinking. "Can't help you there, I'm afraid. At least not off the top of my head."

"Ever heard of Violet Grba? Or Dr. Oscar Flygenring?"

His smile was one of patience and forbearance. "You're making those names up."

"No. Carole Carr?"

"I'm afraid I'm stumped, Milan." He turned on the charm, full wattage. "Of course my brain doesn't function that well on the weekend."

"Shall I make some coffee then?"

He lifted a hand. "Not this late in the day. I'd be up all night."

"A beer? Seven-Up?"

"A Seven-Up might be nice. Is it diet?"

"Sorry."

"Ah. Well nothing, then, thanks." He folded his hands neatly over his little paunch the way he probably did every Thursday evening in his box at Severance Hall, when the Cleveland Orchestra was playing something safe like Mozart or Beethoven, not seeming to be in any hurry to get the conversation started. I guess he was waiting for the conductor to appear.

"You said you wanted to talk to me about something?" I said, jarring him from his reverie.

"Indeed yes. You know, meeting you this week and getting to know you set me to thinking about this . . . unfortunate business." His eyes twinkled, and he gave me an arch wink. "I'm a dangerous man when I start thinking."

I smiled, which wasn't quite the helpless guffaw I think he'd been hoping for, but he went gamely on.

"Our news department is the jewel in Channel Twelve's crown, Milan, and I'm damn proud of it. We don't have a hell of a lot of say about what shows the network sends us, but in a market this size, local news is an area where a station can really have an impact. I'm constantly on the lookout for ideas that will improve our news. We're tied for number-one in the ratings—we have been all winter. But an old ex–football player like you knows what they always say about a tie."

I knew he was dying to deliver the punch line, so I let him.

"They say a tie is like kissing your sister," he explained.

I knew that, an old ex–football player like me.

"So," he went on, "I thought you might be of some help to the station. Get things moving in a positive direction. Give us a new angle."

"I'm not anchorman material, I'm afraid. I'm not nearly as pretty as Vivian Truscott."

Scandalios chuckled. "That's not exactly what I meant."

"Oh." Dreams of stardom dashed.

"A great deal of our coverage, I'm sorry to report, is in the area of the police beat. Crime, in other words." He shook his jowls in Nixonian fashion. "The scourge of our cities. The most serious social problem facing our country today."

I was beginning to wish I'd worn hip boots.

"And that's where I think you might be able to help us. A former cop, a private investigator; you know the ropes. You know the way police departments work. You're trained in the rules of evidence, that sort of thing. And you have connections downtown that any one of our reporters would kill for." He blanched. "Ah, damn," he murmured, clearing his throat and wriggling around in his chair, flustered. "Under the circumstances, that was an unfortunate turn of phrase, wasn't it?"

"I don't quite understand where you're going with this, Mr. Scandalios."

"Very simply put, we'd like you to come to work at Channel Twelve. As a consultant."

"A consultant?"

"Sure. You'd hardly have to do anything at all. Once in a while one of our field reporters might give you a jingle, just to get some background, or maybe to run something by you and see how it feels. And the publicity it would generate—you know, that we had our own police expert—would be invaluable."

He unfolded his hands and aimed a well-manicured finger at me. "And the fact that you aren't with the department anymore, that you're not bound by their rules and regulations and their internal politics, would make you just that much more valuable to us." He relaced his fingers over his belly. "Very valuable indeed."

"Just how valuable?"

He consulted the ceiling, as was his habit. He seemed to derive some sort of inspiration from it. "Let's say . . . a two-year contract. At five hundred dollars per week. That comes to fifty-two thousand over the two years."

"Math wasn't my best subject," I said, "but I can figure that out."

"Not bad money for maybe four or five phone calls a month, eh? If that." He leaned heavily on the last two words.

"Uh-huh."

"And we'd put you on the payroll as a regular employee so you wouldn't get stuck for the double Social Security." His smile became avuncular. "I know how tough and how unfair that double tax is on self-employed people like yourself. The IRS doesn't make it easy on little guys."

"They sure don't," I admitted.

"Of course, we'd want you to sign an exclusive with our station," he said, looking me right in the eye so I'd be sure to take him seriously. "Exclusive at least within the viewing area. We wouldn't want you showing up at Channel Five or Channel Eight, would we?"

"Of course not."

He sat back in his chair, pleased with himself. "So. What do you say?"

"I say," I said, "it's too good to be true."

He nodded, beaming.

"What I mean by that is that there must be a string attached somewhere."

"I wouldn't quite call it a string . . ."

"Why don't you tell me what it is and then we can both decide what we would quite call it."

He hooked an arm over the back of the chair. "We'd like you to withdraw from your commission with Steve Cirini."

"Oh."

"Steve didn't kill Ginger Carville," he said. "We both know that. There isn't enough evidence for the police to make a case against him, and it would save him some money. He hasn't made a nickel in the last week, ever since this whole business started. So how I look at it is, why complicate matters?"

"For whom?"

He was still smiling—at least, his mouth was. But there was little merriment or goodwill in his eyes. "For Steve, and for us—the station. Come on board with us, pick up some fast money, and make it easy for everyone."

"Without the bullshit, Nicky, how *I* look at it is you're offering me a fifty-thousand-dollar bribe to drop Steve Cirini's case. To stop poking around in Virginia Carville's life."

That chased all pretense of a smile away. "Fifty-two thousand."

"And if you ever did call me up to consult on anything at all, I'd be so surprised I'd faint dead away. What I'm wondering now is why."

"I told you," he said. "I dislike complications."

"Maybe you should have thought of that before you started fucking Ginger Carville."

He jerked upright in the chair, and his normally cherub-pink face and scalp turned several shades darker. "You're guessing. You can't possibly know that."

"I didn't—at least not for certain—until you started turning purple. You're a bad liar, Mr. Scandalios, but you're a liar."

"That's a lousy thing to say."

"Screwing around on your wife is a lousy thing to do. And dangling fifty thousand bucks in front of me to keep me quiet about it goes beyond the pale—sorry, fifty-two thousand," I quickly corrected myself. "As you said, that's a nice piece of change. Especially when it's the station's and not yours."

His hands fluttered helplessly in the air. "I never meant for it to get out of hand with Ginger. It was just—one of those things."

"A trip to the moon on gossamer wings?"

His mouth tightened. "All right, then. How much *do* you want?"

"To cover up a murder?"

His visage went from angry to impatient. "I didn't kill her, for Christ's sake!"

"Who did?"

"How the hell should I know?"

"You were sleeping with the woman—don't you care?"

The breath he expelled seemed to deflate him; he looked old and sad. "Of course I care. More than you could imagine. It wasn't what you think. It wasn't just a . . . casual thing. Ginger had become very special to me."

"Spare me the sad songs. I'm tone deaf."

"I'm a married man," he whined.

"Congratulations."

"Have pity, Milan. If this came out—about me and Ginger— it'd just about break my wife's heart."

Sure, I thought. She'd be so heartbroken that she'd probably toss him out like a Tupperware dish full of two-week-old lasagna and take the big Bay Village mansion and an impressive chunk of his seven-figure income in the process. And the scandal about his having a clandestine relationship with one of his female employees, especially in these days when sexual harassment suits lurk in the dark corners of every office in the land, might be enough to get him bounced out of one of the best media jobs in Cleveland. And he'd have a hell of a time getting another one locally.

All the years of schmoozing, all the contacts, all the benefits he'd chaired and sat through while smiling stiffly in a boiled shirt, all the prestige he'd so carefully cultivated—all might suddenly disappear with a giant sucking sound.

I figured a fifty-two-thousand-dollar fix would be cheap.

"Tell you what I'll do with you," I said. "I'm bound by law to inform the police about your relationship with Ginger." I put up both hands to stem his protest. "But adultery isn't a crime in and of itself. I know Lieutenant Meglich at homicide pretty well, and I think I can convince him to keep a lid on it. Unless . . ."

Now his ruddy face turned pasty white. "Unless what?"

"Unless it comes out that you killed her."

He shook his head vehemently. "That's not going to happen."

"I hope not, for your sake. If it does, your wife's finding out that you were cheating on her will be the least of your worries."

Scandalios ran a hand over his face like Brian Keith used to when Mr. French told him Buffy and Jody were being naughty. "This isn't real," he said.

I picked up a pencil and started doodling an empty gallows on my yellow legal pad, but in my mind's eye Nicky Scandalios's head was in the noose. "It's real, all right."

"The job offer still stands, Milan," he stammered. "I'd really appreciate your going to bat for me with your policeman friend. My wife . . . hell, you used to be married yourself. You know how things are."

I knew how things were.

"Well, it still stands. Five hundred a week for two years. To consult." He relaxed a little; now that we were talking money, he was back on his home field. "Not a bad gig."

All at once my sleepless night got to me; I felt tired and irritated. "Don't worry, Mr. Scandalios. I won't tell your wife."

I neatly finished off the thick knot in the noose with my pencil. "And you can put your gig in your ass," I said.

❋　　❋　　❋　　❋　　❋　　❋　　❋

CHAPTER EIGHTEEN

❋　　❋　　❋　　❋　　❋　　❋　　❋

It was one of those shots in the dark that every once in a while pay off.

I suppose I should have figured it out earlier. Ginger Carville had been sleeping with Steve Cirini strictly for the fun of it, and being the person I had discovered her to be, it would have been unlike her to take the risk of getting involved with a married man if all that was in it for her were the same things she could get from Steve, i.e., sweaty and unbridled passion. And unlike Mary, who was with Cirini for the benefits and career advancement it might bring her, an on-air personality like Carville could get all the perks and ego strokes she desired in a medium-size city like Cleveland, where most of the other local celebrities wore jockstraps. It would surprise me if she'd paid for a theater ticket or dinner at an expensive restaurant in the past three years.

So her married lover had to be satisfying other needs. With a lot of women in Carville's situation, I would have just looked up the ten richest guys in town and bounced them around until one of them told me the truth. But ambition is what drove her, not libido and not money, and it only made sense that, with Cirini on the side for the more imaginative bedroom acrobatics, Carville would have chosen to have a clandestine relationship with someone who could advance her career. And Nicky Scandalios, the general manager of her station and one of the biggest power rangers around, was in the perfect position to do that.

When Mary told me he wanted my home number I'd figured he wanted to come clean about the affair and beg me not to blow the whistle on him. But the job offer had come as a complete surprise. It was a neat way to camouflage a bribe.

He said he wasn't Ginger's killer, and although he hadn't exactly proclaimed it with ringing conviction, I believed him. Not that I thought him incapable of it; Nicky Scandalios was a great white shark in an expensive suit. You don't get to be a major player in broadcasting by emulating Mother Teresa. Besides, we're all capable of the most extraordinary behavior when we find ourselves in a corner.

And if nothing else, I had the whole conversation on tape, and now Nicky got equal billing with Steve Cirini on the suspect list; any homicide cop will tell you that whenever anyone gets killed, the first one they look at is always the victim's spouse or significant other.

Driving homeward on Carnegie Avenue, being careful not to exceed the posted twenty-five-mile-per-hour speed limit that catches so many drivers unawares, I pondered the vagaries of modern English usage: what, I wondered, was an *in*significant other?

Nicky Scandalios was a spouse, all right—just not Ginger Carville's. And she might have been blackmailing him in the traditional sense, but it wasn't money that floated her boat. And what she wanted—an anchor job that might lead to network stardom—wouldn't have cost him much to give her.

Other than putting Vivian Truscott's beautiful nose out of joint. As popular as Carville had been with viewers, Truscott was literally revered, and if Nicky did anything to cause her unhappiness and eventual defection to another station, it could easily cost him his job. Local television is a great deal like the movie industry, in that the producers and directors and studio bosses might have a lot of behind-the-scenes power, but it's the stars, the personalities, that audiences tune in to see. As a result, the stars invariably call the shots.

And in the Cleveland market, stars didn't shine much brighter than Vivian Truscott. Nicky's extracurricular personal activities could very well have gotten his professional nuts in a wringer.

Vivian had enough clout at the station that she could usually turn thumbs up or down on who worked on the air and who didn't. But if she perceived Ginger as a threat that, because of Ginger's relationship with Nicky, she couldn't get rid of by demanding her ouster, she might have been tempted to take matters into her own hands. Her Channel Twelve contract was rumored to be somewhere in the vicinity of two million dollars plus, for three years, and that, coupled with her status as a media icon and the reigning queen of northeast Ohio society, was certainly worth protecting.

But did Truscott even know about Ginger and Nicky? She certainly might have—but then nobody else seemed to. The lovebirds had, of necessity, been very discreet.

By the time I got back to my apartment, another disturbing possibility had flapped its wings at me. I'd found out about Vivian Truscott's sex-for-sale past several years ago, although to the best of my knowledge I was the only one in town who knew about it. But Virginia Carville was an investigative reporter—by all accounts a damn good one—and she might have tried to get something on Vivian for leverage purposes and uncovered the same story I had.

And Vivian had all sorts of compelling reasons to keep that quiet. Two million of them.

Sitting in my den with an icy Stroh's and a bag of potato chips, I doodled Vivian Truscott's name on my yellow pad amongst the empty nooses.

For the hell of it, I wrote down Andrew Lemmons's name, too, just because they'd worked so closely together. I didn't think he'd had anything to do with killing Carville—he'd obviously adored her. But maybe there had been some unrequited passion there, maybe he'd found out about her and

Cirini, or her and Nicky for that matter, and exploded in a blind rage. Or perhaps in his own mind, he perceived her preference for them over him as a racial thing and it had momentarily unbalanced him.

Nah.

I could recognize genuine grief when I saw it. Andrew Lemmons's shock and sadness was the real thing.

I was still convinced it was those notes on Ginger's secret diskette about Violet Grba's repressed memory syndrome that had gotten her killed, and neither Nicky, Vivian, nor Andrew had anything to do with that.

Or did they?

I'd think about it tomorrow. Tomorrow was another day. And I couldn't wait for it to happen, because tomorrow would mean Sunday was over with.

I hate Sundays.

For me, this Sunday night in February meant a dinner of peanut-butter-and-jelly sandwiches—I always keep the fixings on hand for when the boys are over for the day—and a glass of milk. Otherwise it was just another night to agonize over the Carville situation. The file folder in my office was labeled CIRINI, STEVE, because he was my client, but along the way he had become a supporting actor.

After I'd stared at the names and unoccupied gallows on the legal pad, I started thinking about Bosko Grba, Violet's father. He was certainly sharing in the largesse that the Phantom Molester was shelling out to his daughter. Either that or the retirement benefits they paid at the steel mills were a hell of a lot more generous than they'd been when my father worked there, if the new Cadillac was anything to judge by. If Carville had been threatening to take the whole issue public and kill his egg-laying goose, he might have motive enough to stop her. And I had personal knowledge that he was a violent man when provoked.

But when I'd mentioned Virginia Carville's name to him he

hadn't even blinked. He only knew her from the TV, he'd said, and had heard she'd been killed. I tended to believe what he said, mainly because I didn't think he was nearly a good enough actor to pull off such a bare-faced denial. He probably wasn't even as good as Nicky Scandalios.

And while Bosko's quick and violent temper might provoke him to throw a punch at a younger man, hitting a woman on the head with a blunt instrument, having sex with her, and then strangling her with her own pantyhose didn't seem to fit the profile of an old man slowly dying of cancer.

Because I'd promised, I made a note to call Marko in the morning and give him the poop on Scandalios's affair with Ginger. That would take some of the heat off my client—and I felt all right about it because it was what I'd been hired to do. But a life had been taken here, and I'm just not the sort of guy who can walk away from that kind of situation and ever be able to sleep again.

The trouble was, I'd managed to dredge up so many people who'd been directly or indirectly involved with Carville, and they all might have had a motive for killing her. But I wasn't making that final connection that would convince me one or the other of them was the guilty party.

I couldn't face watching the movie about the adoptive child and her birth parents, so I paced the living room for most of the evening, smoking cigarettes and listening to music. I'd found a CD by Rosemary Clooney and the late Woody Herman in the Cleveland Heights main library on Lee Road, but this was the first chance I'd had to play it. It was full of the good old stuff, including a favorite of mine, Duke Ellington's "I'm Beginning to See the Light." They don't write them like that anymore; Ellington was an authentic American genius, and geniuses don't come around very often.

I sure didn't fit the category. I'd been working for Cirini for a week now, and all I had to show for it was a fistful of supposes and what-ifs.

Then again, Duke Ellington might not have done any better with the murder of Ginger Carville.

I finally got tired of walking around my apartment. Despite barely closing my eyes the night before, I was too wired to go to bed; maybe if I read for a while, I thought, I could clear my head and be able to fall asleep.

I was chagrined to find that the only book in the apartment I hadn't already read was Rosemary Kelley's *Desire With a Stranger.*

I'd gone through about a hundred pages before putting it aside just a few days earlier, and I barely remembered anything about the plot. So I skimmed the beginning again to catch up, which wasn't too hard.

There were miles of hairy chests and hot, demanding kisses to go before I slept, and I hoped like hell Rosemary Kelley wouldn't follow through on her threat to use me as the model for a character in her next novel. Highwayman or no highwayman, I didn't know how I'd ever be able to look my sons in the eye again if they ever found out.

Despite the frequent and steamy sex scenes, the book wasn't holding my attention, and I let my mind wander during those brief passages when the characters were not thrashing around beneath or on top of the sheets, or on one occasion in a hayloft.

And then, as my thoughts drifted farther and farther away from what passed for the plot of *Desire With a Stranger,* I experienced an epiphany. I tossed the book onto the floor and jumped out of my chair, adrenaline pumping, heart thumping.

Rosemary Clooney wasn't the only one who was beginning to see the light.

✿ ✿ ✿ ✿ ✿ ✿ ✿

CHAPTER NINETEEN

✿ ✿ ✿ ✿ ✿ ✿ ✿

If you're rich enough to afford a condo in one of the glittering glass-and-steel high-rise buildings that line the lakefront on the west side's Gold Coast, you probably think they're nifty. Other Clevelanders curse them for blocking what would otherwise be a panoramic vista of the water. Chicagoans think of the shores of Lake Michigan as their playground, but Lake Erie isn't terribly accessible in the metropolitan area.

But in the tenant parking garage beneath former city councilman Frank Kelley's building there wasn't much of a view anyway, unless you happen to like the rear ends of Mercedes-Benzes and BMWs and Acura Legends and Lincolns.

So, having left my Sunbird in the visitor's parking lot outside, I skulked around the garage with a certain amount of impatience, my hands in the pockets of my coat, as I waited for him to come downstairs. It was eight fifteen in the morning, and whatever warming trend the middle of the day might bring, it hadn't yet penetrated into this subterranean concrete cavern.

I could have waited for Kelley at his law office downtown at the Leader Building, I suppose. But at the office—even in the parking garage—people are geared to solve problems, are ready for them. By bracing him first thing in the morning, at his home, before he'd switched into his business mode, I had the advantage of surprise—as far as I knew he wasn't even aware of my existence. And he certainly wouldn't be expecting the kind of trouble I was about to dump on him.

Reading *Desire With a Stranger* by Rosemary Kelley, I'd remembered that secret diskette. FK INC SPNG-SMR 83, it said. All on the same line. And I'd reasoned that maybe FK INC didn't mean FK Incorporated at all; maybe in Virginia Carville's quaint and cryptic shorthand it stood for FK *incidents* in the spring and summer of 1983. Incidents of gross sexual imposition on a minor child. FK. Frank Kelley.

Violet Grba had said she had been abused by a man who lived in a big house on the west side, and whose wife was always home at the time but busy upstairs.

There are lots of big houses on the west side, quite a few occupied by wealthy men whose wives work upstairs, unseen, while the hired cleaning woman toils with her mops and buckets. But only one of those houses was right next door to where Virginia Carville had lived. And died. It seemed to make sense. Ordinarily a fourteen-year-old child-molestation case wasn't big news, but when it involved a former city councilman and gubernatorial hopeful, it could be a career maker for a journalist. No wonder Carville had kept her notes in code.

I might have been whistling down a rain barrel on this one, but it wasn't costing me much to find out.

At ten minutes before nine the elevator door slid open noiselessly and a man came out. A medium-blue shirt with a white collar and a fairly assertive flowered tie showed at the neck of his black Brooks Brothers overcoat. He had an extremely ruddy complexion, almost bright red, as if he'd been exerting himself—probably by lifting a full glass to his lips on a regular basis. His gray-white hair, combed straight back from his forehead, was a little too long to be fashionable and almost glittered with styling gel. I recognized him from dozens of newspaper photos and television appearances back in the days when he'd been a driving force on the Cleveland City Council. He was portly, close to sixty, and moved with the confidence of a guy who knows he has a six-figure bank account and the world by the short hairs.

"Mr. Kelley?"

He stopped and looked at me with the kind of annoyance usually reserved for a cockroach on the kitchen counter. "Yes?" he said. His blue eyes were somewhat bloodshot, and his voice was raspy, like Uncle Joe's on *Petticoat Junction;* it made me want to clear my own throat.

I walked over to him, hearing my footsteps echoing off the concrete walls and floor. As paranoid about muggers and carjackers as anyone else in town, he cast a quick, nervous glance around the garage, probably wondering if the building's security guard was within shouting distance.

"I'm a private investigator," I said, handing him a card. "My name is Milan Jacovich."

That didn't seem to cut much ice with him. "Are you investigating something in the garage?" he said snidely.

"Not exactly, sir. Can you give me a minute or so?"

He examined the card carefully, running his finger over the face of it to see whether it was embossed. Finding it wasn't, he put it into his overcoat pocket. "This is hardly the time or place," he said. "Call my office and my secretary will set up an appointment."

"It's about Virginia Carville."

A shadow passed across his face. "Jesus, a terrible thing, what happened. But I didn't really know her. I moved out of the house next to hers about a year before she moved in. You'd be better off talking to my ex-wife. Miss Carville was her neighbor, not mine." He started walking briskly toward his car; it was one of the Lincolns. "I do know Mrs. Kelley is terribly distraught over a thing like that going on a hundred feet from where she sleeps."

"You never met Virginia Carville?" I said, keeping pace with him.

"Sure I did. I've met most of the news reporters in town. I

met Virginia Carville my last year on council when she was covering city hall. And I suppose I saw her once or twice when I was visiting my ex-wife—you know, she'd be out in the backyard or out front fooling around with the flowers. But on those occasions I didn't do anything more than wave. So I can't really say I knew her."

He took his keys from his overcoat pocket, pointed them at the door of the car, and deactivated the alarm system, which gave a yelp like a puppy whose tail has been stepped on. "What's this all about, anyway? You're private—who are you working for?"

"I've been engaged by Robert Nardoianni," I said, managing to remember the name of Steve Cirini's lawyer.

"I know Bob very well. But surely he didn't send you to me?"

"No, sir, that was my idea."

"Not a very good one. As I said, I barely knew Virginia Carville, so I'm afraid I can't—"

"Did you know Violet Grba?" I said.

The muscles in his face didn't move at all, but somewhere inside him someone pulled the stopper in the bathtub of his guts and all his confidence was swirling clockwise down the drain. Violet Grba's name seemed to be the magic word.

"I don't believe so," he said stiffly, his breath vaporizing in the cold subterranean air.

"Her mother used to clean your house back about thirteen or fourteen years ago."

He waved a vague hand in the air. "You certainly don't expect me to remember the names of all my ex-wife's cleaning women?"

"Not necessarily. But I'd think you'd remember little Violet. She used to do things for you too."

He blinked his eyes once, mechanically, like one of those live-action figures from The Pirates of the Caribbean at Disneyworld.

"Who did you say you were, Mr. . . . ah . . . ?" He put his hand into his pocket, but instead of my business card he brought out a .22-caliber pistol, holding it hip-high and against his body so no one would see it but me.

I hadn't expected that. "That's not necessary, Mr. Kelley."

"The hell it isn't. You cheap shakedown artist, I ought to gut-shoot you right here."

I looked at the gun. It was the kind people who don't know anything about guns like to have around to make them feel safe and secure. It didn't have much stopping power, but at such close range I was sure it'd do the job nicely; there is little qualitative difference between a big bullet though your heart and a small one. "You have a permit to carry a concealed weapon?" I said.

"No I don't. Call a cop."

I raised my hands to shoulder level.

"Put your hands down, you idiot!" he snapped. "Just keep them where I can see them."

I dropped them to my sides and kept them in full view, fingers splayed. He was very stressed out, and I didn't want him becoming overanxious and pulling the trigger.

His eyes darted around the garage again, and for a moment he looked indecisive. Then he said, "Get into my car. In the driver's seat."

I slid into the Town Car. It had that expensive, fresh-from-the-showroom smell—the smell of what Ricardo Montalban used to call "rich Corinthian leather" in those commercials. The odometer read only 2624 miles.

"Put your hands on the steering wheel."

I did, waiting while he came around and got in the passenger side, the muzzle of the .22 pointed straight at me all the while. He tossed his keys onto my lap. "Start it," he ordered.

I did, and when the electrical system kicked on I got such a loud blast of Wynton Marsalis in stereo that it made me jump. Kelley was a WCPN listener.

He leaned over and snapped off the radio. "Back out. Slow."

Again, I did as I was told, mainly because of the gun he was pointing unwaveringly at my rib cage. Maneuvering the big car out of its slot, I steered it up the ramp and out onto Edgewater Drive, where I turned toward downtown, driving a few miles below the speed limit. We went past his ex-wife's house but he didn't even glance at it.

"Make a left here," he said as we got to West 103d Street.

We came up over a rise and turned onto Cliff Drive, just one short block long, which overlooks the lake and affords the most spectacular view of the glass-and-steel towers of downtown Cleveland anywhere in the area. It really takes your breath away on a clear, crisp night, and in my teenage years I'd been known to take a date there to make out. On a cold gray morning like this one it was only slightly less impressive.

There wasn't much traffic on Cliff Drive. I suppose he was counting on that.

"Stop the car," Frank Kelley said. "Now turn off the engine and then grip that steering wheel, hard, like you were Mario Andretti."

When I did, he reached over with his free hand and patted the front of my coat, sneering his satisfaction when he found my own .357 nestled under my left armpit. He removed it deftly and put it on the floor between his seat and the passenger door. Then, his little popgun still pointing at me, he said, "You'd better start talking, fella."

"That's why I came here, Mr. Kelley. To talk to you. The hardware isn't necessary."

He rapped the knuckles of my right hand smartly with the snub barrel of his pistol. It hurt like hell, and I shook it to make the pain go away.

"I'll decide what's necessary or not, you understand me?" he said, and then jammed the gun into my ribs hard, eliciting a grunt. "Keep those hands up there or you'll get worse."

"Tough guy, huh?" I said through clenched teeth.

"You don't last twelve years on council if you aren't. Now

what is this, buddy? A crude attempt at blackmail? Who do you think you're dealing with? I'll shoot you right through the fucking head, put your own gun in your hand, and claim you were kidnapping me and I shot in self-defense," he said, sneering. "And you know I've got the connections to make that story stick."

"You could do that," I said.

"And I will if I have to. Now what's all this about this Violet whatever-her-name-is?"

"You know damn well what her name is, Mr. Kelley."

He reached out and tried to rap my hand again, and I pulled it out of the way, grabbing the short muzzle of the gun. I twisted it away from him, and then whacked him across the face with my sore knuckles, being careful that I hit him with the back of my hand and not the metal. His head slammed against the car window. His face contorted with terror and complete surprise; this wasn't the way it was supposed to go.

The first rule you learn on the streets is that if you're going to act tough you damn well better *be* tough—otherwise someone tougher than you is going to call your bluff. But then Frank Kelley probably hadn't spent a whole lot of time on the streets, and he wasn't used to handling weapons.

I transferred the gun into my left hand and slapped him again, openhanded, just for the hell of it. He whimpered, shrinking away from me.

"Never pull a gun on someone unless you're ready to use it, Mr. Kelley. Otherwise they'll take it away from you like I just did, and feed it to you."

Rubbing his smarting cheek, he shrank from me, pressing himself against the car door as hard as he could, his bloodshot blue eyes wide with panic. Even though it was not yet nine o'-clock in the morning, I would have bet he could use a quick one right at that moment.

"Don't worry, I'm not going to hurt you," I said, putting my sore knuckle into my mouth and sucking at it for a second. "I'll take my weapon back, please." I put the .22 in his ear and screwed it around a little. "Carefully. Butt first."

His eyes never left my face as he reached down, groped around for my Magnum, and handed it back to me the way I'd asked him to.

I put it back in my shoulder holster. Then I broke the chamber of his gun and emptied the bullets into my palm before giving it to him.

He looked at it as though he'd never seen anything like it before.

"What the hell do you carry that for, anyway?" I asked.

He replaced it in his pocket with an air of weary resignation, shifting his body away from the car door and easing back into his seat. "For security. I used to be on council. I made enemies—naturally," he said sulkily. "What is it you want from me, Jacovich? Money?"

"You're paying Violet Grba enough without me putting the bite on you too."

"You don't know anything about it!" he protested.

"I know an inexcusable and disgusting act when I hear about it, so don't give me any excuses, Mr. Kelley."

His mouth tightened at the corners. "You moralizing son of a bitch!" he spat out. "You think everything is black and white, don't you?"

"I do when it comes to child abuse."

His mouth drooped along with his shoulders; he'd aged ten years since I took his gun away, and he was racing through a few more years every second. "It wasn't like that."

"The devil made you do it?"

His face had gone gray, and sweat popped out on his forehead and upper lip. "My wife . . . she never had time for me. She was so busy being a best-selling author. So busy being successful and—*social!*" He scratched angrily at his nose. "Ours was not a very physical marriage."

"So that made it okay to take down an eleven-year-old girl's underpants?"

Hearing it like that, raw and hard, made him gasp.

"Children are people, Mr. Kelley, not consolation prizes."

"Don't say *children*, like I was some sort of goddamn weirdo!" he screamed, spittle flying from his lips. "It was only that little Violet!"

I was dumbfounded. Knowing what he was, I hadn't thought he could shock me. "Try it once, Mr. Kelley, and maybe you're just philosophically curious. Do it all summer long, you're a pedophile."

He actually hung his head and a strand of greasy-looking gray hair flopped into his eyes. "You just don't understand," he whispered.

"You've got that right."

"How did you find out? She told you, didn't she? Violet?"

"No. She didn't. She didn't violate the terms of your little agreement. And she won't tell anybody else, either, because she wants you to keep paying her whatever you've agreed to. But somehow Virginia Carville found out about it, and she was going to make it into the biggest local story of the year—until somebody killed her."

"Carville knew?" It took a few beats for that to sink in. "Jesus, you don't think that I . . ."

He turned sickly pale beneath his red cheeks, and he opened and closed his mouth like a goldfish. Then his throat started working, his chest and stomach heaved, he jerked open the door and lost whatever he'd had for breakfast. Then he shut the door again, and the stink that rose from him in the closed, stuffy car almost cost me my breakfast, too. I turned the key in the ignition to engage the electrical system and rolled down the push-button window for a refreshing gulp of the cold wind off the lake.

He fumbled around inside his jacket for a handkerchief and mopped his face with it.

"So you've become a major suspect in the Carville thing, Mr. Kelley. And when the police start poking around, it's all going to come out."

He rolled down his own window and leaned his head out, gulping fresh air. I just sat and waited for him to get himself together, rolling the small .22 cartridges around in my hand like Captain Queeg with his steel balls.

Finally he pulled his head back in and rested it against the back of the seat. His nose was running hard and I could smell his sweat along with his breakfast.

"Virginia Carville," he gasped. "She—she knew?"

"Sure. She never contacted you?"

"No. No, I swear to God. What I said was true—I barely knew her. I don't think I've seen or talked to her in at least six months."

"Tell that to the cops," I said.

He burped, and I flinched, afraid he was going to throw up again. "No. No—there's going to be no need."

"Why's that?"

"Because I couldn't have killed her. If I recall correctly, she died a week ago Thursday night."

"You know damn well when she died."

"There you are!" he said triumphantly, or as triumphant as he could get sitting there with vomit on his chin. "I was in Houston when it happened. I gave a speech that night at a law convention."

My heart sank; just when I thought I'd found an answer, the son of a bitch comes up with an alibi. "I suppose you can prove it?"

"At least five hundred people saw me. And I stayed in Houston until Saturday." He burped again, bringing up something that, thank God, he spat out the window. Then he wiped his mouth again. "I can prove that, too."

"You could have hired a hit."

"Don't be an ass, Mr. Jacovich. I'm too well-known in this

town for that." I guess he was feeling a little better; most people don't get nasty when they're frightened. Or when they're guilty. "I'm already paying that little slut a small fortune to keep her mouth shut. Do you really think I'd hand somebody else something to squeeze me with? I make a good living, but there are bottoms to my pockets."

"You didn't think she was such a little slut when she was eleven years old and you made her jerk you off and said you'd fire her mother if she told anyone," I reminded him.

I slumped against the seat back, feeling dirtied by being in the same car with him.

He stared at me for a long while. "You're not going to tell anyone, are you?" He averted his gaze—if I'd done what he had I'd be ashamed to look anyone in the eye too.

"This is a murder case," I said. "The police will have to know."

"It'll *ruin* me. Socially and politically. I have *plans,* Mr. Jacovich. I could be the next governor."

The prospect of that was enough to turn your blood to ice.

"I'd be a damn good one, too. I care about the people in this town, in this state." He clawed open his necktie and loosened the top button of his shirt. "It'll *ruin* me," he said again.

"You should have thought of that when you took advantage of a child."

"It's none of your business anyway! Who do you think you are? God?"

"If I were God, I'd have fried your ass with a thunderbolt back in 1983."

He blew a jet of air through his nostrils. "It'll only hurt Violet," he said craftily. "If the story comes out I won't have to give her any more money. So if you don't keep your mouth shut, she'll be the one who gets hurt."

Sure, I thought. And if I do keep my mouth shut, the people in Ohio will have a chicken hawk sitting in the governor's mansion.

And then I remembered the fear in Violet Grba's eyes when she thought her ride on the gravy train was over. I remembered her father, on his knees in his front yard, spitting up blood.

"You're one sick unit, Mr. Kelley."

"Leave me alone," he murmured.

I shook a Winston out of my pack and lit it. Kelley looked for a moment as if he would protest my smoking in his car but thought better of it. Wisely. I probably would have stubbed it out on the end of his red nose.

He shuddered, putting his head back against the headrest again. "I can't go to the office like this. Drive me back to my place."

"I'm not your goddamn butler," I said with some heat, opening the car door. "Drive yourself."

"Didn't you park your car there?"

"I'd rather walk," I told him, and got out of the Lincoln. "I'd rather walk a hundred miles."

I trudged back around the curve and onto Edgewater Drive, hunching my shoulders against the chill wind off the lake, which went through my clothes as if they were made of the finest gossamer. I'd once heard Vivian Truscott say on the five o'clock news that hunching up makes you colder, not warmer. I hadn't believed her then and I didn't now.

I was breathing deeply, trying to get the bad smell out of my nostrils. The cigarette helped. I enjoy brisk walks, especially along the lakefront, but not in the middle of February. I'd gone about two blocks when I saw Kelley's Lincoln roar past me.

The King of Denial, I thought, watching him disappear in the distance. Just because it happened with only one child many years ago it was somehow not such a big deal, to Frank Kelley's way of thinking. I wonder if people who only rob one bank, only steal one car, only rape one woman, only kill one person can always whitewash it in their own minds, can tell themselves it was a temporary aberration.

After about five minutes I found myself in front of Kelley's house, right next to Ginger Carville's. I stopped, staring hard at both houses, processing what had gone on in each of them and trying to connect the dots.

I briefly considered ringing Rosemary Kelley's doorbell, but I wasn't sure what I would say to her. I had a few questions, but I doubted if she'd answer them. Even if I asked nicely.

I had more important things to do, though, like getting back to my office and letting Marko know about Ginger Carville's affair with Nicky Scandalios, and about Frank Kelley and Violet Grba. And to tell him that for whatever it was worth, I'd deciphered the code on Carville's unmarked diskette.

I shook my head, hearing my own thoughts. Deciphered the code, for God's sake.

Bond. James Bond.

※ ※ ※ ※ ※ ※ ※

CHAPTER TWENTY

※ ※ ※ ※ ※ ※ ※

I had the heater on full blast as I drove back down to Collision Bend; my unexpected morning constitutional along Edgewater Drive had chilled me to the bone. It had also given me some food for thought.

I stopped at Ernie's Restaurant, a little diner on the curve of Canal Road in the Flats and picked up a maple-glazed donut and a large container of black coffee-to-go and drank half of it before I got down the hill. I needed something to warm me up from the inside.

When I got to my office I brewed some more coffee, and when the Braun finished its bubbling I sat at my desk to drink it, still wearing my coat and thinking about some of the things that had come to me after I'd gotten out of Frank Kelley's car and made the long walk back to where I'd left mine. By the time the office had heated up enough to make it livable, I had decided to share them with the police.

Marko Meglich wasn't in when I called. Neither was Detective Matusen. As do many retail stores, the homicide division does a brisk business over the weekend, and Monday morning was never the best time to catch the gold-badge honchos at their desks.

What with my new high-tech electronic office toys, I considered writing up a report and faxing it to Marko but quickly decided that was a bad idea. Frank Kelley and Nicky Scandalios were pretty well known in Cleveland and I didn't want a fax chronicling their sins circulating all over the Old Central before Marko got a chance to see it. The department, like any big-city cop shop, was far too political.

I could have talked to the two investigating officers of record, Detectives Peggy Farmer and Richard Haake, but I didn't know them, I didn't know what their own personal agendas might be. A wily, ambitious officer could do a fearsome amount of damage with such information in hand.

On my own for the time being, I shucked off my coat, and spread the contents of the Cirini file out on my desk.

There were a hell of a lot of suspects, all of whom had more of a reason to want Ginger Carville dead than Steve Cirini. That was the good news. The bad was that I couldn't quite make any of them fit the picture of Carville's murderer.

Steve Cirini was my client, which meant I automatically gave him the benefit of the doubt; I have to proceed on the assumption that my clients are telling the truth, are without guilt, and that I'm working on the side of right, the side of order; otherwise I couldn't ever get out of bed in the morning, couldn't face myself in the mirror when I'm shaving.

It wasn't such a great leap of faith at that. Cirini, being a single guy, had no motive for killing Ginger Carville. She was the kind of woman with whom he could have exciting, freewheeling sex without any real commitment or emotional engagement—something I knew from experience he wasn't getting from Mary Soderberg, unless she had radically changed in three years. With me, Mary had been sexually imaginative, even adventuresome—but in no way like he described Ginger.

So working from the premise that of all the suspects in my notebook, Steve Cirini had the least reason for wanting Ginger Carville dead, I began examining the others.

Scandalios had the most to lose—his marriage and his job, for two instances. But as long as he gave Ginger the media exposure she so desperately craved—certainly no hardship because she was, by all accounts, an asset to the station or the news operation—she'd continue giving him what he wanted.

Vivian Truscott was threatened by the *All About Eve* scenario she'd helped to create with Ginger, but she not only had a fat, long-term contract but the love and goodwill of most of the station's viewers. Murder seemed a pretty radical way of getting rid of what was still only the possibility of competition. And even if Carville had found out about Vivian's past and had threatened to reveal it, there were safer and easier ways to resolve the problem, such as agreeing to let Carville become a coanchor. Certainly to be avoided if possible, it was still a better solution than wrapping Carville's pantyhose around her throat.

Frank Kelley was running scared, but he'd found an effective albeit expensive way of keeping his reputation unsullied, and from his reaction when I told him, he hadn't known beforehand that Ginger knew his dirty little secret. Besides, he had an alibi for the night of the murder—five hundred of them, all lawyers. That disappointed me a lot. I wanted it to be him.

The best motives belonged to Violet Grba and her father. But poor, damaged Violet didn't strike me as the type.

Bosko did. And he might have figured that by getting rid of Carville and making sure the hush money would continue to flow, he was helping his daughter without risking much; he was dying anyway.

He could have gone there to argue with her, plead with her not to mess up Violet's little annuity, and when she refused, perhaps things got out of hand and became violently physical. But would he have had sex with her? I couldn't imagine Ginger Carville taking him into her bed. Would he have raped her—and then strangled her with her own pantyhose? I couldn't believe it of a man like Grba. Still, he was the best candidate I had at the moment.

But I didn't like it.

I began perusing the notes on forensic evidence I'd copied

from the police file, once again impressed with the two detectives' thoroughness, with the way Marko had trained them, just like he'd trained me in my old blue-uniform days. Oil of Olay, L'eggs sheer-to-the-waist, Summer's Eve, etc. Precise and specific.

I closed my eyes, trying to recreate in my mind what the investigators had seen. I'd looked at the crime-scene photos in Marko's office, but now I tried to get a mental picture from the details in the report.

Something curious occurred to me. And if Farmer and Haake were as efficient and thorough as the report seemed to indicate, it meant I had even more reason to be certain Steve Cirini was in the clear.

Who else it might implicate, I didn't know. But I had an idea.

I turned off the coffeepot, activated my voice mail, armed the security system that, if tampered with, would set off a piercing wail that could be heard clear across the river, and drove up the road and across the Eagle Avenue Bridge to downtown Cleveland.

My first stop was the Cleveland Public Library on Superior, where I pored through computerized records of the *Plain Dealer* for the last several years again and came up with quite a few entries for Kelley, Rosemary. As a local celebrity she got quite a bit of ink, mostly of the speech-giving or book-releasing variety, although she seemed to have been active in fund-raising for several worthy causes, or at least to have shown up at a lot of benefits, according to the society columns.

The item that caught my eye, though, was one dated about two years earlier, reporting that she had signed a six-book deal with her publisher for 2.4 million dollars. The article, illustrated with a pretentiously sexy studio portrait that appeared to have been shot through a layer of filmy gauze, as well as a reproduction of the cover of her current book, stated that Rosemary Kelley was one of the top five romance writers in the world, a fact that had somehow escaped me. Then again, that type of book rarely finds its way to my nightstand, but apparently there was a lot of money in heaving bosoms and urgency and "heat."

The ex–Mrs. Kelley was a rich woman in her own right.

Or her own write, as the case might be.

I looked up the entries for Kelley, Frank, too, but he'd kept a fairly low profile locally since retiring from the city council, and his appearances in the pages of the *Plain Dealer* in the last three years were infrequent and not very interesting, and again mostly of the social variety—notes about what boards he served on, what benefit parties he attended and with whom—always a different woman. But I couldn't find anything that resonated for me.

From the library it was only a five-minute walk to the hall of records.

In America, the right to privacy is one of our most cherished illusions; we think no one can crack the facade we present to the world. But the fact is that almost everything about you except your bathroom habits can be found out by just about anyone who knows how. It doesn't take a private detective, but we're the ones who have learned the various information avenues to travel. The date and place of your birth, your income, your various residences, your credit-card purchases, your marriages and divorces and businesses and how much you paid for your home, and your arrest record, if you're unfortunate enough to have one—they are all a matter of public record.

The people of my state were taught this hard fact during the 1992 congressional campaign when one of the candidates dug up the records of her opponent's divorce and, in a shocking invasion of privacy, read some of the juicier portions of the trial transcript in a television commercial. She lost the election, but the lesson was, don't say or do anything you don't want in the papers.

For instance, with only a little help from my grandmotherly friend Renee, who commands the front desk at the hall of records, I was able to find out when and where Frank and Rosemary Kelley of Edgewater Drive had dissolved their marriage because of "irreconcilable differences." What I couldn't learn were the terms of the settlement; if there was a settlement, it had been negotiated privately, out of court.

That fit with Rosemary Kelley's account of a friendly split. But what with her seven-figure book contract and her husband's income as a partner in one of the most prestigious law firms in town, there'd been a hell of a lot of money on both sides of that divorce.

As long as I was there, I asked Renee to pull another file for me, a business file.

If you want to start a business, you need a license, and for that you have to tell the authorities your real name, even if your business itself has a name—like Acme Plumbing or Bugs-B-Gone Exterminating. Or Milan Security.

Or ZZZ Carpet Cleaning.

Lorain Avenue begins at the western end of the Hope Memorial Bridge and runs seemingly forever, all the way out into the western suburbs. Like any long urban street, it changes character every few miles or so, in this case from Puerto Rican to Irish to Slavic. Up until about West 117th Street it's a strip that runs past cut-rate furniture outlets, junk shops styling themselves as antique stores, and more smoky shot-and-a-beer taverns than I could count. The numbered north-south streets that intersect it are lined with old two- and three-bedroom houses built quite close together, many of which have elderly pickups parked in their narrow driveways. It's only a small part of the city, but it's the image of the blue-collar, dirty-fingernail town most people who've never been here expect Cleveland to be.

ZZZ Carpet Cleaning was in an old storefront in an ugly square yellow-brick building just past West Forty-sixth Street, and its name was lettered in gilt across a large, dirty window, the Zs curiously enclosed in quotation marks. I parked my car at the curb and crossed Lorain, my face stung by a fine, cold mist.

At the hall of records I'd discovered that the firm was owned jointly by Jerome and Harriet Zelman and Harvey Zelman, accounting for the three Zs. The way they were listed led me to believe Jerome and Harriet were husband and wife. I didn't know about Harvey.

I also didn't know whether it was Harvey or Jerome I'd seen at Rosemary Kelley's house.

Inside, the one huge room had been converted to several by way of cheap wallboard partitions that stopped several feet short of the ceiling, which was dirty-white and of the old-fashioned stamped-tin variety. The walls had been painted an unlikely baby blue a long time ago. Overhead, fluorescent fixtures hummed intermittently in the key of A-flat. There was a thick, coarse carpet on the floor—very clean, naturally. From somewhere in the rear I heard a man's voice.

In the front of the office was a desk that must have been purchased from a consignment of unclaimed railroad cargo, and two chairs with cracked-vinyl seat cushions and tubular aluminum arms that could have come from a neighborhood barbershop of the Truman era. A coatrack held a blue-and-green man's parka and a woman's long cloth coat in mousy brown.

The woman at the desk was Harriet Zelman, at least according to her nameplate. Looking to be about forty, bespectacled and slightly bottom-heavy, she sported a braided gold wedding ring and had wrists thick enough to belong to a lumberjack, and a supremely forgettable face.

She looked up from the catalogue of solvents and rug shampoos she'd been perusing, and pushed her cat's-eye glasses back up onto her nose. "Can I help you?" she said with something less than enough warmth to convince me she wanted to.

"I'd like to see Mr. Zelman."

Her eyelids lowered slightly as if she was falling asleep.

"Which Mr. Zelman is that? Mr. Jerry Zelman or Mr. Harvey Zelman?"

"I'm not sure."

"I'm not either," she said. She crossed her plump arms across her chest and sat back in her chair; that was all the help she was going to give me.

We both waited for the offstage prompter to tell us who had the next line. Finally I said, "Are either of them in?"

"Jerry's in. He's the inside man, he's always in. Harvey's the field man."

"Maybe I could talk to Jerry?" I dared to suggest.

She looked down at the telephone on her desk. One of the buttons was lit. "He's on the phone."

"I can wait."

She indicated one of the barbershop chairs with her chin. I sat down and looked around for something like a 1958 *Life Magazine* with a black-and-white photograph of Marilyn Monroe on the cover.

"I haven't seen you around before," Harriet Zelman said. "Are you a vendor?"

I smiled at her use of the business-speak word, which has become so common. I always think of a vendor as someone who goes up and down the aisles hawking hot dogs at a ball game. "No, I'm not," I confessed. "It's kind of a personal matter."

"I'm *Mrs.* Zelman," she said, as if that would suddenly get me to spill my guts.

"Is that Mrs. Jerry Zelman or Mrs. Harvey Zelman?"

She gave me the sort of look usually reserved for garden slugs discovered in the salad. "Mrs. Jerry. He shouldn't be too long."

While I looked at the baby-blue wall and listened to the muffled male voice from the back of the establishment, she went back to her catalogue. After about five minutes the voice stopped and I saw the light on Harriet Zelman's phone blink off. That fact managed to escape her attention.

I waited for about a minute. Then I said, "Is Mr. Zelman still on the phone?"

Looking down as though doing so was one of the labors of Hercules, she picked up the receiver and pushed a button. I heard a buzz from the rear.

"Someone to see you, Jerry." She listened for a second, then glanced up at me. "What's your name?"

"Milan Jacovich," I told her.

She considered repeating it, decided it was too tough for her to handle, and instead said nastily into the receiver, "Just come on up here, all right?"

I waited another minute and then Jerry Zelman appeared from behind the partition, proving to be the man who'd barged his way onto Rosemary Kelley's doorstep. He was even wearing the same maroon sleeveless sweater, this time over a white shirt gray with age and a pinkish tie with a too-fat knot.

I stood up to greet him and was instantly sure he recognized me, because the sight of me clearly shook him pretty badly. He took two steps and then froze, remaining motionless for about five seconds. Then he licked his lips and broke into a beaming smile.

"Hey, how the hell are you?" he said loudly, almost sprinting over to pump my hand, all false heartiness. "What a nice surprise!" His eyes were terrified—and pleading. He shifted them significantly toward Harriet, who was sitting where she couldn't see his face. "Have you met my wife?" he said.

"Well, we—"

"Hey, why'ncha lemme buy you a cup of coffee and we can talk?" he said, moving quickly to the coatrack and snagging the parka with one finger. "I'll be back in about fifteen minutes, babe," he said to Harriet.

"Don't forget you have a four o'clock appointment," she said.

"I'll be back way before that," he assured her, struggling

awkwardly into the parka like a kindergartener who had never been taught the Montessori method.

He threw an arm around my shoulders—which wasn't easy for him because I was so much taller—and guided me out the door. Two good old buddies going out for coffee. The masquerade, obviously for Harriet's benefit, was kind of pathetic, but I had to give him credit for quick thinking. I admired the way he hadn't let her find out that he didn't know my name. Jerry Zelman was pretty fast on his feet at that.

We'd walked about twenty yards from the storefront before he dropped his arm from around my shoulder and wheeled on me. "Are you out of your fucking mind, coming here with my wife sitting there and everything?" His voice was ragged, ravaged. All the bonhomie had evaporated, replaced by anger and the kind of deep-down fear that ties knots in the gut. "How did you find me, anyway?"

"If you don't want to get found, don't use your business van to come calling on pretty women."

He threw a fearful look back over his shoulder, the automatic, guilty reaction of a cheater; we were far enough away from his place of business that I could have shouted and his wife wouldn't have heard.

"What is it you want, exactly?" he said nervously. "I figure you're probably pissed off at me, but we both said some things we shouldn't've the other night—kind of in the heat of battle, you know."

He probably assumed I was in a jealous rage and that I'd hunted him down so I could smack him around a little. Good—that'd give him something to think about. I was silent, letting him twist in the wind a little.

"It was an innocent mistake on my part," he said anxiously. "How was I supposed to know you had a thing going with her? I wouldn't have just barged in—"

"I don't have a thing going with her. I'm a private investigator."

He stared at me. A muscle started jumping in his cheek. "Private investigator?" He looked back at his storefront once more, then suddenly at me again, his face crumpling. "Are you working for my *wife*? Did she hire you to—"

"I've never laid eyes on your wife before today," I said. "Or talked to her."

"Then what's this all about?"

"It's about a murder."

His mouth grew slack with disbelief. "What?"

"I'll explain it to you over that cup of coffee. Come on."

We walked for a block and a half in uneasy silence. His fists were jammed into his pockets, and his head was lowered as if he were expecting a blow to the face.

"I don't know from murder," he said at last. "I'm just a working guy, okay?"

"Okay," I said, but didn't give him any more succor than that.

We turned in at a flyblown little coffee shop on Lorain Avenue that I happened to know specializes in chili dogs, although right at that moment chili dogs held little appeal.

Sitting down in a ratty booth, we ordered two coffees from the woman who came out from behind the counter. Jerry Zelman unzipped his parka and with a palsied hand took out a pack of cigarettes and stuck one into the side of his mouth. It took him two matches to light it with his shaking hands.

He gulped the smoke down as if it were hamburger and he was starving to death. "What's all this about murder? I don't know what the hell you're talking about."

"Virginia Carville," I said. "The television news reporter who got killed two weeks ago."

"So?"

"She lived right next door to where I saw you the other night."

He coughed on the smoke, kept coughing until his face was scarlet and there were tears in his eyes. "Oh my God," he said. "Oh my God."

"So I'd like to ask you a couple of things. And you'd better answer them, Jerry, and answer them nicely, or else you'll be talking to the homicide division, and they aren't nearly as good-natured as I am."

"Yeah, yeah, right." The woman brought our coffees, and he was so anxious that he took the cup out of her hand before she could set it on the Formica table. He gulped some down, gasping. "I need a break here, all right?" he said. "It doesn't take a genius to figure out I don't want my wife hearing about Rosie."

"Rosie?"

He nodded. "You know."

Rosie. When she'd been trying to charm me out of my socks she'd told me to call her Ro. I couldn't imagine anyone addressing Rosemary Kelley as "Rosie."

"Maybe your wife doesn't have to know," I said. I didn't much like myself for it, but I wasn't above playing on his fear. Fear can loosen a recalcitrant tongue quicker than booze, money, or even a beating. "It depends on whether you and I can reach a meeting of the minds."

His laugh was hollow and mirthless. "You got the wrong guy, pal. You saw my place. I look to you like a rich man?"

"I don't want money. I want some answers. If I get them without any crap, maybe Harriet doesn't find out about Rosie. If you jerk me around . . . " I took a sip of my own coffee, which tasted vaguely of chili dog, letting the threat hang over him like a guillotine blade. "Do we have a deal?"

"Yeah, sure," he said, his head bobbing the way one of those toy dog's does in the back window of a 1974 Chevy. "Whatever you want."

"I want to know about 'Rosie.' "

"What about Rosie? You probably know her better than I do."

"I doubt that. How long have you been seeing her?"

"Seeing her?" He ran a hand through his hair, flattening it. "I'm not seeing her. I don't even know her last name."

I lit one of my Winstons to mask the taste of the chili-coffee. "You're kidding me."

He shook his head. "I swear to God! It was only a one-night stand."

"What night?"

"You mean the date? Hell, I don't know."

"Think hard, Jerry," I said. And then added, "You'll be sorry if you don't."

He did think. "It was on a Thursday night. A week ago Thursday."

The hairs on the back of my neck prickled. "You're sure?"

He nodded. "I work late most Thursdays, doing the accounts and stuff. Sometimes I stop and have a drink before I go home. To unwind, y'know?" He held his coffee cup with both hands, possibly gaining comfort from its warmth. "So I was in this bar, and—"

"What bar?"

"How the hell do I know? Just a bar."

"Come on, Jerry, you said you sometimes stop and have a drink after work. Don't tell me you don't know where."

He looked away. "Draper's Tavern," he said. "It's on Clifton."

I didn't know the place, but then I do my drinking on the east side.

"So, you're in Draper's. Go on."

"So she comes in there."

"What time was this?"

"Eight thirty, nine o'clock. No, it must've been after nine because *Seinfeld* was on."

"That's a funny thing to remember."

"Not really," Zelman said, "because it's my favorite show, and I hadn't seen that episode. But when a woman who looks like Rosie starts coming on to a guy like me, you don't care about watching a TV show."

"*She* started coming on to *you*?"

His eyes became narrowly nasty, his masculine pride getting the better of his fear. "You saying you can't imagine that, huh? What am I, chopped liver?"

"I'm not saying anything. You're doing the saying."

"There's lots of women wouldn't mind crawling into the kip with me," he boasted, and then looked around suddenly, as if afraid Harriet was listening. Catching himself, he hurried on. "But that doesn't mean I mess around on my wife, because I don't. I mean, we work together, we live together—screwing around is just too damn hard to work out."

"But it wasn't hard with Rosie?"

He waggled his head from side to side. "I guess I was taking kind of a chance, sure. But she's a knockout."

"I noticed," I said.

"Yeah. Well, so anyway I'm sitting there and she comes and sits one barstool away from me, and she smiles at me and starts talking. You know."

I knew.

"And the next thing is, she's asking if I want to go home with her."

"And you wanted?"

He ducked his head. "Shit, yes. Wouldn't you?"

No, I thought, that particular offer had in fact been tendered and I'd turned it down. "So what happened?"

"Whattaya think happened?" He drew himself up in his seat as much as he could; he'd discovered his dignity somewhere. "I'm not gonna go into details. You get off on hearing shit like that?"

I leaned forward just a little. "Try not to get me pissed off, Jerry. I'd have to complain to Harriet."

His dollop of new-found confidence instantly evaporated, and he licked his lips. "I thought we were doing this on a friendly basis."

"To have a friend you have to be a friend," I said, remembering something a kindly old nun at Saint Vitus Parish had told me when I was eight years old. "So you and Rosie went back to her place? What time?"

"Nine thirty, quarter to ten, I guess."

"You work fast."

"*She* worked fast."

"And you never saw her before?"

He bobbed his head in affirmation, trying hard to convince me.

"Isn't that kind of reckless in this day and age, Jerry? Having sex with a perfect stranger you just met in a tavern."

"I used protection!" He said it with something akin to pride.

"How come you had condoms on you? You said you don't cheat on your wife."

"I don't!" he protested. "She had a box right in her dresser drawer. In fact, she was pretty insistent about my using one."

"And then what?"

He rolled his eyes. "Then nothing. The whole thing didn't take ten minutes."

"Not very romantic, was it?"

He shrugged. "I got the idea she was in kind of a hurry."

"That's too bad," I said. "What about afterwards?"

"Nothing. She told me to go home, so I put on my pants and did."

"No afterglow, huh?"

"What?"

"Never mind. When I saw you at Rosie's house the other night, you said you didn't have her phone number."

"I didn't. I swear to God. She didn't give it to me."

"Didn't you ask for it?"

He shook his head.

"So you were out of there at what time?"

"I don't know exactly," he said. "Ten fifteen at the latest. I know I was home in plenty of time to watch the eleven o'clock news."

"Where do you live, Jerry?"

"Ohio City," he said.

Ohio City isn't more than ten or fifteen minutes away from Rosemary Kelley's house on Edgewater Drive. "You always play around that close to home?"

"I don't play around at all!" he said.

"That's why you thought your wife had hired a private detective, huh?"

He pulled at his cheek. "You don't let up, do you?"

"Why did you come back to Rosie's the other night?"

The corner of his mouth twisted unpleasantly, and one eyebrow climbed lasciviously toward his hairline. Jerry Zelman is one of those guys who finds it hard to talk about sex without leering like a prepubescent middle-schooler. "Why do you think?"

"Ten minutes and that's it, and you came back for more?"

"A woman who looks like that, all she's gotta do is show up," he explained.

"You've stepped in some pretty deep shit, Jerry. The night you were at Rosie's house, Virginia Carville got herself murdered right next door."

"I *told* you, I left early," he blubbered. "What I read in the paper, Virginia Carville did the newscast that night at eleven."

"You think the police will believe you?"

"The police? Why do I have to talk to the police? Jesus, I didn't kill anybody—all I did was get laid." He was practically hyperventilating.

"Sometimes that's enough," I said.

CHAPTER TWENTY-ONE

I stopped at a stand at the West Side Market and picked up two bratwurst sandwiches to eat back in the office. By the time I got there it was after five o'clock. Across the river I could see commuters making their daily exodus from downtown like refugees fleeing a plague city, and in the western sky the pewter light ran from the approach of night.

But I was raring to go. Puzzle pieces were falling into place for me. It was a crazy scenario, one I was having trouble believing myself, but I was going to stick with it until something made me do otherwise. I didn't have proof—but maybe I would soon.

I checked my voice mail. There was a call from Mary Soderberg, and another from the plumbing supply factory manager wanting to know how the work was progressing on his security system. He sounded anxious, and I didn't blame him. I'd pushed him onto a back burner ever since getting involved with the Virginia Carville killing, and he was too valuable a client to let get mad at me.

There was also a hang-up.

I microwaved and ate the two brats, washing them down with a Stroh's from my little refrigerator that looks like a safe. The building was pleasingly quiet; my tenants had long since gone home.

Poor Jerry Zelman, I thought. He was in it up to his eyebrows, and while I believed that he had nothing to do with Carville, he was still going to take a lot of heat, if what I thought I'd figured out was true. He and I were never going to be best friends, but I couldn't help feeling a little sorry for him; the last time I'd looked, being an adulterer and a jerk was not a capital crime.

Marko still wasn't back at headquarters when I called. Maybe he'd gotten lucky and broken a big case. I found myself hoping it was the old man's, the one I'd seen on East Thirty-ninth Street when Marko had taken me along with him and Detective Matusen. The sight of the body lying in that neat bedroom had been irritating my stomach lining for a while now. It was making me question whether I shouldn't have stayed on the force the way Marko wanted me to, so I could do something about terrible tragedies like that. Making me wonder whether keeping the world safe for Steve Cirini and guys like him was really the most noble of callings.

But that morning I'd seen something in my notes on the police report that I thought cleared him. I felt guilty for having taken so much of his money and spent so much of my own time when it had been right there in the police report all along.

I even thought I'd figured out who killed Ginger Carville. But that wasn't my job. My job was to get Cirini off the hook. And I was thinking I had done that.

I called him and told him so.

"God, that's great!" he said. "How can I ever thank you, Milan?"

"Don't thank me yet. I still haven't talked to the homicide cops, and I'm not sure they'll buy what I'm selling."

"Which is what?"

"It doesn't matter right now. Tell me again what happened when you got to Ginger Carville's house the night she was killed."

"I told you."

"Humor me. Tell me again."

He sounded annoyed. Now that he thought he was in the clear he was reverting to his accustomed arrogance. "We met outside at the front door. We went in, we went upstairs, we screwed."

"More details. You met, you went inside . . . "

"Christ, Milan!"

"Just do it, Mr. Cirini. It's your ass that's on the line."

A put-upon sigh. "Okay. We started kissing and stuff at the foot of the stairs. We both took off our coats and dropped them there. We went upstairs, kind of slow, because we were messing around on the stairs. We finally got into her bedroom. She took off her blouse and I pulled down her pantyhose. Then I took off my—"

"All right, fine," I said. "Remember all that, just the way you told me. Practice it if you have to. And don't go into work in the morning until you hear from me."

"Why not?"

"Because I said so."

"So—uh—what're you going to tell the police to clear me?"

"In the morning," I said.

I hung up before he could argue.

I waited an hour, smoking Winstons and pacing across the hardwood floor, reviewing my notes for the umpteenth time. I had to be sure I was right; I didn't want to make a complete idiot of myself in front of the police. Finally I called Marko at home, but he wasn't there either. Maybe this Brittany business was getting serious.

"Mark, it's Milan," I told his answering machine. "Don't pick up Steve Cirini tomorrow morning until you talk to me first. He didn't do it, okay?" I looked at my watch. "It's ten after seven. I'll be at my office until . . . let's say nine o'clock. Call me."

I hung up, sat back, and stared at the phone, willing it to ring. When it didn't, I decided I'd keep myself busy until Marko called.

I pulled the vacuum cleaner out of the closet, plugged it in, and ran it across the floor, wondering at the occasional metallic clicks that went racketing up the tube. Maybe paper clips, or tiny pebbles I'd tracked in from the gravel parking lot, or even, God forbid, a stray coin. I needed all of those I could get.

It's a big office, bigger than the apartment where I'd worked for so long, and it took a while to clean it. I had just about finished when the telephone rang. I picked it up and said, "Milan Security," and there was a click. It irritates me when people aren't even courteous enough to say, "I'm sorry, I must've dialed a wrong number."

Then again, I thought, maybe it wasn't a wrong number at all.

I put the vacuum back in the closet. The light through the windows was all but gone now, and I turned off the overhead and watched the river traffic in the dark. The ice on the water had broken up a week or two before, and I hoped it wouldn't return until next winter. The Lake Erie shipping, while not yet in full swing, had picked up considerably. I always watch the ore-carrying behemoths with something akin to awe, especially as they painstakingly negotiate the hairpin turn of Collision Bend.

Finally I turned on my knockoff Tiffany desk lamp and pulled out the security system plan to work on. I owed the plumbing guy that much.

About forty-five minutes later the downstairs door creaked open, and I heard footsteps ascending the inside stairs. They sounded a lot like they were made by high heels.

It was pretty late in the day for uninvited guests. I felt around under the desk with my foot until I found the little kick-switch on the floor that activated the tape recorder.

Rosemary Kelley opened the office door. She was wearing a fingertip-length black leather jacket over tight-fitting black leather slacks and a red sweater, which surprised me. She should have known bright red is not the most flattering shade for redheads. Black knee-high boots with two-inch heels and a black leather clutch purse completed milady's ensemble.

"Hello, Mrs. Kelley."

She pouted prettily. "I told you to call me Ro. All my friends do. And I put you in that category, Milan. I was hoping I'd find you here tonight."

"You were pretty sure you would."

A faint smile.

"You called the office a little while ago and hung up when I answered, so you knew I'd be here. I've actually been expecting you."

She decided to ignore that. "Aren't you going to invite me to sit down?"

I was going to—honest. But she did it anyway, without waiting to be asked. "Your office is charming," she said, taking it in with a languorous glance. "It could use a little color, some art prints or posters—maybe a Hopper. But it has such possibilities." She turned her head and looked out the windows. "Fabulous view. I think Terminal Tower is so beautiful at night when they light it up." The smile escalated to high-beam. "This is the perfect place for such a romantic fellow."

"Yeah, that's right," I said. "The highwayman, wasn't it? In your next book?"

"Oh, you'll be there, all right."

"My own little slice of immortality."

"That's the way most people feel," she said. "My fictional characters are almost always based on people I know, and even when I portray them in less than a favorable light, they're all flattered just to be in the book."

I waited.

"But I'm afraid you're not going to be the hero anymore, Milan."

"Oh?"

"No," she said, suddenly a disapproving Sunday-school teacher. "You spoiled it."

"How did I do that?"

She shook her head sadly. "You just about scared the life out of poor Frank this morning. He's been throwing up all day."

"He's delicate," I said.

Her eyes got steely, turning the dull green of a military tank. "As a matter of fact he is, though you wouldn't think it to look at him. Delicate and sensitive. Don't be so quick to judge, Milan. Anyone can make a mistake."

"That's what you call sexually abusing a child? A mistake?"

"That happened a long time ago. And he's been paying for it."

"I know," I said.

"How? *How* do you know? How did you find out?"

"About your ex-husband? It's a long story, Mrs. Kelley."

She waved a hand in front of her face. "Don't tell it. Not to me, or to anyone else. It won't do anybody any good, and it will hurt a lot of people. Me, Frank, that girl and her parents. I just don't see the point."

"Virginia Carville saw the point, though, didn't she?"

She didn't answer.

"I don't know exactly where or how she found out, do you? A leak in the psychiatrist's office, or maybe on Frank's own lawyer's staff. Reporters have their sources. And for a local journalist, an ex–city councilman and future candidate for governor being exposed as a pedophile and a blackmail victim is one hell of a big story. Too big for Ginger to be bought off like Violet Grba."

She crossed her legs, and the leather of her boots creaked. It was a comfortable sound. "How about you, Milan? Can you be bought off?"

"I'm afraid it's gone too far for that, Mrs. Kelley."

"Ro," she chided me.

"Ro," I repeated. For a moment there was no sound except the ticking of the clock. Out of the corner of my eye I could see a tugboat creeping by outside on the river.

"You knew about it, didn't you?" I said. "Even while it was happening. You knew what was going on between him and your cleaning woman's little girl."

She opened her purse and took out a pristine tissue, with which she dabbed at her nose. "I happened to take a work break and came downstairs for a glass of lemonade at the wrong time. I saw them. It absolutely revolted me."

"And you didn't do anything about it?"

"I spoke to my husband about it, yes."

"You just spoke to your husband about it?"

Her chest rose and fell along with her shoulders. "It seemed harmless at the time."

I almost came out of my chair. "Harmless!"

"Harmless to me, Milan," she said firmly. "We all tend to look at things from our own sometimes narrow perspective. Frank is a normal man with normal needs, and I didn't care to fulfill them, because he's not only a clumsy and insensitive lover but he's hardly what anyone would call—prepossessing. And to be honest, I've always considered sex pretty much of a bore."

"You get enough of it through the books you write?"

"Something like that," she admitted. "For me, if it's a choice between leaving it in the bedroom or putting it on the page, that's no choice at all. So I wasn't really jealous of Frank, not in the traditional sense. I didn't give a damn what he did or with whom."

"One of those modern marriages," I said.

"Call it what you want to. But if he'd taken a mistress, there was a chance he'd fall in love with her and leave me. I didn't want that. I hadn't yet become a best-selling author, you see, and Frank, as a wealthy lawyer and political power here in town, kept me in quite handsome style. So keeping quiet and allowing him to simply fool around with that rather homely child seemed to be a way of keeping everybody happy."

The bratwurst sandwiches were battering at my gag reflex,

and I had to swallow several times. "Everybody but the rather homely child."

"Don't be so dramatic. People like that are survivors. They're ill-bred and ignorant and dirt poor, so they have to be resilient or they'd be shattered. Frank didn't hurt her. He never—penetrated her. And I know he was buying her very nice little presents. Books and records, pretty clothes, things her family could never have afforded. So for me it was the lesser of two evils."

At least she got one word right.

"But you eventually divorced him," I reminded her.

"I no longer needed him. My books bring me plenty of money. And I'm even famous in some circles—among the five percent of adult Americans who read more than two books in a year. So I told you the truth: I couldn't possibly live with a man who didn't read what I wrote." She gave me a winsome smile. "You read my book, though, didn't you, Milan?"

"Without even moving my lips."

"Did you enjoy it?"

"Sure," I lied.

She laughed gaily. "You're so gallant."

"When you divorced Frank, you got a pretty handsome settlement, didn't you?"

Her eyes opened in some surprise, but she was pretty well stocked in the self-control department, and she recovered quickly. "I got the house," she said.

"You got more than that, Ro, I think. In return for your silence. That's why the divorce settlement was handled out of court, wasn't it? So there would be no record."

She started to say something, but I rolled right over it.

"Your husband's high-rise condo isn't cheap, but it's hardly a mansion on the lake, is it?"

She tossed her head. "He's not suffering."

"No," I said. "Most people in the world—especially the ill-bred and dirt poor and ignorant ones—would probably trade lifestyles with him in a minute. But between what he's giving you and what he's paying the Grba family, he's hardly living as well as his income would allow."

I could tell from the tightening around her eyes that she was growing impatient. "Cut to the chase, Milan."

"All right. If the story about what he did to Violet Grba ever came out, not only would he be finished socially, politically, and probably as an attorney, but you'd be finished too. If your devoted readers found out that a famous novelist, who writes about love and romance and bravery, knew her husband was molesting a little girl and did nothing about it, your riches and fame and your book sales would dry up like a three-week-old cold sore, and the closest you'd come to the best-seller list again is if you used it to swat your cat off the furniture." I rocked back in my chair. "The cash cow would die on you, Ro."

"What an unpleasant expression," she murmured.

"And then Ginger Carville found out about it. That's why you had to kill her, isn't it, Ro?" I continued. "To keep the story quiet."

"Why would I kill her? And how was I supposed to know she'd found out? Do you think she'd come and tell me?"

"She'd come and double-check what she'd gotten from her sources, because that's the kind of responsible reporter she was."

"I think the wrong one of us is the writer, Milan," she said in a voice like an old paper bag. "With an imagination like that . . ."

"It didn't take much imagination, frankly. Just a lot of plodding and asking questions and making puzzle pieces fit."

"Your little fantasy is quite absurd. Ginger had engaged in some sort of sexual activity before she was killed; according to the news reports there was semen in her vagina. And I'm afraid I couldn't quite pull that off." She leaned back in the chair, relaxing, exuding confidence. "If I were you I'd go looking for that horrible little man who runs her TV station. I know she was putting out for him. I used to see him getting out of his car, looking furtive. Afraid. I recognized him because he puts his own ridiculous face on television all the time."

"Nicky Scandalios? You'd better rethink that particular plot, Ro. It has a few holes in it."

"Oh?"

"Nicky has a wife that he wants to keep. And while lots of married men have affairs, I don't think too many wives are so understanding that their husbands can be out at two o'clock in the morning without a good explanation. And that's what time Ginger was killed."

"I suppose I ought to be taking notes—all this would make a marvelous book."

"Take all the notes you want to."

"What about the other one she was humping?" Rosemary Kelley said. "The curly-haired one who looks like a waiter in an Italian restaurant?"

I'm ashamed at how much pleasure that gave me. "Steve Cirini is his name, and for a while he was the police's number-one suspect, because he admitted he was with her around midnight that night. They had sex as soon as she came home, almost did it on the stairs. And then he left, because their relationship didn't include cuddling and falling asleep after sex nestled together like spoons. That's how I know it couldn't have been him who killed her."

"And what led you to that particular little deduction, Mr. Holmes?"

"The police report," I said. "She had showered that night after Cirini left; the towels and the shower curtain were damp. She'd also used a douche afterward—there was an empty Summer's Eve container in the wastebasket. But as you pointed out, there was semen present. So whoever killed her did so long after Cirini was gone."

"This is all very interesting, Milan, but it still doesn't explain why you're accusing me of something so monstrous. It certainly wasn't *my* semen inside her, now was it?"

"As a matter of fact, in a sense, it was."

She laid her forefinger aside her jaw and cocked her head archly. I think she'd seen Vivien Leigh as Scarlett O'Hara a few times too many. "And how could that be, pray tell? I'd never pass the physical."

"ZZZ Carpet Cleaners," I said.

She took her hand away from her face, frowning the way some people do when they get a sudden and unexpected chest pain.

"You said it yourself, Ro. You were never that interested in sex. But yet on that Thursday night you went into a sleazy tavern, the kind of place a woman like you wouldn't be caught dead in. You picked up a strange man at the bar, a guy wearing a wedding ring, so you could be sure he'd keep his mouth shut. And after a few minutes you had him follow you home and go to bed with you."

"I told you before," she said, trying to look pathetic, "I was lonely. No, I don't care for making love that much. But every so often every human being just wants to feel a pair of arms around them. Sex is the price women have to pay."

"For ten minutes."

"Pardon?"

"You only had sex for ten minutes or so. That's how long he said it took. I talked to him this afternoon. His name is Jerry Zelman, in case you didn't know, and his wife's name is Harriet."

She sighed. "Was it as long as ten minutes? The poor slob, he's the original minuteman. I'm afraid he was a big disappointment to me. That's why I was so appalled—and embarrassed—when he came back the other night while you were there. He was the last person in the world I wanted to see again. But I still don't see how this makes me a murderer. And while it hurts me that you think that I could do such a thing, it also makes me very angry. I'm afraid if you persist in this, my attorney—"

"Your attorney is going to be way too busy to bother about me."

"I behaved in an unladylike manner—I've admitted that. Maybe I was indiscreet. Slutty, even. Maybe what I did was dangerously foolish. But—"

"He said you made him use a condom."

"Of course I did! Give me credit for at least a little sense!"

"Why would someone who doesn't like sex keep a box of condoms in her dresser drawer?"

"Because Mr. Triple-Z isn't the first stranger I've taken into my bed!" she said, finally angry, her beautiful skin drawn and pale. Beads of perspiration dotted her upper lip; she looked almost ill. "God, this is humiliating and distasteful! Do you think I wanted to risk getting AIDS? That I wanted his—his come inside me?"

"No," I said. "I think you wanted it inside Ginger Carville."

CHAPTER TWENTY-TWO

Outside the window, the wail of a ship's horn cut through the silence, echoing under the bridges and off the riverbanks, the kind of sound that makes your ribs vibrate. Rosemary Kelley sat across from me, as still as death, her green eyes hooded, her jaw set like concrete. Only the faint rise and fall of her chest indicated she was anything more alive than a beautiful mannequin.

Then her expression brightened a little. "Does it matter," she said, "that the little bitch was trying to blackmail me?"

She'd obviously decided to be philosophical about the whole thing.

"I don't believe that, Ro," I said. "Ginger Carville came to you with the story for you to confirm or deny. If money was discussed at all, it was probably your idea, because people like you and your ex-husband think everyone and everything is for sale. But an ambitious young woman like Ginger didn't give a damn about dollars. She wanted fame and power and maybe a shot at a network job, and a big story like this one could give it to her. That's when you decided to kill her."

"Go on," she said, so softly I could barely hear her.

"You waited until Frank was out of town, so he'd have an alibi. You went out to Draper's Tavern—the kind of place where you'd surely not be recognized. And you hit on poor stupid Jerry Zelman. You took him to bed and literally milked his semen into a condom, and then you sent him home."

She looked away, nodding ever so slightly. "I hated having him touch me," she whispered. "Even now, just thinking about it makes me feel creepy. I hate it that I had to let him."

"After he'd gone, you got dressed and took the condom next door to Ginger's. I don't know how you talked your way up into her bedroom, but you did. You hit her on the head with something, probably something else you'd brought along, and when she was unconscious you wrapped her around around her neck and choked the life out of her. Then you emptied the contents of that condom inside her and came back home. And probably went to sleep. How'm I doing?"

A tremor ran through her body and she bent forward in her chair as if she'd been seized with a terrible abdominal cramp. "It was the most disgusting thing I've ever had to do in my life," she said. "I've never touched another woman—there. And I've never touched a dead body, ever. I used surgical gloves, but it was really quite dreadful."

"The semen was a good touch," I said, lighting a cigarette. "It got the police looking everywhere else but at you—a woman. Just from what you saw out your window you knew she was sleeping with both Nicky Scandalios and Steve Cirini, and you figured they'd be the top suspects."

She inhaled deeply, her breasts thrusting against the red turtleneck. "You're smarter than you look, Milan." She offered a wan smile. "I thought you were a big, dumb, earnest guy who was out of his league with me. The kind of man I can usually wrap around my little finger." By way of illustration she curled a strand of hair around her finger, then playfully flicked it away. "I don't even have to do anything. A little glimpse of cleavage, a little too much thigh when I cross my legs, and men like you start slobbering."

"You have a pretty low opinion of people, don't you, Ro? 'Men like me.' 'Ignorant, ill-bred people' like the Grbas. Your ex-husband. Jerry Zelman, Steve Cirini, Nicky Scandalios. And

Ginger. To protect your career you snuffed her out like you were stepping on a roach."

She nodded agreement. "And the thing is, Milan, you'll never be able to prove it."

"Sure I will," I said. "You ought to stop writing about the eighteenth century, Ro. We're almost in the twenty-first now, and times have changed. There's a little thing called DNA testing. It'll take them a couple of months, but they'll test that sperm and find out the odds are two hundred million to one that it came from Jerry Zelman."

"They'd have to find Jerry Zelman to make that connection. And they won't."

"You don't think I'll tell them?"

"I know you won't," she said, and pulled a Glock nine-millimeter out of her purse. "Put your hands flat on the desk in front of you, Milan. Unlike Frank, I know how to use one of these."

I did what she told me. The gun she was aiming right at my chest had considerably more stopping power than her husband's .22, and she did seem to know what she was doing. At that distance I had little hope she'd miss.

"You know," she said, as easily as if we were discussing the weather or a good movie she'd seen, "before I start writing a book I take lots of notes. Ideas for scenes, character traits, things like that. I find it's really helpful when it comes time to put the whole thing together."

"I know. I took a creative writing class at Kent. But the professor didn't usually use a gun to get a point across."

She smiled. "I'm sure not. But I'll bet you do that too, Milan. Make notes about your cases and study them to help you make sense of everything."

I nodded, and her smile disappeared as quickly as it had come, like a random flicker of moonlight on the river that flowed past the window.

"I want those notes. All of them. Right now. Everything that pertains to me, to Frank, to Ginger Carville. Give them to me."

I didn't move.

Neither did the gun barrel. "Milan, you know I'll kill you if you don't. I'll shoot you right now. In the stomach, so you'll be a long time dying."

I looked quickly around the office for some sort of escape hatch, my gaze finally settling on the refrigerator.

Her eyes followed mine. "Of course," she said, fooled as were most people by the look of the thing, "they're in the safe, aren't they?"

"Isn't that where everybody keeps important papers?"

"Get them."

I took my hands from the top of the desk.

"Slowly!" she barked. "I'm sure you have a gun of your own in that desk drawer, but don't try me." She jumped to her feet and extended both hands in front of her in the police-academy-approved firing stance; the muzzle of the Glock was about six inches from my throat. "I killed Ginger Carville without any compunctions—and I *liked* her."

"And here I thought you liked me too," I said sadly.

"Wishful thinking on your part, then."

I stood up slowly, holding my hands out belt-high. I believed that she could handle the gun, but I wasn't sure how her nerves were going to hold up. I slowly crossed the room to the refrigerator, then turned back to look at her.

"Open it up, dummy!" she said.

"You're not thinking very clearly. This has gone too far now. If Ginger Carville found out about all this, and then I found out, eventually somebody else is going to, and it'll come back to you and your ex-husband."

"Frank had nothing to do with it! He didn't even know about Ginger. He's a weak, pathetic excuse for a man; he wouldn't have the guts to do what I've done."

"Make it easy on yourself. Let's call the police together."

"Let's open the safe together instead."

"You're making a big mistake, Ro. I'm trying to help you."

"Do you want me to kneecap you, Milan?" she said, changing to a one-handed grip and lowering the muzzle to aim it at my legs. "Shoot you in the knee so you'll never walk right again? I'm losing patience—fast."

I sighed. "You're the boss," I said.

She nodded. "The one with the gun is always the boss."

I squatted down in front of the refrigerator, hiding the door with my body so she couldn't see that the dial on the front of the door was a fake. I fooled around with it a little.

"Hurry up!" she snapped.

"Sorry. I'm a little nervous, my fingers aren't working right."

"If you don't make it snappy, nothing's going to be working right," she warned.

I fiddled around for a few seconds more, then swung the door open. I reached in and put my hand around a nice cold bottle of Stroh's. I couldn't think of a moment when I'd wanted one as badly. Then I swiveled around on my haunches and threw it at her as hard as I could.

I'd aimed at her head, but when I played football I was a defensive lineman and not a quarterback, and my throw was woefully inaccurate. The bottle hit her in the left breast, and she stumbled backward, screaming in pain and surprise. Then it bounced onto the hardwood floor and shattered with a pop that was lost in the roar of the Glock.

I'd turned away instinctively—a good thing, too. Instead of my taking the bullet in the abdomen, the slug ripped a blazing furrow along the fleshy part of my left buttock.

It felt like a white-hot sword.

I lunged toward the desk just as she fired again, blasting a pane of glass out of the window. With my arm I knocked the phony Tiffany lamp onto the floor, where it broke into smithereens, so that the only illumination in the room was the light from the pink-gray city sky outside, and the reflection of the floodlights on the facade of Tower City across the river.

I somersaulted over the desk and onto the floor behind it—groaning loudly as I landed on my ravaged butt. Her 9-millimeter coughed again, and I felt the impact as the bullet thudded into the thick cherrywood that was all that was between us.

Rising painfully to my knees, I yanked open the top drawer and scrabbled in it for my .357. My fingers closed around the grip, and it felt familiar and comforting in my hand.

I thumbed the safety off and squeezed the trigger, pointing the Magnum toward the ceiling—a warning shot just so she'd understand that the playing field had been leveled and she wasn't the only one packing heavy artillery. At the very least it would give her something to think about.

The gun sounded like a howitzer next to my ear, and loosened plaster cascaded down on me like a spring snowfall. I didn't dare raise my head yet; she knew where I was but I didn't know where she was.

The office was filled with the unmistakable stink of cordite. On the river a boat horn blared again, but even with the broken window I had trouble hearing it through the ringing in my ears.

After a few moments I was able to make out stumbling footsteps rapidly receding down the stairs. I was relieved she was going, and surprised, too. I guess she'd decided she didn't want to shoot it out with me, no matter how good she was with a gun.

In one way, it didn't matter a damn whether or not I caught her and brought her down. I had the entire conversation on tape, and the gunshots too, and if they weren't enough to convict her, they were certainly enough to get Steve Cirini off the griddle. But if she wanted to kill me badly enough—and she'd given me every reason to think she did—she'd come back for me—and for all I knew burn down the building to get rid of my files.

I had to catch up with her before that happened. I straightened up, ready to follow her, and stepped in a puddle of beer. My left leg buckled under me—it felt as if the left side of my butt and thigh were on fire from the inside. I grabbed the desk for support, almost dizzy with the pain. When my head cleared I staggered across the room and hurled myself through the door and down the stairs, holding onto the wall for support. Every step was like a branding iron, and I was aware of something warm and sticky running down the back of my thigh.

I heard a car engine start up.

When I finally stumbled through the door and into the parking lot, her white Saab was roaring out onto Carter Street, spewing exhaust as it bumped over the low curb. Limping as badly as I was, I knew that before I could reach my own car, unlock it, get in, and drive off after her, she'd be long gone, up the winding hill and out of the Flats, into the busy downtown area adjacent to Jacobs Field. Once she got up onto Carnegie Avenue she could either take that east, Ontario Street north, the Hope Memorial Bridge to the west side or jump onto any one of the three freeways that converge conveniently just across the street from the ballpark, and I'd have lost her.

Except that the boat horn that had shaken the panes of my office windows had announced the approach of an enormous oil tanker traveling upriver toward Lake Erie to the bridgetender at the Eagle Avenue Bridge. Bells were ringing, red lights were flashing; the safety barriers came down as the great bridge started to rise.

The Eagle Avenue Bridge spans the Cuyahoga at Collision Bend; it rises vertically thirty or forty feet on counterweighted pulleys to allow the big ore boats to pass beneath it. The bridgetender's shack is built directly above the roadbed in the middle of the bridge; I could see the bridgetender in the light of his little room, white-haired and chubby-faced, wearing a black sweater and a Cleveland Cavaliers cap, completely unaware of the drama unfolding below him as he and the bridge ascended.

The Saab almost hit the barrier before screeching to a halt. Rosemary Kelley ground the gears into reverse, and the car jerked backward into the trunk of a towering oak tree. The motor died, the driver's door flew open, and she was out of the car and running, down the little knoll that slopes from Fire Station 21 to the river, and into the darkness.

I had little choice but to follow her, but my bad leg crumpled under me again and I tumbled down the little hill, rolling over and over, clutching my Magnum, knowing the safety catch was off and hoping I wouldn't accidentally shoot myself.

There are wooden benches down at the base of the grassy knoll near the water's edge, where in warmer weather the firemen take their lunch breaks and watch the ships go by, and my momentum rolled me to within a few feet of them. Shaking with the pain, I used one of them to haul myself up to a standing position, staggered down to the water's edge, and started off around Collision Bend on foot.

Now I knew how Hans Christian Andersen's Little Mermaid must have felt; every step was agony. Of course the mermaid suffered under the curse of a sea witch, and I had only been shot in the ass.

I could see Rosemary ahead of me; the lights from the monster ship only thirty yards out into the river illuminated her, creating almost a nimbus around her slim black-clad form. She was picking her way along the rocks and broken slabs of concrete and masonry that form the riverbank's revetment, arms extended on either side for balance, and having plenty of difficulty in her high-heeled boots. I could see she was still holding the gun.

I could feel that I was still bleeding a lot. I didn't have such an easy time of it on those rocks myself.

"Ro!" I shouted.

One of the sailors on the rear deck of the tanker must have thought I'd yelled "Yo," because he looked down at me and gave me a friendly wave as the big ship moved on toward its eventual destination, Lake Erie. From that distance and in the dark, he didn't see Ro and probably couldn't tell I was carrying a .357 Magnum.

Rosemary Kelley made her way under the bridge, slipping and falling forward onto her hands and knees as she did so, which let me close some of the distance between us. She quickly straightened up and looked back at me, firing the Glock. The muzzle flash blazed orange in the dark, and the slug hit the rocks somewhere behind me and ricocheted off into the water. I jerked away and lost my own footing; I didn't want to land on my gunshot wound again, so I put my free hand out behind me to break my fall and split my palm open on the sharp edge of a broken concrete slab.

I gritted my teeth against this new pain and clawed my way upright again, sucking on the gash in my palm and almost reeling from the agony in my buttock and thigh. I could see Rosemary some forty yards ahead of me, and as I watched, she made a sharp right turn and began scrambling up the bank again, almost on all fours, and disappeared from my sight. The great ship had passed beneath the Eagle Avenue Bridge with another dolorous blast of its whistle, and the old steel bridge began its creaking descent.

When I turned and started climbing up the incline myself, the novelist was already at the crest, a stark silhouette against the pinkish-gray light of the winter sky. For just a moment I had a perfect shot at her, and I raised my gun from my side and took aim. Then I lowered my hand again. Not in the back.

But I had to stop her. I knew the Flats better than she did, but it was dark and deserted now, and there were too many twisting streets, too many quiet, shadowy old buildings where she could hide—or wait to ambush me.

She had all the advantages, it seemed. In my current condition I couldn't outrun her and she knew it. She wouldn't afford me the same consideration.

At the crest of the rise she turned again, crossing Eagle Avenue and heading back toward the firehouse, the way she'd come. By the time I got back onto level ground, though, she'd stopped, seeming disoriented, like a fox who hears the approaching hounds giving tongue. Looking around frantically, her long red hair whipping in the cold river wind, she made a sudden decision and started running directly toward the bridge, tottering on her high heels. On the other side of the river there are fewer side streets and more hills and gullies and boulders and trees. Perhaps she thought there was safety in that.

The bridge was still several feet in the air, but coming down, and she darted around the wooden barricade and ducked under the network of cables stretched across the roadway, their fluorescent orange-and-white-striped warning plaques glowing, and made a flying leap up onto the descending slab of steel and concrete.

She got both arms up onto the bridge. She must have gotten rid of the Glock somewhere along the way, because she was clawing at the pavement with both hands, her boot-clad feet flailing as she tried to haul herself up to safety.

But she didn't have the strength, and she didn't make it. As I watched in horror, the bridge came down to meet the roadway, practically cutting her in half.

I hope I live long enough to forget the sound of her screams.

CHAPTER TWENTY-THREE

I spent the next three weeks wearing oversize slacks with baggy seats that I'd bought at the local Big Man's Store, and sitting on what proctologists call a doughnut, a device usually reserved for those recuperating from hemorrhoid operations, to protect my stitches. It felt like a potty seat and was uncomfortable as hell. It's a good thing I possess an innate sense of dignity.

Mark Meglich was predictably furious about the way the whole thing had gone down, but when I pointed out that I'd tried in vain to call him all that day, he softened a little. And after listening to the audiotape I'd made of my conversation with Rosemary Kelley, he bumped it upstairs to his superiors, and the Cleveland Police Department officially closed the Virginia Carville murder case.

It made all the papers and local TV news shows, of course. Even Ed Stahl did two columns on it. I wasn't surprised. Virginia Carville had been a local celebrity; so had Rosemary Kelley. The fact that one had been murdered by the other, especially in such lurid fashion, made it one story no reputable news organization could afford to pass up.

The motive for the killing was also the stuff of which headlines are made. Frank Kelley would not be going to the governor's mansion. Not in this lifetime.

Unfortunately he wouldn't be going to prison, either. Although the statute of limitations had not expired, as Ginger

Carville had feared it might, without Violet Grba's testimony there was no criminal case to be made. And she refused to press charges. I couldn't prove it, but I imagined another large sum of money changed hands.

Kelley took early retirement from his law firm and exchanged his Gold Coast condo for a smaller one down in Naples, exiled, for all intents and purposes, from Ohio, the state he might have governed.

Bosko Grba died of stomach cancer early the following July in the oncology ward of the Cleveland Clinic. Shortly thereafter his wife sold the house on Track Road. Like so many immigrants from Eastern Europe, the Grbas had a horror of debt and had paid off their mortgage many years before, and with the money from the sale and whatever Frank Kelley had given them to avoid criminal prosecution, Mrs. Grba and her daughter Violet bought a nice yellow-and-white tract house in Garfield Heights. I haven't heard anything of either of them since.

I didn't give Marko the tape I'd made of my conversation with Nicky Scandalios. His affair with Ginger Carville never became public knowledge, and as far as I know, Mrs. Scandalios never found out about it either. In September a small cable network originating in Virginia offered Scandalios the position of CEO and general manager at a substantially higher salary plus stock options and bought out his contract with Channel 12. Once in a while I'll catch him on TV doing promotional spots and public service announcements—still trying to make himself as big a star as the on-air talent he employs, still oozing warmth and sincerity.

Jerry Zelman wasn't so lucky. Since it was his sperm that had been used by Rosemary Kelley to mislead the police, he spent a lot of time down at the old rock pile on Payne Avenue answering questions, and while his name was never made public, his wife Harriet's discovery of his one-night stand was unavoidable. I heard they went to a marriage counselor for a few months before she filed for divorce. Their business is now called Harriet's Carpet Cleaners. I don't know what became of Jerry. Or of Harvey Zelman, either.

Steve Cirini was welcomed back to his desk, and his Channel 12 coworkers threw a big party at the Watermark restaurant on the east bank of the Flats to celebrate his innocence.

Under considerable pressure from the local chapter of the National Association for the Advancement of Colored People, Channel 12 News hired an African American woman from KABC in Los Angeles to replace Ginger Carville on the news staff.

Andrew Lemmons was offered the position of senior news producer, but the memories were too painful for him to deal with, and that fall he took a similar job in Detroit. I had lunch with him the week before he left.

Vivian Truscott won the fourth of her local Emmy awards for excellence in news broadcasting. The citation specifically mentioned her coverage of the Virginia Carville killing.

Carole Carr was interviewed by Lesley Stahl on *60 Minutes* when she became involved in the case of a Pentecostal minister in Mentor, several of whose former parishioners suddenly remembered being abused by him in the late eighties, when they were children, and all of whom were being treated by Dr. Oscar Flygenring.

It was a long time before I was able to drive over the ramp and across the Eagle Avenue Bridge again. For about four months I came down to work the long way.

I'm happy to report that the reason I couldn't get in touch with Marko to tell him about the Kelleys that day was because he had indeed cracked the case of the elderly man who'd been murdered in his bedroom on East Thirty-seventh Street. Kids. Kids looking for drug money. For their trouble they'd found twelve dollars and change in the old man's house. It's a good thing Marko caught them; at that rate they'd have to murder an awful lot of people to keep themselves in crack.

"Animals!" he had said when he told me about it. "Wild dogs on the street wouldn't do that! Punks! I'd like to line 'em all up against a wall." And he made a gun of his thumb and fore-finger and swept it from left to right.

He was right, of course, certainly from a law enforcement officer's perspective. The evil twins of drugs and poverty have produced a generation of murderous children. Kids who kill for the price of a rock of crack, who kill for a Chicago Bulls Starter jacket, a dirty look or a perceived slight. It's scary out there.

But for all their savagery, are they any worse than people like Rosemary and Frank Kelley? Is it somehow less terrible to kill for higher stakes, for big money and big prestige and a shot at the governor's chair? Is it better if the killers have college de-grees and stock portfolios and best-selling novels and homes on the lake? If they go to church and pay their taxes and hob-nob with judges and cardiac surgeons, if they own VIP boxes at the Jake and the Gund Arena?

The punks who killed the old man had taken a life, all right. But so had Rosemary Kelley.

As for Frank Kelley—well, he'd only stolen one.

The east-side Heights being akin to a middle-size town, I run into Nicole Archer from time to time, shopping at Russo's or in line in front of the Cedar Lee. We're always pleasant and civil to one another, and violently uncomfortable.

It was nearly noon, eleven days after Rosemary Kelley had died at Collision Bend, and I was sitting at my desk, wriggling uncomfortably on my doughnut. Pain had transformed itself into soreness; improvement enough so that I could work again.

The bullet that had given the smart guys a lot to laugh at, that made me the target of a lot of leers and wise-alecky one-liners, had in fact come perilously close to killing me. So I let my highly entertained pals have their fun. I considered the al-ternative.

I'd replaced the fake Tiffany lamp with a ten-dollar goose-neck from Just Closeouts on Mayfield Road. The shot-out windowpane had been repaired, but I hadn't done anything about the desk. The bullet hole in the front panel gave it a certain character, I told myself.

We were enjoying a rare day of late winter sunshine, and I'd opened a couple of windows to let in some badly needed fresh air, cold as it was. I would have liked it even more if sitting could have been accomplished with anything approximating comfort. I was putting the finishing touches on my security plan for the plumbing supply company; toilets, after all, have to be protected.

Workers in the wrought iron shop downstairs were clanking away, so I didn't hear Mary Soderberg until she opened the office door and walked in.

I wasn't particularly surprised to see her. The week before she'd called to thank me for my efforts on Steve Cirini's behalf, but we both knew she had a lot more to say to me. I just wasn't especially looking forward to whenever she would decide to say it.

Truthfully, I'd been dreading it.

And now here she was in my office, unannounced, her hair pulled back into a French twist, her ever-changing eyes a dark, bluejay blue today, and I knew whatever there was that simmered between us was about to reach a roiling boil.

"Hello, Mary," I said. "On your lunch hour?"

Her face was drawn, tight, and she looked older and more tired than I'd ever seen her. "No, I'm out making calls all day today, and I was in the neighborhood, so . . . "

"Want some coffee?"

"I guess so."

"I'm afraid you'll have to get it yourself." I nodded toward the coffeemaker. "I'm not getting up and down too well these days."

It took her four long-legged strides to get to the Braun,

where my second pot of the day was on the warmer. She filled a mug and carried it back to the chair opposite me.

"Okay to put it right on the desk?" she said.

"There's a bullet hole in the desk—I guess a coffee mug won't hurt it any."

Running her fingers almost tenderly over the gouge Rosemary Kelley's bullet had made in the front of my desk, she sat down without removing her coat and took a baby sip of her coffee. "So how are you, Milan? How's your . . . ?" She colored a little.

"How's my ass? As well as can be expected, I guess. How's yours?"

The smile she tried to force wouldn't hold; instead she began crying, grasping the edge of the desk with both hands. So much for me always being able to make her laugh.

I didn't know what to do. To avoid just sitting there, I leaned forward, wincing with the effort, and put my hand on top of hers, patting it gently.

The tears spilled out of her blue eyes, streaking her face with mascara. She turned her hand over and squeezed mine. She didn't speak. We just sat there like that, holding hands, until she'd cried herself out.

"I've screwed everything up," she said finally. "I screwed up my whole life."

I couldn't argue with that.

She was fumbling around in her purse, looking for a tissue. I opened the bottom drawer and handed her the box I keep in there in case of such emergencies. She took it gratefully, pulled out several, and went to work on her eyes and nose.

"I've told Steve we're finished," she said when she'd gotten herself relatively under control. "I don't want to live like that anymore."

I didn't know whether congratulations were in order or not, so I didn't say anything.

"Steve was a mistake," she went on. "Right from the beginning."

"We all make them, Mary."

"But this was a three-year mistake," she said as if she couldn't believe it. "Three years of my life."

"The trick is not to make the same mistake again. There are so many new ones out there, just waiting to be made." I smiled to take the sting out of it.

"The worst part is that mistakes hurt other people too." She looked down at her knees. "I hurt you."

"I got over it."

Her eyes bored into me. "Did you? Did you really?"

This was worse than I'd thought it would be, this inescapable meeting that I'd known for a week was coming. "Eventually," I said.

Her fingers went to the French twist at the back of her head. "Would it matter if I told you that I've never really gotten over you?"

"Matter?"

"Almost right away I realized what I gave up, Milan. I felt really lousy about it. And I've been living with that."

I squirmed miserably on my doughnut. My uneasiness was escalating toward an anxiety attack.

"I don't much like the taste of crow," she said, "so you must know how important this is to me." She inhaled enough air to blow out the candles on an octogenarian's birthday cake and plunged ahead. "I'd like for us to try again. You and me."

There it was between us, almost tangible, making my mouth go dry and my throat hurt.

"Mary," I said, "this is a rebound."

"No." She shook her head resolutely. "I've been thinking about it for a long time, long before I ever found out about Steve and Ginger. I've never really stopped thinking about you. Your kindness. Your—decency."

I searched for a response but not a single thing occurred to me, so I pushed myself up out of my chair, wincing. I walked unsteadily over to pour some coffee that I didn't really want and stayed there, watching the Cuyahoga snake by my office window. In our town winter is never really over until May, but this day was so sunny and cheerful that despite their chilled fingers and hearts, Clevelanders could almost believe in spring.

"And you haven't stopped thinking about me, either," she said. "I know. I can tell by the way you look at me."

"I'm not looking at you at all."

"Then do."

"Mary . . ."

"Look at me and tell me you don't want me anymore, Milan. If you can say it, I'll go away."

I turned to look at her. I thought of the way it had been with her, for a while. I thought of how it had been with Nicole, and how very similar it had been when they'd both glided noiselessly out of my life.

I thought about *alone*—the icy precision of the word.

"If by want you mean desire," I said, "I can't tell you I don't. If you mean do I want you back in my life, do I want to be in love with you again . . . "

I fumbled in my pockets for my smokes until I realized they were on the desk.

"We could start slow," she suggested. "Feel our way. Try extra hard to be very, very kind and loving. Get to know each other again."

"We know each other pretty well already. I haven't changed any." I smiled gently. "And neither have you."

She bowed her head, and I went haltingly back to the desk for a cigarette.

"Is it Nicole?" she said.

"Nicole is out of the picture."

"Well then, why?"

"Because it won't work any better this time," I said. "I'm still Stroh's beer and klobasa sandwiches and movies on Saturday night at the Cedar Lee. Still—what was it you called me? A judgmental son of a bitch. I'm still the guy you traded in for life in the fast lane."

"I've already admitted that was a mistake. Can't you forgive me for it? After all this time?"

"Forgiving has nothing to do with it. You're feeling needy now, and abandoned, and I seem like the answer to you—but I'd only be a Band-Aid. We're too different. Nothing has changed, and if we try again it'll end the same way, except this time we'll really wind up hating each other."

"I wouldn't want that," she said without raising her head.

"We can't go back, Mary. Those bridges are burned."

She looked up at me, her eyes big and wet, and for a moment I thought she was going to cry again. But I was spared that.

"Are you sure?"

No, I thought.

"Yes," I said.

"You don't want to make the same mistake twice, is that it, Milan?"

I lit a Winston so I wouldn't have to answer. Neither of us spoke for almost a minute.

"Well," she said finally. "I guess this was a mistake too."

"Thanks for trying."

"You have to try." She stood up. "I'm thinking about going back to Boston. I know I could get a job at one of the local stations there—everybody knows me."

"Boston," I said.

"This hasn't turned out to be a good place for me."

I wondered for a panicky moment what Cleveland would be like without Mary. And then I realized I'd been living in Cleveland-without-Mary for a long time now.

She glanced at the photographs of my sons on the shelf behind my desk. "My sister had a baby last year."

"I didn't know that."

"A little boy. Carl, they named him, but his father calls him Carlo."

"Congratulations," I said. "You're an aunt."

"That's exactly the point," she said. "I think I'd like to really be an aunt, be there and watch him grow up, help her out baby-sitting and things. And my mom isn't getting any younger."

Neither am I, I thought.

"So, Boston."

"I hope you find what you're looking for," I said. "In Boston or wherever."

"I found what I'm looking for—and I threw it away. Now you're doing the same thing. We aren't so different after all, are we, Milan?"

She opened her arms and I hobbled over to her and hugged her good-bye, feeling the contours of her body along mine, so familiar, through the fuzzy edges of memory, and yet now so very strange. She put her head back and kissed me, gently at first, and then her lips opened and she whimpered in the back of her throat, her tongue searching hungrily for mine.

We stood that way, pelvises straining together, for a long time, and then she broke away, breathing hard, and peered at me, but whatever she thought she might see in my eyes wasn't there.

She smiled sadly, dropping her head a little. Then she looked back up and gave me the tiniest of waves. "See ya," she said, and turned and walked out of the office.

I waited until I no longer heard her footfalls on the stairs, until I couldn't taste her tongue anymore, couldn't smell her perfume in the air.

See ya. Wouldn't wanna be ya.

I eased myself back onto my flotation device, finished the

coffee left in my cup, and went back to work for the toilet manufacturers.

The gulls cawed noisily as they swooped over the water around Collision Bend; it was lunchtime for them, too, I guess, and they were gossiping about the events of the morning.

"Schmuck! Schmuck!" they seemed to cry.